ONE OF US

M.M. SHORT

outskirts press

This is a work of fiction. The events and characters described herein are imaginary and are not intended to refer to specific places or living persons. The opinions expressed in this manuscript are solely the opinions of the author and do not represent the opinions or thoughts of the publisher. The author has represented and warranted full ownership and/or legal right to publish all the materials in this book.

Outskirts Press, Inc.
http://www.outskirtspress.com

ISBN: 978-1-9772-0060-0

PRINTED IN THE UNITED STATES OF AMERICA

Dedication

In remembrance of those who left behind wives and children, mothers and fathers, brothers, sisters, friends and neighbors, who marched off to fight in foreign lands and seas for someone else's freedom, never to return.

Contents

1

"Up The Ropes!"

June 6, 1944
0710 Hours
2nd Ranger Assault on Pointe du Hoc

The landing craft crashed through angry swells and waves, waging a horrible psychological battle against the men inside. They huddled against the walls of the craft, flinching as ocean spray fought its way inside. Only the uneven strain of the motor offered any hint as to what was just outside as it fought its way through one wave and then another.

They have already lost two of their craft and the men inside, victims of shore fire and the cold eye of Fate. Still, many men cannot resist the urge to look over the edge of their boat, eastwards toward Omaha Beach, where the hypnotic hum of heavy fighting echoed across the waves. It makes some men anxious while others are just curious. They're here to fight. They're ready. So they look towards the sound of the fighting instinctively. They try to catch a glimpse of the shore, to see how close they are. And maybe what they would be facing when they got there.

Sergeant Garr is the ranking NCO of the landing party. He is able to process any grim reality about the upcoming fight. What is worrying him now is the lateness of the hour. They had sailed too far to the east, mistaking Pointe de la Percee for Pointe du Hoc. He also knew that the reinforcements were waiting for a signal from Colonel Rudder that would, no doubt, arrive too late.

"Get your head down!" he shouted. Instantly a few heads here and there ducked down and resumed their position against the wall of the boat. It continues to pitch as it crashes though more swells. The uncertain droning of the engine echoes an oily chorus as it changes pitch with every dip of the craft just before it rises again with the next swell.

Then it seems to shift lower, like a downshift. And the direction changes.

"Second Rangers!" Sergeant Garr calls out.

The men shift in place, weapons pointing up, readying themselves for the dash across the sand. The cliffs of Pointe du Hoc now hover before them, the top visible even to those laying low inside the craft.

"Move hard across the beach!" Garr shouted. "Spread out and don't stop to trade shots with Krauts on top! Get to the wall and wait for the rockets to fire!"

The engine's hum lowered and the direction shifted just a little to one side.

"Ten seconds!" the pilot shouted.

Garr moved into the middle of the landing craft and gave his final instructions.

"Keep the sand out of your action! Remember! Move hard to the cliff wall and wait for the rockets to fire! Then up the ropes!"

His words died with the sound of the craft coming to a halt. The hatch was spun open, sending the door splashing to the surf. Men began to pour out even before it was fully down.

“Go! Go! Go!” Garr shouted as he began pushing men forward. He followed on the heels of the last man and together they broke for the cliff wall.

A sporadic fire broke from the top, blowing the sand up and screaming off of rocks. There was a sickening sound of breaking flesh and bone as the man ahead of Garr went down, then another further up. Then another…and another. The men dodged their way over rocks brought down from the cliff by the preceding naval fire and large puddles that turned out to be small ponds when they filled with water.

At the wall Garr came up on a Ranger who had stepped back a few paces and was firing upwards. Garr grabbed him up and threw him against the wall.

“Whaddid’ I tell you!? Whaddid’ I tell you about standing off and trading shots with the Krauts!?”

The Ranger stood back and straightened up. His face was flushed, his jaw set. He started loading a new clip into his M1 carbine.

“Sorry Sergeant!” he said angrily, slamming the clip into place. “But they’re killing our guys! I’m not going home alive or dead without firing back!”

Garr stared back. There was no time for this discussion. The rules of engagement for war always seemed to bend this way and that. Besides, he liked the Ranger’s reasoning. Then he noticed that elements of Dog Company were landing with Easy and Fox companies. Dog was supposed to land on the other side of the Pointe but Rudder must have been impatient to get the show started, or so Garr thought.

The rockets fired, sending ropes screaming their way to the top. Rangers began to cluster to the base while Germans atop the

Pointe continued to fire down. Not wanting to wait any longer, Sergeant Garr gave the order.

"Rangers! Up the ropes!"

Rangers that were waiting their turn stood back and fired upwards, letting their carbines run dry before retreating back to the cover of the base. German stick grenades began to pepper the narrow beach concealing the Rangers. The explosions blew men apart from the wall to the waters' edge. Spoiling for a fight, men try to get onto a rope but many fall useless to the ground when pulled on. The Germans are cutting the lines.

With mounting casualties Garr calls for a radioman but there is none around. Finally, disobeying his own command he steps out onto the beach and starts firing his submachinegun against the defenders of the Pointe. But it all seems futile. Ropes are falling to the ground on the left and right. His platoon getting chewed up, men falling everywhere, all seemed to be lost. Garr began to wonder what the life expectancy would be on this narrow pocked beach. There would be no rescue and no reinforcements. It was up to them to fight their way through.

Just then a hot thunder roared overhead. It scorched a lightning ride over the beach and slammed onto the top of the Pointe. Then another and another. Dirt and rock began to fall like a stinging sleet. Garr collapsed against the cliff wall and strained his eyes seaward. It was a naval bombardment.

"Thank God…for Guardian Angels," he muttered.

Then a Ranger pulled on his web gear to get his attention.

"Hey Sarge! The guns knocked a piece of the wall down! We can crawl up! Defilade all the way!"

Defilade. No one could shoot at them from the sides. What could be better?

"Do we still have the commando ropes?!"

"Roger that, Sarge."

Garr ripped his spent magazine from his weapon and stuffed it into his shirt. Then he slapped a new one in and charged the weapon. They would fight their way out after all.

"Second Rangers!" he screamed. "Follow me!

Garr scrambled up the cave-in, the walls on either side shielding him from fire coming from the top. Behind him, a line of Rangers crawled frantically in an attempt to keep up. Their boots slipped in the softened and increasingly damp limestone, pieces sent crumbling to the floor below as heavy combat boots bit into anything that offered resistance, propelling the Ranger toward the top.

At the top, Garr held up just below ground level. Then, his breaths coming in rasping heaves, he rose up and pushed himself the last bit, enough to bring himself over the top, leaving one leg behind. He raised his Thompson submachine gun and sprayed the area, sweeping a fiery half-moon across the top of the Pointe. He was the first to arrive and he was eager for payback.

He couldn't discern any return fire anywhere on the Pointe. He scrambled the rest of the way up and fell to the ground as he worked a new clip into his weapon. Rangers poured over the crest behind him like a swarm of really pissed of hornets. Garr spread them out with hand signals while he watched for any arrivals coming from the other ropes. Incredibly, he saw two other lines start to produce Rangers. Somehow they had been neglected by the German Infantry.

Watching his force build up behind him, Garr scurried over to the cliff edge and looked over. There was a glut of Rangers still making their way to the top. There would be no room for them when they reached the top.

"Rangers!" he screamed. "To the guns!"

All at once the men rose up as one, like a beast with a thousand heads, bristling with spikes that moved this way and that. On his left Garr saw Rangers coming over the edge. Then, to his right he saw another line pop up. There was sporadic fire coming from inland defenses but it wasn't enough to stop the invaders. Just shy of the first bunker the fire had become strong enough that the Rangers stopped to make a brief battle line. They opened fire on instinct, not needing any orders. The resistance waivered noticeably and the Rangers picked up again and charged in.

Making the first casement, Sergeant Garr and several Rangers poured in, firing blindly as they entered. It was all useless, though. There were no Germans in the bunker. And what was worse, their objective was missing. Instead, they found themselves looking at a telephone pole pointing out of the casement.

"Where's Corporal Murphy?!" Garr snapped.

"Right here, skip!"

Garr turned to face his Corporal. He could see the same confusion in his eyes.

"There's supposed to be a gun in here, Sarge," Murphy said.

"Well, there ain't one in here now! Listen, you take two squads and you clear the Observation bunker, got it?!"

"Got it!"

I'll take the rest and see about the rest of these gun positions! Move out!"

Murphy disappeared, taking two squads with him to the Observation Bunker.

Reenergized with the idea that there were other guns that were still to be discovered, Garr's men streamed out of the first bunker like bees with a damaged hive. There were supposed to be six in all. Intelligence had confirmed that. One of them had to be here. But as Garr and his men hit the open air again they could see two other groups coming out of the only remaining casement. They weren't acting like they found anything. One Ranger held his rifle in one hand but his free hand was held out in disbelief.

Where the hell are the goddam guns? he thought.

Garr held his men up. The four other gun positions were open pits. He could tell they were just telephone poles made to look like guns. That was it. There were no guns on Pointe du Hoc. Garr looked around for the Command Post but couldn't make it out. He wasn't sure how this was going to affect the mission. The guns were still the target but where? If the Rangers start out inland which way do they go?

Do we still cut the Coast Road, he thought. *Or do we look for the guns?*

At that moment there was a devastating fire from the right flank. A handful of Rangers went down in an ugly rippling sound of bullets tearing into the dirt, gear and men. Garr and all the men around him hit the dirt and crawled behind whatever they could find that would keep them alive.

"What the goddam hell is that!? Garr screamed.

"AA battery!" a Ranger called back. "The AA battery on the West side! It's still in action!"

Garr cursed in disgust. He had forgotten all about the AA battery because it wasn't part of his mission. The AA battery was Dog Company's problem. The only thing was, Dog Company was supposed to land on the other side of the Pointe and take it out.

But they landed on this side instead.

"Corporal Murphy!" Garr screamed.

"Yeah, Sarge!"

"You take six or seven and swing wide left! Get on the other side of that hedgerow and then make your way toward the battery! I'll take another six and swing along the cliff side! We'll be in the open so I am giving you five minutes to get into position. After five minutes, I attack! Got it!?"

"Got it!"

"When we move, you lay down suppressing fire!"

"Will do!"

Corporal Murphy grabbed his men and was off to the left. Garr started to return fire in an attempt to occupy the AA battery. It was a 20 mil gun that proved to be too much for any type of frontal assault without a second action on the flanks. It would have to be a see saw attack until one group got close enough to throw a hand grenade.

It was a long five minutes.

When the gun turned inland and started firing Garr knew Murphy had succeeded in drawing its attention. He raised up and started toward a barbed wire that lay between him and the battery. Garr's men followed on his heels. Knowing when the gun would be re-directing its fire to his side would be the main concern. It may stop firing to turn, or it may just turn in place and keep firing.

With his boots falling hard as he streaked forward, he noticed the shell strikes starting to move in his direction. That was all he needed to see. He hit the dirt and flattened out, confidant that his men behind him would do the same. Then they opened up as best they could, the 20 mil scorching up their position, churning grass, dirt and rock into the air and sending it streaking the air in all directions.

The fire shifted again and Garr rose up and started off. He heard fire from Murphy's team on the left so he knew they were still in action. He didn't look back on his men, he knew they were there. He just didn't know how many. When he reached the barbed wire the fire paused, just a touch, but it was enough to force the men to the ground again. They hit with a rippled thumping sound, waiting for the inevitable raking from the 20 mil. But it didn't come. After the short pause it had resumed taking on Murphy's crew. Garr rose up again and started off, oblivious as to whether or not any of his men were following suit. He fell on the barbed wire, flattening a section of it. His men followed, using his body for a spring board as they vaulted over the wire. He counted six as they ran over him. His team was still in play.

Garr was up again, a little too slow in freeing himself from the wire. The battery now turned to meet Garr's team, shooting up the pock marked terrain in front of him. Coming loose at the last instant he collapsed forward and fell into a bomb crater left by the naval bombardment just as the gun raked the turf in a beast-like hunt for anything living. He heard his men behind him. They were calling out, screaming, trying to get synced up with the rest of the effort. But Garr was too busy catching his breath and steadying his nerves. They were either there…or they weren't.

Then the fire shifted over to Murphy's team once more.

Jesus, he thought. *This gun was supposed to be gone!*

Up again and charging, he could see that they had gotten to the nearest edge of the hedgerow. The battery would have to focus on them. With his heart racing Garr rose up again and charged while firing short bursts at the battery. He had a crazy idea of going head to head with the 20 mil but it disappeared when the barrel swung his way. He dove onto the ground once more and rolled into another bomb crater. Reloading, he raised the submachine-gun up above ground level while he stayed well into the crater and let his clip fly at the battery. At this close range, this was as suppressive a fire as he could manage. He picked up the sound of fire from his rear, from his own men, prompting him to bring his weapon down before they shot his arm off. As he did he rolled onto his back and loaded another clip and ripped the charging handle back, loading the weapon once more. But then there was an explosion. He knew it was a grenade. He recoiled. Raising up he saw it was effective enough to make the final assault.

"Let's go, Rangers!"

And with that both teams charged the battery, firing weapons as they came. When he was close enough he fired his clip into the battery and finished what the grenade had started. All the men that were left arrived with weapons pointed into the battery. But the only thing that was there now was smoke and death. The gun's barrels popped and cracked from the heat. All the men were still. The battery was silenced.

"Where's Corporal Murphy?" Garr asked finally.

"He's gone, Skip."

Garr turned to look at his own team. There were only three left and one of them was wounded and laying back about thirty yards. Garr sent a man back for the medic.

"Who threw the hand grenade?"

"I did Sergeant," a Ranger said reluctantly.

"That saved a lot of Ranger's lives. What's your name?"

"Johnson. Private First Class Walter Johnson."

Garr nodded.

"Well, you're now Corporal Walter Johnson. Who's left on your team?"

Johnson turned to point to a smaller Ranger standing next to him.

"Tescovitz here and me are the only ones left."

Garr nodded again.

"Right. Fall back and rejoin the effort. We still have some buildings to clear."

Garr motioned in the distance where the rest of the battalion was still securing the remaining bunkers and gun emplacements. This part of the mission was over. The next part would be gathering up and identifying the dead Rangers.

Ranger Command Post

"I need casualty reports and we need an ammo check!"

All the platoon leaders stood silently while Colonel Rudder issued orders. The mission was still on. The guns were still to be found and the Coastal Road had to be cut. Sergeant Garr had been summoned specifically by Rudder, though he did not take part in the briefing.

"Questions, gentlemen?"

No one spoke up.

"Then you have your orders. I will need your numbers and your estimates by twelve hundred hours. Dismissed."

As the officers dispersed Rudder motioned for Garr to come forward.

"Yes sir."

"Sergeant Garr. You and your men took out the AA battery on the west side of the Pointe?"

"Yes sir."

"The report I have here is that you lost seven men with one wounded?"

"Eight men. Sir."

"Eight men," Rudder echoed distantly. He then took to shuffling the rest of his papers into his message bag before straightening up and looking directly into Garr's eyes.

"That was a tough call. It was the right call. I'm sorry that you had to take that on. But it saved a lot of Rangers' lives."

Garr stared back.

"Yes Sir."

Rudder delayed just a little, as if waiting for Garr to voice a complaint, challenge his decision to land on the wrong side with Dog Company, or anything else. But Garr said nothing.

"Dismissed, Sergeant," he said at last.

Garr started to leave but then stopped himself.

"Excuse me sir…but I thought I would ask one thing, things being what they are."

Rudder looked up.

"Alright Sergeant. Go ahead."

"Is it safe to assume that we will not be reinforced as planned, sir?"

Rudder stared back for just a second. Then, his head lowered as he slung his message bag over his shoulder, he heaved a sigh and answered.

"Well, you'll learn this from Lieutenant Hill in about thirty minutes, anyway. Yes, that is correct. We will not be reinforced or resupplied on schedule. We missed our window to call for the reinforcements. C Company is already ashore on Omaha and they are getting hammered. We are going to have to hold on until Fifth Rangers arrive."

Rudder began to gather his things as if to leave but Garr cut him off.

"There are no guns on the Pointe, sir."

An uneasy silence invaded, leaving the two men staring at each other for a moment. Garr resented the delay and the apparent poor planning on the resupply. And he resented Dog Company screwing up the timing and not landing where they should have. And then no guns to capture.

A new burst of gunfire in a forward area broke the stalemate.

"Thank you, Sergeant," Rudder said as he turned to leave. "That will be all."

Garr unslung his weapon and adjusted his helmet strap. The obvious question as to what they would do when the ammo ran out had already been answered. There was no retreat.

"Yes sir," he rasped in disgust.

At the perimeter Garr was briefed by Lieutenant Hill about the coming actions. They should expect a counter attack. They were still going to go for the guns, wherever they were and they were still going to cut the Coast Road and set a roadblock. The guns would be first, though.

Garr listened mindlessly, taking it all in like so much machinegun fire. There was nothing to be done now anyway. They were here. They couldn't withdraw and the Germans were coming. He had to come to grips with the fact that he was bitter. He was bitter for Rudder screwing up the landing. For taking Dog Company ashore on the wrong side of the Pointe. And for getting Garr's people killed when they were confronted with the sudden reality of it all when the AA battery opened up on them.

But then again, he also had to admit that there were Dog Company casualties expected in that attack on the battery. Had Rudder made the right decision to land Dog on the east side of the Pointe after making everyone so late? Didn't Rudder have the argument with the commander of the flotilla to turn west and head away from Pointe de la Percee and towards Pointe du Hoc?

And finally, was it reasonable to assume that Rudder had hopes that the naval bombardment had taken out the battery and that the best course of action, given the lateness of the hour, was to land all the troops as soon as possible and commence the attack in earnest in the shortest amount of time? Didn't that give them the best chance to signal for the reinforcements to come on? Was Rudder human and was he allowed, and expected, to make mistakes? And, as Garr finally reconciled, was he willing to fight for Rudder still, and follow his orders to the utmost? The answer to that was yes. And so Garr elected to keep his head in the fight and let the mistakes drift away with the rest of the smoke. War is war. And commanders only pretend to plan its outcome.

Receiving his orders, Sergeant Garr gathered his men.

"Fox Company! On me!"

The bulk of Fox Company moved in and gathered around Garr, their faces ashen and dirty.

"Listen up…we have the west section of our perimeter. We will take an initial position on the hedgerow that extends from the battery…"

Here he stopped. The battery was the one he and his men had

just taken out only an hour earlier. The hedgerow was the one that Murphy was killed fighting in.

"...to the first out building right here in front."

"We gettin' reinforced, Sarge?"

Garr stared back.

"No," he said reluctantly.

"Shit! We're not?!"

"Listen! We don't have time for this! No, we are not getting reinforced! Not as planned! Stop worrying about reinforcements and start worrying about the counterattack! It's coming! And we better be goddam good and ready! Now...you done?"

The Ranger got quiet but the look on his face spoke the truth about his real feelings.

Getting himself under control, Sergeant Garr addressed the men again.

"We'll be reinforced. Just not as planned. We have to adjust. We have to flex with the changing conditions. That's what makes Rangers unstoppable. You take away our food. You take away our water. You take away our ammunition. You even take away most of our men...and still you lose. That's a Ranger. Everybody onboard?"

"Rangers!" The group echoed.

"We are expecting a counter attack. We will repulse this attack. We will hold this ground. We will prevail against the enemy if we have to go to the bayonet. We will be reinforced and resupplied. But now...we dig in. Questions?"

There were none.

"You have your orders! Disperse!"

He watched the Rangers spread out and start work on their defenses. Then he started at the left end of Fox Company's line over at the first row of out buildings and worked his way down the line, giving instructions, pumping the men up and inspecting their work, until he ended up on the far right, which ended along a hedgerow. It was the same one that Corporal Murphy had used to screen the movements of his team assaulting the AA battery. There he had his last men dug in, leaving the far right wide open. He felt confident, though, that there would be no advance along the narrow area between the end of his right flank and the cliffs. At least none that wouldn't be spotted in plenty of time to come up with a response. Still, he was bringing with him one more Ranger from another platoon in Fox Company.

"Who do we have here?" Garr asked.

Two men looked up, stopping their digs long enough to recognize Sergeant Garr.

"Private First…I mean….Corporal Walter Johnson and Private Tescovitz…"

Garr recognized the man he had promoted to Corporal just a few hours earlier. It was like looking at Murphy all over again, even though he looked nothing like Murphy.

"Walter Johnson. Right. Look, since you two are a little thin over here on the far right I'm going to give you Provenzano on the B.A.R."

"Okay," Johnson replied.

"Sonny….over here."

Sonny Provenzano, native of Brooklyn, dice thrower, card player, teller of tall tales and renowned expert with the Browning Automatic Rifle jumped into a foxhole.

"He'll give you guys some extra fire over here."

"Right Sarge. We'll hold tight," Johnson answered.

"We'll hold 'til we're cold, Sarge!" Provenzano sang.

Garr only nodded. He wasn't in a joking mood.

"Just hold. And try to stay alive."

"Say, you're...you're Tescovitz, right?" Provenzano asked. "Aren't you the guy they call Tesla?"

"That's me," Tescovitz answered. He was going over his carbine and hadn't bothered to look at Sonny.

"Yeah...you're the real smart guy...that's what I heard."

Tescovitz looked over at Sonny, a weak smile on his lips. After what they'd been through he wasn't sure how someone could be so casual, even light hearted, but then again you have to keep the edge off. You can go a little crazy sitting in a foxhole waiting for someone to start shooting at you.

"Hav," he said reaching out to shake Sonny's hand.

"Hav...yeah. I'm Sonny."

"Right," Tescovitz quipped. "And here we are in sunny France. Who invited the Germans?"

"Germans? Who are they?" Sonny answered as he started a function check on his B.A.R.

"They're the ones in grey."

"Oh yeah! Now I remember."

Sonny leaned forward a little to see Johnson about ten feet away finishing up his hole.

"Now...you know who that guy is, right?" Sonny cracked, pointing to Johnson.

Tesla looked over for a second as he made himself more comfortable in his hole.

"Yeah…that's Walter. Walter Johnson."

"I know, I know," Sonny cracked impatiently. "But he doesn't go by that name! Didn't you know that?"

Tesla could only sigh.

"You call him Walter Johnson when you're back on post, ya' know?" Sonny continued. "Like, when you're back in the world."

"Back there you call me Corporal Walter Johnson," Johnson called out, obviously overhearing the foxhole chatter. Sonny looked once in his direction before continuing.

"Yeah, well, anyway…he's got this nickname, too. We all have them."

"You don't, Sonny," Tesla replied.

"Yeah, yeah…but I was born with a nickname! It's not like my name is 'Charles' or 'Bartholomew!'"

Tesla laughed. "Bartholomew…that's good…"

They smiled quietly. Any reason to crack a smile was good on the Pointe.

"So what's Corporal Johnson's nickname?" Tesla asked.

"You still don't know?"

"I guess I dropped it in the sand somewhere," Tesla said in frustration. He leaned back in his hole and started to clean sand out of the action on the carbine.

Sonny laughed.

"Everyone calls Johnson 'Hall.' You know…Walter Johnson…Hall of Fame…? Baseball? Hall of Fame?"

Tesla was blank at first but then the light came on.

"Oh, yeah…Walter Johnson. He pitched for…"

"—Washington. Washington Senators!" Sonny said in a sing song voice. "Great pitcher! Hall of Fame, man! So everyone calls Johnson here 'Hall' for the Hall of Fame!"

"Did you pitch baseball, Walter?" Tesla asked.

"Did he pitch baseball?!" Sonny shot out. "Man he was going to be a pro! Walter Johnson II! Can you imagine it? Can you imagine some guy coming back to baseball, pitching like Hall here pitches, with that name? Can you imagine that? The sports writers will run out of ink covering that! That's history! History, man!"

Tesla smiled as he stared at Hall, expecting him to clarify all the news from Sonny.

"Yeah, I pitched baseball. Was doing ok until this shit broke out."

"Where'd you pitch?"

"Semi Pro. Barn Stormer type baseball. There was some scouts from Cincinnati that were interested."

"So what happened?" Tesla asked, stumbling into the obvious.

Johnson glanced at Tesla, half thinking he was being put on.

"Well, first the Japanese bombed Pearl Harbor and then Hitler declared war on America. Cincinnati's phone call was cut off by Uncle Sam and they sent me here."

He stared back at Tesla who was nodding his head.

"Right," he said and he went back to inspecting his rifle.

"Yeah…I can see it now," Sonny said aloud. "Walter Johnson on the mound! Again! That would make history."

Sergeant Garr showed up an hour later, checking his line again. Colonel Rudder had sent one group inland to find the guns, which they did. They were unguarded. Thermite grenades took them out and the Rangers were making their way back to the

Pointe. With no reinforcements, though, the expected counterattack had to be soon.

"Sergeant Garr!" Sonny called out.

"Are we dug in, gentleman? Are we ready?"

"Hundred percent, sarge," Sonny answered. Tesla and Hall raised their hands to show 'ready.'

"Those Germans gotta be on their way," Tesla remarked.

"Yeah. Soon," Garr answered as he jumped into Johnson's foxhole.

"You gonna' fight here, sarge?"

"Might as well. You fellas are pretty thin over here, and I don't like the open area between here and the cliffs."

So he settled in and re-checked his Thompson.

Each man waited silently, their thoughts private, while they gazed ahead into the countryside that the counterattack would produce. The only sound was the occasional clinking of metal from the rifles and gear. Then a sneeze, a cough, someone clearing their throat. Sergeant Garr spoke first, breaking the silence like a machinegun shooting up a silent movie.

"Sonny!"

"Yo, sarge!"

"You switch places with Johnson. I want the B.A.R. over here."

Hall glanced at Sonny as the two slowly began to trade places. Once in the foxhole Hall took it up with Garr.

"You want both automatics in the same foxhole?"

"If the Germans try to come through by way of the AA battery, we might need some heavy auto fire to suppress and keep control of the right flank. There's too much open area on the right. I know. I'm breaking the rules. But it's my call."

Hall looked to his right and behind, past the destroyed AA battery and out onto a small plain that ran to the cliffs. Nodding in approval he settled in with Tesla.

"Hey, sarge. Can you do us a favor?"

"There's no reinforcements. There's no resupply, Sonny," Garr droned, anticipating a smart ass request from the guy from Brooklyn.

"Yeah, yeah…I heard that part. But maybe you could call Johnson by his nickname? We call him Hall. That way there's less chance of confusion. Okay?"

"Now why would you call him that?"

"Dig in, sarge, here it comes," Tesla said laughing.

"Because of his name and because he's a pitcher for real, see? Walter Johnson is in the Hall of Fame. So-"

"So because he has the same name you call him Hall for short? Short for Hall of Fame?"

"Yeah…yeah that's it exactly."

"You a pitcher, Johnson?" Garr asked, his gaze covering down on the right flank. "I mean, Hall?"

Hall smiled and nodded quickly.

"Yeah, sarge, I pitched for a few years…barn stormer team in Pennsylvania."

"Right. You threw the hand grenade."

Hall stared back a second or two, then nodded.

"Yeah."

"Well," Garr started. "That makes sense I suppose."

Everyone got quiet again. There was no reason for it, other than that's what they wanted or that's just the way it worked out. Everyone just went about doing nothing, watching the line… waiting.

Then Tesla and Hall became occupied with a bee that had taken an interest in their foxhole. Tesla took to swatting it away but it would always return. Finally he took to waving his helmet at it but that was futile as well.

"Just ignore him," Hall said impatiently. "He'll go away."

"Yeah…just as soon as he bites my lip off. I don't go for bees!" And he took to swatting at it again with the helmet.

"Put yer' goddam helmet on Tescovitz!" Garr growled. His mood worsened as time wore on, dragging his men closer and closer to a collision with the German Army.

"Hey! Maybe it's a German bee. Maybe it's spying on our position!" Sonny cracked.

Hall held out his hand while Tesla put his helmet back on. The bee swirled around then darted away only to return again. This time it hovered over Hall's hand for a few seconds and then landed.

"Look at that!" Tesla exclaimed. "Man can bring a bee in for a landing!"

Garr and Sonny watched from the other hole while Hall turned his hand this way and that, allowing the bee to take a stroll.

"He's gonna' sting you, man!" Tesla droned.

"Let 'im," Hall replied. Then it happened. The bee stung, causing Hall to jerk ever so lightly.

"He got you! He got you, didn't he!?"

"Yeah…he got me," Hall replied.

Then the bee flew off and disappeared forever. Hall went back to his rifle and the boredom of watching the line.

"How can you do that?" Tesla asked in disbelief.

"Bees don't bother me," Hall said casually. He checked his carbine once more, for the hundredth time. It was still locked. Loaded. Clean. Ready to kill someone.

"Oh man! If that thing had speared me I would have needed a medic!" Tesla cracked.

"Bees don't bother you, Hall?" Sonny asked.

"Nah. I could get whacked a dozen times and it wouldn't bother me. I dunno' why…or why not."

"Hall," Tesla began. "If I got whacked a dozen times I would have to-"

"Hey Tescovitz!" Garr shouted. "How about if we drop the goddam bee scare and get back to something that doesn't drive me crazy! How about that?! What say we watch the goddam line!?"

Tesla shrank back in his foxhole, suddenly very conscious of his bee phobia.

"Okay, sarge," he said weakly.

There was a short silence.

"Hey sarge," Sonny began, his voice very low and respectful. "…again…about the name confusion thing…"

Garr leered at Sonny, who was facing him due to his new seating assignment.

"Sonny…"

"Yeah sarge..."

"Get yer ass outta this hole and go find out about chow."

"Yeah sarge."

Sonny worked his way out of the hole and was off. Hall really didn't want to say anything but he was, after all, a Corporal now.

"I didn't think there was any chow, except for what we were carrying on our own, skip."

"Let him find that out," Garr snapped.

"Here they come!" Garr shouted.

Instantly gunfire erupted up and down the line. Sonny jerked himself around to face the front and opened up with the heavy thumps from the B.A.R. Hall and Tesla fired furiously, their clips expiring with a little '*cling*' sound as they fired.

Garr found himself glancing to the right rear as he fought on. He didn't know why but he was suddenly very afraid of the counterattack coming from the direction of the AA battery. It appeared empty, though, so he had to devote all his attention to the front. Shots started to whiz over their heads as the German infantry found them. There's was a logical spot to try to force a breakthrough being as they were at the extreme end. The thing was, Garr wasn't convinced the Germans knew that.

Explosions to the rear and then the front clouded everyone's marksmanship. It wasn't for certain if there was armor present or not. That could spell disaster for Rudder's position. But it couldn't be debated now. The infantry had to be dealt with. The armor would be compromised without them.

"Reloading!" Hall screamed.

"Reloading!" Tesla echoed.

"You two better pace yourselves!" Garr hollered. He didn't want a foxhole going dry completely. Better if one kept the firing up while the other reloaded.

"They're moving up!" Sonny screamed. Then he let more go from his automatic rifle.

Garr then unloaded a quick burst of his clip in the same direction, giving up any interest in the right flank beyond the AA battery.

"Short bursts!" Garr screamed to Sonny. "Short bursts!"

If Garr and Provenzano went dry it would compromise the

defense considerably. If the whole position went dry it would end up being a bayonet defense.

Just then there was a terrible explosion directly in front. Hall and Tesla ducked down instinctively before raising up again. Then another blast sent them down into their hole again.

"Jesus!' Hall cried out. Then he raised up and was firing as he did so. If he went dry then so be it. But he had taken all he was willing to take. He emptied his clip.

Cling!

Then Tesla raised up and started firing while Hall reloaded. All the while the two automatics were boiling away just ten feet away. Everyone was bracing for what must be a hand to hand affair. It didn't seem likely that the ammo would hold out, or that the two foxholes on the far right could hold against a concentrated attack.

Hall was down again, reloading as fast as he could while Tesla kept the fire going from the hole. Sonny and Garr poured out their biggest concentration of fire when the German infantry massed in the front. It was more a matter of showing off the firepower then aiming at anyone. But then the German stick grenades started arriving. There was several explosions that sent everyone down into their holes. When they cleared there was another wave. Garr knew that the infantry was making their final push behind the grenade attack.

"Be ready for close contact!" Garr screamed.

Just then Tesla raised up to fire. Hall dropped down to load his last clip. But when he started to raise up he heard something. It wasn't the same as the other sounds. This was close. In the foxhole close. When he looked he saw a German stick grenade lying in their fox hole just behind Tesla.

"Lookout!" Hall screamed as he pushed Tesla out of the way, sending his last shot skywards. Grabbing the grenade by the handle he was able to fling it out of the foxhole just as Tesla collapsed against the side of the hole. Hall grabbed him by his web gear and violently dragged him down in the hole, collapsing on top of him.

"What the hell!?"

Then the grenade went off a short distance in front of their hole.

Another heavy burst from Sonny and Garr seemed to end things. The attack thinned out. The firing slowed. As the German withdraw began the crew became uninterested in firing at fleeing Germans. Exhausted, they collapsed in their foxholes. They were out of breath. Their hands shook. Sweat poured off their faces like rain.

It was several minutes later, their breathing still heavy, when everyone started to check on each other. Garr wanted an ammo check. Hall and Tesla were quiet. Sonny was griping about running low on ammo.

"That was a grenade…a grenade in our foxhole," Tesla rasped.

Hall could only stare back.

"You saved our lives. You saved my life."

"You…woulda' done the same," Hall answered weakly as he collapsed in the deepest part of the foxhole.

"Yeah…but you did. You saved…both of us," Tesla gasped. He collapsed against the rear of the foxhole and sank down next to Hall. Putting his hands on his forehead, he pushed his helmet back until it toppled off his head and rolled onto the ground.

Nodding, Hall could only do the obvious. He checked his

ammo, reloaded as best he could with what was left and leaned back and closed his eyes. He didn't need to see what was transpiring now. He could hear everything. Sonny was muttering to himself, a vain attempt to reconnect with a saner world. Garr was reloading, stopping only to ask Sonny if he was alright. Tesla was weeping. Hall understood. Everyone dealt with combat in their own way. Some men, like Sergeant Garr, tried to carry on like it was just another day at the grind. Others muttered unintelligibly about simple things like needing more bullets. Still others wept. Hall retreated to baseball, remembering his days on the mound and wondered, even here in a foxhole on a lonely chunk of rock in France, how he could finally master a split finger fast ball. It wasn't bravado. It wasn't mental instability. It was self-defense.

The Second Rangers endured four more attacks. They were relieved two days later by 5th Rangers approaching from the East. By then they were out of food and almost dry of ammo. Of the two hundred and twenty five in the original strike force, ninety were still standing. Four of the ninety occupied two foxholes on the far right flank.

2

Rain Delay

Atlas Town, Pennsylvania
Present Day

Jonny Morris swung into the parking lot of the Atlas Globe with his radio blasting and his windows rolled down. It was a John Fogerty song called Centerfield. Jonny sang along as he whipped the old Chevy Impala into a parking space.

"Put me in coach! I'm ready to play…today! Put me in coach! I'm ready to play! Today! Oh…look at me! I can be! Centerfield!"

By the end he was doing more shouting than singing. Everyone in the lot could hear him but that's what he wanted. Today he was up. It was a crisp Fall day. Baseball was getting down to the wire. Pittsburg was in the hunt for a pennant. He was feeling good. He still played a mean baseball game at twenty five himself. It didn't seem like he lost anything since his college days. Then he was known as Masher Morris, for the way he treated a certain baseball in a game during his sophomore year. It was a reputation that served the psyche real well most of the time.

He turned the engine off, letting the radio die at the same time. Then he swung the door open and practically leaped from his seat to start off across the lot, slinging his backpack over his shoulder as he went. He didn't lock the door. Striding across the lot he waved to some and called out to some others. It was getting easier to feel good these days. He was starring on the local softball team, he was writing his sports articles for the Globe and the Nationals were coming to Pittsburgh for a critical three game stand with the Pirates. And he was going to be there. And for all three games if he could help it.

Everything seemed so right this day that he let his full six foot frame out as he strode into the front door. No walking slumped over today. No staring at the ground as he cruised underneath the statue of Atlas holding up the world, the words *Atlas Town Globe* etched at the base. He glided through the front doorway without touching it, benefitting from the effort of the person who went ahead of him, the same person he then passed in the hall and beat to the inside door of the Globe. Swinging the door open he tumbled into the office like a drunk crashing a party. Yep, things were looking up. Baseball was big again. He was big again. He even had his favorite buzz cut that made him feel like the players of old, like Mantle or Maris. His muscles still showed. He was slim. Fast. Could still field a wicked hot grounder, throw hard from any place on the field and drive the ball deep. Everything was clicking even though he didn't know why or how. But they were. So he just went with it. Masher Morris was back.

He always knew he would get over her. He just needed some time.

"Hey Betts!" he called out as he reached his desk. Slamming his backpack down on top he gazed over her way with the biggest smile he could work out of his face.

"Aren't we cheery?" she called back.

She was really Elizabeth Ann Carlson. She ran the office of the Atlas Town Globe for Ron Faber, owner and senior editor. She was about 50, though no one could, or would, say for certain. She was attractive with an old style hairdo from the 40s. She wore those classy dresses and was always accompanied by some dreamy perfume that interrupted the thought process with distraction and dreams. She had a kind of Hollywood appeal but she wasn't pushing it. She would look you straight in the eye and tell you what's what or she would gaze back at you like she was settling into your eyes, as if daring you to think that she was flirting with you. She did a great job in the office. It could hardly run without her. Everyone called her Betts.

"Yes we are! We are cheery today!" he answered without looking.

The office had just started to get busy. There were only six other people who worked there, seven if you counted Luther, the maintenance man. He was a baseball player in his day, too. But Faber had everyone working a little bit of everything. Jonny was into Sports for the last few months. He was good at it. People wrote in and said as much so the boss turned him loose to write at will. It increased subscriptions and that meant advertising. That meant money.

"Someone's a little too happy!"

Jonny looked up to see another young guy plop down on top of his desk. It was Sammy Diver who drove the truck delivering the Globe all over town. Jonny gave in to temptation to play games with the name three months ago when Sammy came on board.

"Diver the Driver!" Jonny shot back. "Yes, I am a little too happy."

"Why so? I think I know," Sammy echoed with a tone loaded with humor.

"Because I'm Jonny Morris! Masher Morris! In the flesh!"

"Nah-nah-nah," Sammy answered. "It's the weekend. And the Nationals are coming to Pittsburgh…"

"Ah! You caught me!" Jonny cracked, holding his hands out in defeat. "Yes, it is the weekend and yes, the Nationals are coming to Pittsburg!"

"And you are going to be there?!"

"And I am going to be there! Right again!"

The two of them shared a short wave of bar room guffaws and then resorted to the mandatory high fives with all the extra stuff that goes with it. Sammy started off, walking backwards while he flashed the thumbs up sign to Jonny, turning at the last moment to head for the door only to stop and chat up Betts at her desk.

Jonny threw himself into his chair, letting it roll him away from his desk before he pushed himself back and started banging on the keys of his keyboard. Even logging in was pleasant this morning.

When his system started to come up he started his ritual. First, he would visit the coffee bar in the corner of the office. Then he would look to see if anyone brought in donuts. Someone did. He ate the first one while sipping coffee and talking to Freddy Walker who covered weather and local news items. When that was done, he grabbed the second donut, topped off his coffee and returned to his desk, waving to Betts again as he navigated past the tables of printers, servers and cubicles that by now were filled with people visible only by the tops of their heads as they went about clacking away at their keyboards.

“Okay,” Jonny said under his breath. He started his mail application and began to go through his mail to start the day.

“Sexual harassment…delete…ethics…delete…whistleblower rights…delete…another sexual harassment…delete…manage my portfolio…delete…ah! Receipt for my reservation in Pittsburgh. Save…and print.”

When he hit print he looked over at the printer to make sure it was responding. When it spit out the receipt he got up to retrieve it.

“Pittsburgh, here I come,” he said as he slid back into his chair, letting it roll him away from his desk again. Then it hit him. Air that suddenly circulated about him like a hood that was thrown over him in an instant. It was the only aroma that could defeat the allure of morning coffee.

“Hello Betts,” he said.

“Hello Jonny. Got a big weekend planned?”

She knew he did. This was just her way of starting a chat session. But having a chat session with Betts was usually pretty cool. He had to make a better effort not to gaze at her chest this time, though.

“Yeah. A big weekend. Pittsburgh and—”

“The Nationals,” she interjected. “Yeah…I got that part of the story. I got another story for you. Do you want to hear it?”

“Another story?”

“Yep.”

“Fire away.”

“She called again last night,” Betts said in a hushed voice. “She was in a bad way. I mean…a real bad way.”

A wave of silence erupted like the Kraken rising from beneath the waves without making a sound.

"Now I know you don't want to hear this," Betts said defensively. "I wouldn't mention it if I didn't think there was a need."

Jonny could only stare back. He knew what this was all about but he didn't want to hear it right now. He had his receipt. He was just about to go into Ron's office and ask to leave early. He was going to promise to write a human interest piece about the game as an extra. About what exactly he had no idea.

"I don't want to hear this, Betts," he said rubbing his forehead.

"I know you don't! But I get the calls at all hours! You two are still my friends! So I am getting the calls. She wants to talk to you. So why don't you just…call her?"

Jonny went back to his computer screen, answering as he pretended to return to work.

"Can't call her. That ship has sailed."

Betts stood there, watching. Then she took a deep breath as she shook her head.

"I'll just forward her calls to you," she said.

"It all goes to voice mail."

"Then it'll fill up your voice mail!" she snapped.

"Betts! Listen!" Jonny said as he got out of his chair. "I'm sorry she's calling you. Tell her to stop. Tell her to stop bugging you. Tell her to go back to the guy she hooked up with at Green's Bar. Tell her anything you want but don't tell her that you'll talk to me about this stuff again!"

The two stood there in a wordless air, letting the remnants of the conversation drift away as echoes in a vast cave.

"Well okay, then," she said caustically. "So you don't want any news that's uncomfortable." She backed off and turned to leave.

"Oh, by the way," she said turning back to face him. "Ron

wants to see you. This morning." She turned and started walking away but turned back again after only a few steps.

"This morning, Jonny. By that I mean now."

And she was gone.

He sat there a few moments, looking at his desktop. It was an action shot of Bill Mazeroski hitting that momentous home run off the Yankees in game seven of the 1960 World Series in Pittsburgh. But he couldn't look at it for long. The Senior Editor was waiting.

"You wanted to see me, boss?"

Ron Faber looked up from his editorial he was typing and waved Jonny in at the same time.

"Close the door."

As Jonny swung the door closed he glanced around Faber's office. It was a compact affair, loaded with filing cabinets, a printer, a few extra boxes of printing paper lying on the floor and his really cool desk with all the accessories on top, military stuff like the hand grenade with the label on the pin that read '1' and the sign beneath that read 'Take a Number.' He was a gruff looking guy, no nonsense type with thinning gray hair somewhere in his early sixties. He had a little of the middle age spread but still muscular, big in the chest and arms, eyes that had a tendency to stare.

"Jonny Morris!" he boomed as he sat back from his keyboard. "I heard you had a big night with the bat last night!"

"Three for four. Three runs batted in. Made some plays at second that Mazeroski would have liked! We're in the hunt for the playoffs!"

Faber laughed.

"Bill Mazeroski," he mused as he sat back in his chair. I was ten years old when he hit that home run. Heard it on the radio."

"You heard it live?!"

"Well, yeah man! Not like seeing it live, though."

"Man, to even hear that live, that's a great kick for a ten year old!" Jonny wisecracked. "Makes me wonder what you did for an encore at twenty!"

Faber stared back almost as if he didn't recognize Jonny all of a sudden.

"At twenty I was in Da Nang."

Jonny stared back, suddenly caught in his first clumsy moment of the day.

"Oh…right."

He shifted in his seat, desperate to get the discussion back on the rails.

"Betts told me you needed to see me asap."

"Yeah," he said slowly, sifting through some papers. When he found a certain one he leaned back and scrutinized it briefly, adjusting his glasses with one hand so he could get the right part of his bifocal on the text.

"I have a special assignment for you—"

"You remember I agreed to write a human interest article this weekend?"

"Human interest article…this weekend? What's the angle?"

Jonny was stuck. He didn't have an angle. He was getting a little disgusted with himself now, being as he was now 0-2 in Faber's office.

"You don't have an angle. So we go with my plan."

Jonny sighed.

"Okay, boss. You have something in particular you're looking at?"

"Yep. It requires a little travel."

Travel was good. Jonny Morris was a man on the road waiting to happen.

"Where to?" he said anxiously.

"I need you to go to…" Faber took a moment to read through his document, then, putting his finger on the page to mark his place he looked up at Jonny.

"Smicksville."

Jonny stared back a moment, working hard to conceal his grin.

"What-ville?"

Faber looked up, an impatient look on his face and his eyes doing that staring thing.

"Smicks…ville," he said slowly.

Jonny straightened up in his chair.

"What's in Smicksville?"

"There's a funeral and a memorial. But it isn't an ordinary funeral. There's a vet from World War Two that passed away and there is going to be a gathering of his close friends who served with him. I want you to cover it."

Jonny thought for a moment.

"Wouldn't Fred be a better fit for this?"

"No."

"He does all the human interest stuff."

"No."

"C'mon, Ron! Fred does the local stuff!"

"This isn't local! It's Smicksville. About two hours away."

Faber straightened his glasses on his face.

"Besides, he doesn't do all the local or all the human interest stuff. Weren't you going to write me a human interest piece this weekend? In Pittsburgh? That's closer than Smicksville. But you had no angle even by today. Friday. Now you do."

Jonny sighed.

"Okay," Jonny grumped in reply. "I can leave first thing Monday morning…or possibly late Sunday evening…"

Jonny looked up to see Faber shaking his head.

"What?"

"You leave tonight. The viewing is tomorrow. Funeral next day. I think that's in Williamsport. Then a memorial service on Monday in Smicksville. I want you to be there for the viewing and the Memorial. You can skip the funeral if you want. Then you can write your article."

"Ron," Jonny said in disbelief. "I am headed to Pittsburgh tonight for the series with Washington."

"Jonny, you're headed to Smicksville for a viewing, funeral and memorial service. There are other three game home stands you can cover."

"This is a big home stand! These don't happen every day!"

Faber threw his glasses down on his desk. Jonny had gone to the well once too often.

"As a matter of fact, Jon, they do happen every day. Every day during baseball season there are three game homestands. So...are the Pirates out of the race if they drop all three?" he shouted.

"No."

"Are they a shoo-in if they win all three?"

"No," Jonny sighed.

"Then it doesn't matter if they split 1-2 or 2-1 either? Right?"

Jonny slumped down in his chair. Just a moment ago his life

was arcing skywards and headed to Three River Stadium. Now he was going to Smicksville for funerals and viewings. His mood was taking a cold shower.

Faber took a breath, rubbing his forehead and then picking up his glasses.

"I want you on this story because you write a very particular way," he said coolly. "I don't want sawdust on this piece. I want the real thing. The real story, with all the nooks and crannies that go with it. The people stuff. You write that covering sports. But sports is just sports. This is real. These men are real. They fought a war. I know all about that. So I know there's a story there. You find it. You write it. Make the senior editor happy. Thirty or forty years from now you'll remember what you wrote and why. You won't have a clue how Pittsburgh did on that three game home stand. And you won't care."

"I don't know what you want from me," Jonny said shaking his head. "I write sports."

"Bullshit. You've been writing sports. But you wrote for real before that. Remember that first article you showed me before you started working here? That piece about people getting thrown out of their homes for failing to pay property taxes? Remember that? You were pretty indignant, as I recall. You said it was an insult that government screws up the economy, watches tons of jobs go overseas and then throws people out of their homes because someone in India has their job. Remember that?"

Jonny could only sit and listen. He remembered the article. It was a hundred years ago now, though.

"Now listen up," Faber went on. "I know there's something going on with your personal life. I know that can affect people. But enough already. Get over the dark clouds or whatever is going on with you, resolve the problem and get back to being you! Move forward for Christ's sake!"

Without saying a word, Jonny nodded and got up. He turned as he started to open the door.

"Travel Pay?" he asked.

"As always."

"What about my reservation in Pittsburgh?"

"Cancel it. I'll reimburse you for any fees you incur."

"Tomorrow morning soon enough?"

"No. Tonight. I want you in Smicksville tonight. Get your room and start looking for all the people you are going to want to talk to."

Like the bartender and a waitress Jonny thought.

Jonny turned and left, making sure the door slammed behind him.

Faber went back to his editorial.

"I damn sure don't want you drinking yourself stupid down at Green's bar tonight and blowing the assignment," he muttered.

Smicksville, Pennsylvania

Jonny whipped his Chevy into the parking lot for Tally's Tavern. It was ten at night on Friday but it might as well been Tuesday morning. There were six cars in the lot besides his. He couldn't hear any music coming from inside even after he switched his car off, killing the radio. His mood was already dark for having to make the trip but it got even darker when the radio reported the Nationals on the verge of taking game one in Pittsburgh.

He sat back in his seat gazing straight ahead at Tallys. It seemed that he needed to get his game face on just to sit somewhere to eat a cheeseburger and drink a beer or two in Smicksville. Especially when beer and hotdogs at Three River Stadium taste so much better.

And that still goes even if the Pirates lose.

Reluctantly he dragged himself from the car and lazily pushed the door closed. He didn't lock it. Then he started the short but tortuous walk across the gravel parking lot on his way to the front door. He was trying not to feel sorry for himself, and trying not to think of what Betts told him earlier. He was just getting convinced that he was over her.

"Lorraine," he said with a sigh. Then he pulled the door open and readied himself for the local culture. Maybe there'd be a television on the wall, at least.

"What'll it be?" the bartender asked. Jonny took one look at him and instantly let his first impressions run wild.

This guy was an earthy type with a careworn face and tired eyes. His brown work shirt with *Lou* stitched into the breast pocket told Jonny this guy was a sure local, the type who was a part of this little town as much as a foundation is to a house. Of course, he might have come home after years abroad, a world traveler that tired of moving around, deciding instead to put roots down in the quietest town he could find. He might be looking to escape his past of living a life of other worldly adventure. Maybe the money ran out. Or maybe he had family here. Maybe he was looking for someone. Maybe he was hiding from someone.

And I'm just getting started, Jonny told himself. *I could have written that human interest piece on one beer and a burger and two more minutes to make it all up.*

"Kitchen open?"

"Yep. Need a menu?"

"Nah. Cheeseburger. Lettuce. Tomato. Fries."

"Cheddar cheese. American cheese or—"

"American cheese."

"Drink?"

"Beer."

"We have—"

"I'll take whatever kind is the closest tap to me."

The bartender laughed.

"Now that I haven't heard before!"

Jonny watched while the bartender poured his first glass. Maybe he was Tally. Jonny wasn't going to ask. But this guy with the jeans and brown shirt, work shoes that did a *thump thump* as he walked behind the bar, the not quite clean shaven face and the salt and pepper hair looked like he sprouted from the floorboards of Tally's Tavern. He had to be a local. Maybe he never went anywhere in his life.

When he returned he slid the glass of beer in front of him.

"Let me know what you think of that," he said as he turned to start the food order.

Jonny took a hit from the mug, a long, desperate pull intended to save him from the obscurity of a far off town at the edge of the world in the middle of Pennsylvania. When he set the mug down he didn't let go of it.

"There ya go!" someone at the end of the bar shouted. Jonny strained an eye to make out enough to tell him that the Pirates weren't going down easily.

Christ. That's where I should be he thought. The excitement of the game filtered down to his end of the bar but he wouldn't let it affect him. Even if the Pirates won, which they weren't going to do, he would still be here in Smicksville sitting in a dark bar with no women and no music. The only distraction was a professional baseball game that he was supposed to be at but wasn't. But there was a half dozen men down at the end that were watching like they were sitting on the third baseline. Their eyes were glued to the big screen mounted just above the bar.

Well, he thought. *might as well settle in, be miserable and drink the pain away.*

"Yeah! Yeah! Go!"

Jonny turned his head instinctively and tried to make out the excitement going on in the game. He was too far away. He craned his neck to catch a piece of the action without getting up. He could see the Pirates were putting men on base but he couldn't make out the situation, how many outs, balls and strikes, who was up and, come to think of it, he still didn't have a place to stay tonight.

He spun himself around on his chair, taking his mug of beer for the ride. Tallys was a quiet place, even with the television. Jonny guessed that the jukebox wasn't filled with heavy metal, if it played at all. The ceiling was low. There were pictures on the side wall at the other end but he couldn't make them out but several had stars mounted on the wall directly above the picture frame.

The front had all the windows and six booths with a lamp that burned a single 40 watt bulb beneath a glass shade that reflected red, green and yellow. There was a single couple in the booth at the end. They were quiet. Middle aged. Probably been in Smicksville all their lives. There had to be a lot of that in this town.

Turning back around he waited for the bartender to finish whatever he was doing under the bar. When he popped up again Jonny got his attention.

"Say…Lou…got a minute?"

Lou wandered down to Jonny's end wiping his hands in a towel.

"What'cha need?"

"I need a place tonight. Something in town if possible. Is there a motel or hotel?"

Lou thought a moment, taking the time to glance at the clock on the wall.

"Well, if you want in town…there's the Marple Hotel. But you need to be there by midnight. Ida usually locks up by then."

"Yeah! There's one! There's one!" someone shouted at the end of the bar.

"What happened Joe?" Lou called out to one of the men watching the game.

"We got one! Down two now!"

Lou turned back to Jonny.

"If you like I can call Ida and tell her she has a guest on the way. How about it?"

"Sounds good. Where's the Maple Hotel in town?"

"Marple Hotel. Goin' in on Main Street you see the library on the left. It's two blocks past that. On the left. It has a sign lit up when it's open. But I'll call and she'll wait. Not too late, though. Okay?"

"Got it," Jonny answered as he drained the last of his mug. When he set it down Lou grabbed it and started to fill it again.

"I guess the closest tap works for you tonight."

As Lou disappeared on his way back to the kitchen Jonny turned his attention to the baseball action at the other end of the bar. The game had suddenly gotten real tight judging by the occasional outbursts of beer laced guffaws. Again he thought of moving down to that end but he resisted. They weren't his crowd. But just then another great holler burst into the air like fireworks. It hung for several seconds as the action unfolded. Someone hit one in the gap. Jonny could hear the stadium going crazy over the noise from the men going crazy at the end of the bar. Then their voices suddenly became desperate, their hands waving in one direction or the other before dying away with a groan that reminded Jonny of a wounded lion. Someone doubled in the tying run but was caught off the bag in a base running error. Suddenly the baseball end of the bar was a wild soundtrack of 'what-ifs' and 'almosts.' Some pounding on the bar and some mild street talk. The Pirates had almost managed to pull it off. But it was going extra innings.

Shit. I could have been there... he thought with disgust.

Then Lou arrived with dinner.

Later, sometime around the eleventh inning, Lou wandered over to Jonny's end. He was pointing at the hands on his watch, telling him that midnight was the cutoff for the Marple Hotel. Jonny raised his hand in acknowledgement.

"Is it always this way on a Friday night here?"

"Well," Lou said as he glanced around. "I'm missing a few of my regulars. They usually come in with wives and girlfriends, boyfriends and so on."

"Oh," Jonny answered. "Something else going on tonight?"

Lou chuckled.

"Well, actually they're in Pittsburg tonight at the game. I doubt the screen would offer much compensation!"

Jonny groaned inside.

"Oh….yeah. That must be great…"

"Say," Lou said breaking in. "what're you doing in Smicksville on Friday night, going on Saturday morning?"

Jonny drained his mug once more and slid it away towards Lou.

"I'm covering the memorial service for a World War II vet," Jonny droned.

Lou started to pour the next draft.

"Oh…Hav Tescovitz? You covering that for a newspaper or something?"

Jonny nodded.

"The Atlas Globe."

"Atlas Globe…where's that?"

"Atlas Town."

Lou slid the fresh mug in front of Jonny.

"Now that's interesting. I wouldn't expect Atlas Town to be interested in a Smicksville vet."

"You'd have to know my senior editor."

Lou laughed.

"Did you know this…Hav Tescovitz?" Jonny asked.

"Not real well but I knew him. He came in here a few times with his wife."

"Really? Did you talk to him? What was he like?"

"A real sweet guy. His wife too. He always talked plants. You know, shrubs, flowers, growing tomatoes and so on. He grew some outrageous tomatoes."

"So he was well known for having a green thumb."

"Oh hell yeah. He won some recognition from the Horticultural Society of Pennsylvania, I think."

"Yeah? How'd he do that?"

"You know, I can't recall. Let me ask down at the other end. Hey Joe!"

A guy at the end reluctantly turned his head around, being heavily influenced by the game.

"Yeah, Lou?"

"What did Tescovitz do to win that award from the Horticultural Society?"

Looking back at the game once, the man turned to answer.

"He grew an annual…that…uhhh…behaved like a perennial."

Lou turned back.

"Yeah, I'm not much on flowers or gardening. I had to go to the authority. Joe's wife is big into that as well.

Jonny thought for a moment. He was trying to dig up an angle with Tescovitz's horticulture and the war but it was escaping him at the moment.

Then he heard the latest update from the game. It was going to the bottom of the twelfth inning.

"Well Lou," Jonny groaned as he slowly rose from the bar-stool. "I don't want to be late for Ida Marple."

"Ida Wolley."

"Huh?"

"Her name is Ida Wolly. She owns the Marple Hotel. It's been the Marple Hotel for about a hundred years," Lou said with a friendly laugh.

"Oh. Yeah. Well, Ida Wolley then. I'd like to stay for the game but this could take all night."

"Ok, Atlas Town Globe! Come back and see us!"

"Jonny left some money on the bar for a tip and started for the door. When he was halfway through and almost out of earshot of the game he heard the last joyous yawp of the evening. He stood there briefly trying to make out what was on the screen. After listening to the celebration for a few chaotic seconds he figured that the Pirates had come up with a walk off home run from the lead-off hitter. Jonny recalled the historical shot by Mazeroski in the '60 series against New York. It was almost like an echo in his ear even though he wasn't even alive when it happened.

"Looks like you saw the whole thing after all!" Lou called out to him as he stood there clapping his hands and laughing to the rafters.

Jonny nodded, doing his best to forget the irony. Suddenly though, he wasn't bitter. The Pirates had won. It was a great come from behind win for a team that was going places. Waving good-night, he walked out and let the door close behind him.

Mazeroski Magic.

Cruising down the darkened Main Street, Jonny was straining to spot the police lurking around a corner. He had a good bit to drink and it wouldn't set with Faber if he started his stay in Smicksville by getting arrested. But after a short while he was able to convince himself that there wasn't a cop in the same time zone as this town. So when the library came up he started counting blocks.

Well, he said it was lit up. It shouldn't be too hard to spot, he thought.

But after two blocks he failed to see the lit sign that Lou spoke of. That's when he got a little stressed. He turned the music down and frantically looked at his watch and caught the time. It read 1207.

"She wouldn't lock up over 7 minutes?!" he snarled. He decided to crawl along another hundred feet or so before turning around. But just when it seemed that he had somehow missed his sign he caught something breaking through the dark. It was a small light, about 40 watts, shining through a sign that hung on an old iron post. Not a neon ad that was 15 or 20 feet in the air like he was expecting. There was tree branch that glided back and forth as the wind willed it, making it even more unlikely. It read 'Open.'

Jonny stopped the car in the street unable to make himself believe that this was the place. It was an old Victorian style house with gables and peaks stabbing at the evening sky, narrow windows at the top that pretended to scrutinize every visitor or passerby, what looked like a car from the 1940s parked in the driveway and a pile of steps that took you from the street up to the front door.

"So I'm staying with the Addams Family?!" he crabbed to himself. "Jesus, Ron. Are you trying to piss me off?!"

He slammed on the brake as he parked, making a quick shriek with the tires. Letting the radio play a few seconds, he kept the beat with the music on the radio while he readied himself for Ida Wolley. But not long. After all, it was now 1209.

"You're late," she said, holding the door as Jonny came through.

"Sorry, I missed it coming through the first time."

"You missed it...," she said suspiciously. She took a moment to turn a large lock on the front door, which gave her trouble at first and then with her other hand she flipped a switch. Jonny assumed that she had turned off her 40 watt bulb on her sign out front.

Ida Wolley was a seasoned, somewhat cynical woman of sixty or so. Her hair was formerly black but was now turning an ash grey. She was dressed in a bedtime coat of sorts and sported a cigarette dangling from her downturned lips. She was obviously worldly, Morris guessed. Outspoken and maybe even a little combative. He figured all that out for himself. And all before she said much of anything.

"Tell me, how do you miss the only hotel in town, with a light on in front, in the middle of the night?"

She stood there gazing him down, even though she was a full foot shorter than he was.

He stifled a laugh. His intuition had served him well.

She smiled finally and started leading him inside.

"You've been too long at Tallys, that's what your trouble is!"

"Guilty!" he answered.

When she got to the steps she stopped and turned.

"Well, here's the rules...no women...no drink...no loud music. You're on the second floor. Room number two."

She handed him a large metal key that was almost as long as his hand and nearly as heavy. He waited a second, in mild shock at seeing a metal key and not an electronic key card. He looked up as she started to turn away. Seeing as he appeared frozen in place, she turned to face him once more.

"Well I'm not going up there, dear. You can find it by yourself, right?"

"Right," he answered thinly. He started up the stairs but stopped himself.

"You have wireless here, don'tcha?"

Ida stopped and turned.

"Wireless what?"

He shook his head and laughed to himself. Really, he should have known.

"Ahhh,..nothing. Goodnight."

Ida turned and started again down the hall.

"Welcome to Smicksville," she said as she drifted away down the hall, a trail of smoke staying behind to guard the way.

In his room he threw the key on a small dresser. It made such a racket that he had to make a mental note that he wasn't carrying a card key but a fairly large piece of scrap metal.

"Hope I didn't wake the guests," he scoffed. "especially the ones that only come out at night…"

He laughed aloud, shaking his head in disbelief over his arrival in Smicksville. When the humor subsided he looked around for the television. There was a small one in the corner, looked to be about a 24 inch screen. He thought better of it.

"Mail," he said resignedly. Kicking his shoes off and stretching out across the bed, he pulled his laptop from its case and opened it up.

I've got mail, he sang to himself. He tapped the top of the computer impatiently waiting for the screen to produce the goods. But when the mail app came up there was nothing to see. Suddenly the logic of that struck him like a messenger bringing bad news that was not unexpected. He was, after all, in Smicksville and the Marple Hotel had no wireless. No wireless anything.

I've got no mail, he sang again.

Thinking what to do next, he then opened up a folder that he kept under the Inbox. After some clicking there was that little *Baroop!* sound that he had programmed to go off every time there was unopened mail in the folder he was in. He stared at the screen for a few seconds. There was a ton of unopened mail. Mostly from her. He closed the app.

"Better set an alarm," he mumbled. He looked around and saw the clock on the nightstand. After briefly scrutinizing the alarm setting procedure he pushed the clock away in disgust.

"Is there one thing in this place that is 21st century…besides the calendar?" he cracked impatiently. He decided to use his watch. He could program that in his sleep, which was not far off. Besides, his watch alarm made a *Baroop* sound as well. He programmed it for 8 AM.

Baroop! Baroop! Baroop! Baroop!

Jonny came to as if he had just washed ashore from a tragic shipwreck. Gathering his waking skills, he cleared his eyes and frantically gazed at his watch. Somehow a vision of a very unhappy Ron Faber loomed in his mind.

"8:30!" he rasped. Suddenly he was in the shower, which was more like an anointing, then he ripped a toothbrush from his overnight bag and gave the teeth a once over. He threw his cloths on and stood adjusting his tie and debating himself whether or not he should opt for mouthwash as well.

I'm not on a date! came the frantic thought. *Just don't make out with anyone!* He splashed some cologne on and, grabbing his laptop, without the case, and his notebook and pen he was out the door. He didn't bother to lock it.

He pulled up across the street, his tires sliding a bit on some gravel in the road. He strained his eyes to make out the name of the funeral home that the Viewing was being held.

"Gantz Funeral Home," he said aloud. "This is it!" He killed the radio with the ignition and struggled to get out of the car as fast as possible. It was a few minutes after nine o'clock in the morning.

Inside there was the expected funeral music played, mournful droning of a single high pitched organ, and a small multitude of people whose presence was betrayed only by an irregular hum, scraps of conversation at the very bottom of the human ear. Jonny looked around, trying to get his bearing and his senses in full reporting gear. When his eyes had adjusted to the dimness of light and the air of quiet grief, he gazed at the display in the ante room. There were several photos of a young man, taut…and smiling, at the very onset of his youth, posing in military dress, posing with family, with friends. And then there were the photos, now aged and turning a little yellow of him with his comrades in full combat gear, his Brothers in Arms. Photos with unknown faces looking back through time, from unknown places in the world, the scar of war all around them. Yet even War was powerless to douse the optimism, the joy, even if only momentary, of the young men staring back at the camera, their hopeful grins on their faces exuding the confidence and panache of a generation. It was all a long time ago in a society that lived a long time ago, one whose numbers had by now nearly vanished.

Then there were the flowers. Not the typical array of flowers for remembrance or grieving, but a seemingly endless march of color, shape and aroma that confronted the visitor like a frontal attack in war. Instinctively he reached for his cell phone and started the camera app. Though he had never done so before, he was drawn to the display. It had to be captured. It would go with his article. He used the Wide Angle.

Eventually he was able to draw away from the back with its photos and flowers that stretched all the way to the front where the casket was. He made his way up the side, slowly taking in the faces of the visitors, imagining where they had come from, what their names were, how they knew the man. Were they family? Friends? Neighbors? He forced his mind to start turning angles in his head, trying to generate ideas for what he would start writing this evening. At the front he could make out who he assumed was the widow and family or close friends. It would be tricky approaching them. It wouldn't do to just jump in there like Jimmy Olsen cub reporter. But the viewing was only an hour and it was already nearly nine thirty in the morning. So he decided to make his move. As he made his way across the front of the Viewing he noticed Ida Wolley sitting two rows back. She noticed him but said nothing. It was just as well. He was heading over to the family.

"Missus….," Jonny said, taking a second to check his notes for the name again. "…Tescovitz?"

A small white haired lady stared back at him, her aging eyes attempting to make sense of the voice addressing her.

"Tescovitz," she answered thinly, traces of a once thick European dialect still present. She was slight, very slight, in fact. She couldn't have been more than five feet, maybe an inch more. Seated she was almost doll-like, a present for a five year old waiting for daddy to come home. She had snow white hair topping off her black dress. There was a veil but it was pulled back at the moment. Her face had thinned with age, revealing sharp cheekbones, thin lips and eyes that smiled sadly, defeated by the inevitability of time.

"Yes," Jonny answered awkwardly. "Sophia Tesco—witz?"

"I am Tzofiya Tescovitz," she answered. Her voice was light but old world, with a heavy accent.

"OK. Uh, I'm Jonny Morris…from the Atlas Globe…"

"The…what, dear…?"

"He's from a newspaper, mama." A sixty-something lady sitting next to Sophia Tescovitz came to the rescue. She was only slightly larger than Sophie. Her hair was honey brown going gray and it was drawn up in what looked like an old world fashion. She wore black as well.

Next to her sat two elderly men and one younger man, maybe a teenager. They took small notice of the conversation going on right next to them. The two older men were Hav's brothers, maybe. The boy, a nephew. Or would that be a grandnephew?

"The Atlas Globe is very interested in running a story about your husband, Hav Tescovitz."

Sophie nodded politely. The woman seated next to her leaned in and got her attention.

"They want to interview you mama."

The two had a short conversation while Jonny waited. One of the elderly men turned to look at him. His gaze wasn't unfriendly but it wasn't exactly a basket of cheer either.

"Hello. I'm Sarah. Sophia is my mother."

The two shook hands briefly.

"Would it be possible to interview your mother this weekend?" Jonny asked. "And maybe other family members as well?"

Jonny turned to motion to the other three seated next to the women.

"Well, let me ask…I think so…hold on…"

Sarah turned back to Sophia and the two resumed their hushed discussion. Jonny strained to appear that he wasn't listening while, in fact, he was straining to hear everything that was being said. When Sarah finished speaking with her mother she stood up and spoke with the men. That conversation was equally difficult to hear. So Jonny wrote it off and just waited for the answers to come.

"Can you come this evening? Around six o'clock?" Sarah said, interrupting her conversation with the others.

"Six. Yep. I can make that."

Sarah returned to the men and then back to Sophia. When everything seemed to be finalized she straightened up again and spoke once more with Jonny.

"Well," she said with a quick smile. "That wasn't so easy!" Jonny laughed dryly. Then Sarah continued. "Ok. Come tonight at six. We're on Story Road, second right going east out of town. After that, we're one mile on the left. Small white Cape Cod with a broken white fence. You can't miss it!"

Jonny scribbled the directions down in his notebook, nodding as he went.

"Can I get the names of the other family members?" he asked, pointing to the three men.

"Oh! Sarah answered. "You want to interview them as well?"

"If it's alright with everyone."

Sarah glanced over at the men.

"Well, these men are from my father's time in the war. We consider them family but—"

"Oh!" Jonny blurted out. "That's great! Can I speak with them as well?"

"I suppose so…," Sarah answered slowly. "They'll be there anyway. Can't make them talk if they don't want to!" she said with a sarcastic grin.

"No problem," Jonny answered. "But….wait…this young man sitting here. He couldn't have been in the war. Who might he be?"

"Oh," Sarah answered sheepishly. "No. He couldn't have been. This is Walter. He's named after his uncle…or…great uncle. He was with Hav when they attacked on D-Day."

"Is he here today?"

"Is…he here…," Sarah asked with some confusion.

"Walter's Uncle. Walter Senior."

"Oh, no. Sorry. Walter Senior is gone now. Sorry."

"That's alright."

"But here is Charlie Garr, father's Sergeant in the war…"

Jonny shook hands with Charlie.

"And here is Sonny Provenzano. He was there, too."

Jonny shook hands again.

"And you are Walter Junior," Jonny said to the youngest member of the party.

"Yeah," he answered faintly. "Walter Johnson."

"Right. So your father's brother was with Hav on D-Day?"

"That's enough…!" a sudden voice echoed. When Jonny looked over it was Charlie Garr stretching out his hand and giving the 'halt' sign. "We're having no interviews now."

Jonny nodded and slowly backed off, packing his notebook away. He had broken a cardinal rule. He let his emotion run wild in front of him. Now he might have an enemy in at least one of the interviewees. He waved farewell to Sarah and Sophia, holding up the directions he had jotted down. Sarah waved a very cautious hand back at Jonny. She was very conscious of Charlie Garr's displeasure with the reporter.

Jonny quietly left the viewing, not speaking to anyone. Outside he went over his notes once more as he made for his car. When he got in he started it up. The radio came on with the start of the engine. As he finished looking over everything he had written in the funeral home he noticed the radio playing a familiar song. He recognized it. An old one from The Flamingos called I Only Have Eyes For You. He drifted in the melody for a moment or two. It had been their song. Disgusted he punched the next number on the radio starting a new station. The next song was better. An old Beatles hit.

"I....should have known better!" he sang as he pulled away. "...should have known better with a girl like you!"

3

The Story Road Beginning

Heading east out of Smicksville the town disappears quickly. Down the road, around a bend and the trees and bushes take over everything your eyes see. A lonely countryside appears out of nowhere, though you aren't really surprised to see it. It's as if there is no Smicksville and no town at all for hundreds of miles.

"Story Road," he called out as he made the right hand turn. Then it was a short mile, more like half a mile really, and he found the Cape Cod with the broken fence on the left hand side of the road. He pulled in, shut the car off, killing the radio and got out.

"You made it, Mister Morris," Sarah said as she held the door open.

"I did!"

She led him inside to the living room where everyone was sitting and chatting. Sarah introduced the reporter to Sophia again, just to make sure everyone knew each other. Then to Charlie Garr, Sonny Provenzano and Walter Johnson Jr., the grand-nephew of Corporal Walter Johnson.

"Mister Morris," Sarah began. "I'd like you to meet Connie Provenzano. She's Sonny's wife."

"Hello," Jonny said politely as he took her hand. Connie was as frail as Sophia. A little taller but obviously very weak. She merely held onto Jonny's fingers a little and then let go. She was sitting next to Sophia on a sofa while Sarah was on Sophie's right in a chair. The two war veterans were seated together on a smaller couch on the ladies' left.

Then Sarah spoke quietly to Morris.

"Sonny is a bit hard of hearing. Ok?"

"Sure," Jonny answered with a smile.

"Mister Morris," Sophia began. "we have coffee. And drink. Would you care for any?"

"No. Nothing, thanks."

"I'll have one," Garr said mechanically. He grabbed a whiskey bottle on the small table and filled his glass. Then he filled Sonnys.

"Oh," Sophia began. "Then, have you had dinner? We ate but there are leftovers…"

"No thank you, Missus Tescovitz. Really. I ate earlier." The fact was he hadn't eaten too recently. But he didn't want to get distracted from his work. He had plans to get everything he needed here and beat a retreat to Tally's Tavern, or somewhere else, and start typing his article amidst cheeseburgers, fries and beer. Besides, he had already impressed himself by remembering to pronounce Sophia's last name correctly. Was the second Pittsburg-Washington game on television?

"I thought we could begin the interview?" he said as he situated himself, powering his laptop up and starting a recording session.

There was a short silence. Sarah leaned over to her grandmother, apparently to remind her why Morris was there.

"Yes, I remember dear," she said. Then, turning to Morris, she fixed a friendly stare on him and signaled ready with her hand.

"Ok," he said excitedly. "You don't mind if I record this, right?"

"No," Sophia answered.

"Jonny Morris, at the home of Sophia Tescowitz, Story Road, Smicksville Pennsylvania."

Sophia looked back and forth between Sarah and Morris obviously confused.

"Are you…asking me?"

He looked back, a bit startled until he understood that Sophia was not a technologically versed human being.

"Oh no! I am just getting my recording ready!"

Assured, Sophia sat back and waited.

"You might want to sit closer," Garr said. Morris nodded quickly and pulled his chair in so he was sitting very close to Sophia.

"Sophia Tescovitz, your husband was Hav Tescovitz?"

"Yes."

"When did you meet?"

Sophia thought for a moment, a distant smile appearing like a ghost ship across her face.

"We were High School sweethearts," she said. "Hav asked me to his Junior Prom dance. We dated after that."

"When did you marry?"

"1940," she said slowly.

"And then he went off to war? He was drafted?"

"No."

"No?"

"No, he wasn't drafted. He signed up after Pearl Harbor."

"Ohhhh," Jonny replied.

"We all did," Garr interjected. "All across the country."

"I see," Jonny said. Then Sonny broke in.

"There were guys…that…there were guys, ya know? That couldn't go. Ya know? There was something wrong with them. Right?"

"Yeah," Garr added.

"These guys…they couldn't go…so they killed themselves. Right? They killed themselves because they couldn't go."

"Yeah," Garr repeated.

Jonny glanced over at Sophia who was nodding very slightly. The conversation was making her sad so he moved on.

"Your husband was sent to fight in Europe, correct?"

"Yes. They sent him to fight at Normandy…with the…rest of the 2nd Rangers."

"You remember his unit?" Jonny asked incredulously.

"Yes. Hav was 2nd Ranger, Fox Company. He was a rifleman."

Nodding, Jonny moved on to the next question. He was impressed with Sophia's showing so far but he was afraid that he would exhaust her knowledge too quickly or tire her out. He didn't want that.

"What did Hav say about the Normandy battle? Anything?"

"Hav didn't fight at Normandy. He fought at Point Du Hoc."

A little exasperated, Jonny was kicking himself for not learning more about the battle before the interview.

"It was all known as D-Day, Mister Morris," Garr added. "But Normandy is usually reserved for the beach battle."

"The 2nd Rangers weren't at the beach?"

"Yesss," Garr added again, though there was some impatience in his voice. Jonny caught a glimpse of Sarah who was getting that *'uh-oh...now he's done it'* look on her face. Garr continued.

"2nd Rangers fought at the Pointe, OK? All except Charlie Company. They landed on Omaha."

"It was a mistake," Sonny said. "Charlie Company was being held in reserve…until the landing…the landing was determined to be…ya know? Determined to be feasible. But the assault got started…too late…"

"Too late," Garr echoed.

"Their supply…went to Omaha as well," Sophia added. "My Hav…and Charlie and Sonny…and Walter here—"

Sarah turned to look at her mother. She leaned over to speak to her but everyone could hear.

"Mama," Sarah began. "Walter didn't go…"

"What…?"

"I said, Walter didn't go. That Walter is gone now."

"Sophia looked over at Walter. He smiled thinly at her but said nothing.

"Oh…oh, of course not. I'm sorry."

"Maybe…maybe the interview is goin' on too long…" Sonny said as he tried to speak with some confidentiality. His hearing problems, however, caused him to speak louder than needed. His remark was easily overheard by everyone.

This made Jonny panic. Despite Sophia's apparent absent mindedness, she was fairly savvy as to what happened on that day of the invasion. He was intrigued and wanted more. He decided on a reporter's ploy, of sorts, in a last ditch attempt to keep the interview going. He would divert his attention to Garr who was more on top of things, Sonny Provenzano would catch a little as well and then he would return to Sophia for more on her husband.

"Well, I only have a few more questions…perhaps I should just move along and finish up?" He looked at Charlie Garr after he said this. He was the man who could sway this activity one way or the other. Garr reluctantly nodded in approval. So he re-positioned his laptop with the microphone and began again.

"You were in charge of the landing at…Point Du Hoc?"

"I was the ranking NCO."

"Exactly what went wrong with the landing?"

Garr took a swallow from his drink. Looking at Morris like he was a beach that needed invading, he began, his voice more mechanical then human.

"Rudder was late. His boat Captain steered for Point Du Percee. To the East. It was too late to make up the time."

"So the landing was late? And that's why you missed your chance for reinforcements?"

"That's right. We had to make the call by 0730 hours. We didn't get started until almost then."

"Then Rudder went up the wrong side of the Pointe," Sonny added woefully.

"Why did he do that?" Jonny asked.

"Because he was…he was late, ya' know? He didn't want to lose any more time."

"So that was a good thing, right?"

Morris looked at both men who were saying nothing. Finally Garr spoke up.

"Maybe. Since we weren't getting any reinforcements

anyway…he could have stuck to the plan. But it was his call. He went up on our side—"

"And forgot the AA gun, ya know? It was there waiting for us on the right flank when we started inland. It was waiting for us, ya know?"

Morris thought for a moment, taking all this in. He had never known there was so much more to D-Day.

"An AA gun is….?"

"What?" Sonny asked.

"Anti Aircraft," Garr interjected.

"Oh, yeah," Sonny said softly. Anti Aircraft…"

Morris stared back uncertain as to the relevance. Garr picked up on it.

"It was there waiting for us, like Sonny said. It cut my guys up pretty good. Lost a lot of good men."

Morris nodded. Suddenly Garr's real personality was coming to the surface. He would figure prominently in the article. Faber would be ecstatic.

"Uh, I suppose it's safe to say that there were several casualties in this fight?"

Garr said nothing at first. He appeared mesmerized by the drink he was pouring. But it was obvious that the question went deeper than expected. It brought back bad memories.

"Ninety were left," he said distantly. "Ninety out of two hundred and fifty…"

Garr choked up some when he said that. Morris let it pass before continuing.

"They all died on the Pointe?"

Garr looked up as if shaken from a daydream. He downed his drink and poured another.

"What? Oh, yeah…the Germans counterattacked. Man did they…each time our little circle got smaller and smaller…ammo got less and less…guys got less and less…"

"I read earlier," Morris began thoughtfully. "that 2nd Rangers also destroyed some guns. Didn't you say there were no guns? Or did I hear wrong…?"

"Nah. You heard right. That was the first morning. Some of our men went inland. Found the guns about…ahhh—"

"About a mile or two away," Sonny added wistfully.

"Yeah, they were a mile or two away…" Garr's voice trailed away. He was drinking pretty heavily. Morris would have to pick the pace up.

"How did they—"

"Thermite charge," Sonny interrupted. Suddenly it appeared he could hear a pin drop during a thunderstorm. Morris caught a quick smile on Connie Provenzano's face.

"I suppose you've heard these stories several times, Missus Provenzano?"

"Well," she answered, her voice drifting across the room like a wisp of smoke from a cigarette. "I was just thinking how…how Sonny's hearing improves when we talk about D-Day."

Morris smiled.

"How about that, Mister Provenzano? Your hearing improves when you talk about the war?"

"What?"

Morris did a short double clutch. Then he repeated the question a little louder.

"Does your hearing get better when you talk about the war?"

"No. I don't like to talk about the war, ya know? I don't like to talk about it unless I'm with the people that were there."

Morris didn't respond. Connie was right. His hearing was different when Garr was talking. Not so good at other times.

"So," Morris started, a little desperate to begin a fresh angle. "Did the four of you form a bond, of sorts? After fighting at Pointe du Hoc?"

"We formed a bond during the fight. The man in the foxhole with you is your friend. He's your brother. He's your father. Your son. Your Guardian Angel. Yeah, we formed a bond."

"All four of us, ya know?"

"That would be you two, right? And the uh, Walter Johnson and Hav Tescovitz?"

"Yeah," Sonny added. Then he finished his drink and completed his thought. "the four of us. We was on the right flank, ya know? Sometimes…sometimes I feel like…I feel like we're still there, ya know?"

Sonny glanced over at Garr who was nodding his head. And pouring another drink.

"How do men like you, men who have fought these terrible battles, feel about the word 'Hero'?"

Morris felt this was one of his cornerstones of his article. The answer he got here would be key. At the same time he was beginning to feel guilty about leaving Sophia out of the loop but it was a difficult thing, balancing a person's stamina against the need to get a story. He resolved in his mind to get back to her after this question. If only he could.

"The heros…" Garr began, his voice sounding increasing awash in alcohol. "are the ones that didn't come back."

Morris let the words hang in the air. Sonny was nodding sadly. Connie was getting teary eyed. Then there was Sophia. He was, after all, supposed to be here for her. But there was one person he hadn't spoken to yet. Walter Johnson Junior.

"So you're Walter Johnson. Relative of Walter Johnson, 2nd Rangers?"

The young boy stared back. He was atypically subdued. Not like a young man of his age.

"Yeah. I guess so."

"Now, how old are you?"

"I'll be nineteen next month?"

"So, Walter Johnson of the 2nd Rangers is not your uncle, right? I mean, you're too young to have him as an uncle."

"Yeah. I just call him uncle. Uncle Walt. He's…more like… a…great uncle…or something."

Morris nodded.

"Do you have memories of him from, things you have read or—"

"Nah. I get all I need from Sergeant Garr and PFC Provenzano."

"Oh! You address them by their rank?"

"Yeah. Always."

Morris glanced over at Garr and Provenzano.

"How about that? That work for you fellas?"

Garr smiled at Walter. Sonny stared straight ahead. Without looking Garr answered Morris's question.

"It's Ok. He's one of us."

"Yeah," Sonny rasped.

Connie grasped Sonny's arm as he began to tear up. Morris moved quickly to Sophia to finish.

"Sophia. Sorry to not get back to you! I have just one more question and then we're done."

Sophia smiled faintly and nodded.

"What do you remember most about Hav? Is it that first dance? The military experience? Your personal lives after the war?"

Sophia thought for the longest time. At one point Sarah leaned over to see if she was alright but Sophia held her hand up to signal she was.

"I remember," she said faintly, her accent piercing the air like a shard of sunlight through a dark cloud. "the day he left. It was overcast. There was some rain. I was cold. He was in uniform. I knew I would never see him again."

"Uh-huh. And how—" Morris began but Sophia cut him off.

"I remember…the day he came home. It looked like him… but it wasn't him. His eyes were…different. And he was different. He was hurt. He would stay hurt for the rest of his life. I knew that then. I remember that. And I remember…all the times in between. I wouldn't change any of that…even if I was to be made young again."

Sophia's answer hung in the air like a mist. Sonny and Connie were still. Walter was still. Sarah was gently rubbing Sophia's back. Charlie Garr had stopped drinking.

"I think that will do it," Morris said.

As he began to gather his things Sarah rose and left for the kitchen. Everyone else kept their seats. When he was all packed up Morris stood tall and waved farewell to everyone.

"Goodnight Mister Morris," Sophia said.

When he turned to leave Sarah was there to take him to the door.

"She alright, isn't she?" Morris asked of Sophia.

"Yes. Yes she's fine. She is ready for bed, though."

"I'm sorry that this went on for so long. I tried not to tax her too heavily."

"Yes. Well, she always likes to talk about her Hav. She'll be excited to see the article!"

"I'll give it my best. I think it will be a strong one."

"Good. Goodnight Mister Morris. Thank you for coming."

"Goodnight."

Driving back to Smicksville Morris began to turn his thoughts over in his head. It seemed he had enough on the main battle, the people, all except Walter Johnson. He also forgot to get any pictures. And then he remembered that Hav was known for his flowers. He needed to get some on that.

"So much to remember. I'll need to write this down when I get to Tallys."

He drove on. The radio was playing. It was tune by Philomena Begley called *'Start Living Again.'* He didn't recognize it.

4

Connie Provenzano

The game was on at Tally's Tavern. Pittsburg was behind again. But Jonny Morris was suddenly not interested. This time he grabbed a booth along the far wall with the framed photographs of servicemen hanging just above. The one above his booth had a black star mounted just above.

As he opened his laptop he could hear pieces of the game from the bar, scraps of conversation from the men watching. He glanced at the screen once but then he heard his laptop beep. Needed charging. He opened his laptop case and grabbed the power cable. Luckily there was an outlet on the wall under his table. While it charged he started to make a list of things in his notepad about issues and angles still to be resolved for the article.

"Booth this time, eh?"

Morris glanced up and saw Lou standing by.

"Yeah. Got some work to do. But I am hungry as a big dog, Lou!"

"What'll it be?"

"Two double cheeseburgers. Fries. Beer."

"Two doubles," Lou repeated. "Fries. Beer. Coming up."

Lou disappeared around the end of the bar and Morris went to work. He already knew how his article would end. It would end with Sophia's answer to his last question. It was a winner. As he scribbled away in his notepad his thoughts raced along, pushing his curiosity deeper and deeper, discovering loose ends to his article that he never expected. His questions started to pop up from everywhere and nowhere. It was like a repeat of the time he wrote the prize winning article about the people losing their homes to the tax man. What was the name of that article? He struggled to remember. Then it came to him. *Taxed Into The Street.*

Lou returned with the beer and just that quickly disappeared again.

No waitress, Morris thought.

He sat quietly for a moment, recalling his obsessive approach to a five thousand word treatise on the plight of lower class working people whose homes were being stolen by a man at a desk.

Takers tormenting the makers, he thought.

Jonny Morris felt the old familiar grip on his soul, the one that overshadowed everything else including the commotion at the end of the bar over the baseball game. His waking world mindset was being overrun by that sudden and unexpected pulling sensation that always took him for a deep dive into an article that was now becoming a tale. One that told stories that people hadn't heard. He had to start listing his curiosities.

Why is Charlie Garr still bitter? Was it the AA gun, or is it something else? How do Tescovitzs flowers play into this? How can they be MADE to play into this? Who is Walter Johnson? How does Walter Junior fit in? Where do these people live now?

Scribbling with his pen, his head being held with his free hand, Morris saw the parade of faces of the people he was getting ready to dig into. He was not looking forward to going back to Story

Road but he would if he had to. He couldn't let go now. He was hooked. He decided that he would make his point of entry through Garr. That would give him the other angle for Hav Tescovitz, a military angle. But Garr would be tough. Even though he was sixty some years older he still had the look of a killer. Not so with Provenzano. He had softened some. But Garr would go back to the Pointe and scale that cliff again. Fight again. Kill again. He had to be careful with him if he decided to bore down. You never know what you are going to find when you go too deep.

Just then Lou showed up with dinner.

"Here you go....Two doubles, Fries and Beer."

"Thanks Lou," Morris answered as he cleared his computer gear away.

"Say Lou, can you tell me anything about the men in these old photos?"

Lou scanned the wall and nodded.

"I should say so. I hung 'em. Let's see...first, all the ones with the dark star above were killed in action. The ones with the silver star survived to return home. The one above your booth is Joe Rake. He was killed at Anzio."

"Ok. So where were all these guys from? There looks to be about ten..."

"Well they were all from Smicksville."

Morris looked up in bewilderment.

"All of them from...here?"

"Yep," Lou replied. "Smicksville had a few more people in it back in the 1940s. All of them...are from here or...just outside of town."

Morris sat back.

"The bone of America," Morris muttered.

"What's that?"

"Oh, nothing. Just something for my article that I'm writing."

"Oh, that's right. You're the guy from the Atlas Town Globe. Writing about Tescovitz?"

"Yeah. Just spoke with his widow and some vets. Did you ever hear of Charlie Garr, or Sonny Provenzano? Or Walter Johnson?"

Lou shook his head.

"But I can tell you how to find out. Contact the Department of the Army. Or call the Veterans Office in Saint Louis. They keep all the records."

Morris nodded.

"That's a good idea, Lou. Thanks."

Morris resolved to do just that. But there was still a funeral and a memorial service to attend. He might get his answers then and there.

The next day, Sunday, was the funeral and interment. Morris had learned that the body was going to Williamsport for burial. He decided not to attend. He didn't want to come off like the paparazzi. Instead, he would work his article and his ideas. Try to get some support from the Globe and try to find a place that had wireless.

He pulled his Chevy into a gas station on Main. It was full serve, which surprised him but then didn't surprise him. When it was time to pay he chatted the attendant up.

"Is there a place, like a restaurant or café that has wireless?"

The attendant thought for a moment, taking the time to look up and down the street.

"Used to be the bakery on Elm," he said almost to himself. "But they closed. I think now the only place around here is the Carriage House."

"Carriage House. Where's that?"

"Five miles south on 953…after Grant Road…on the right. Can't miss it. You can get breakfast there and they have wireless."

Finally.

As he sped south on 953 he cranked his cell phone up and called Ron Faber at home. It was almost ten in the morning so he should be up and about. But the phone rang and rang at the other end and never picked up, which really annoyed Morris.

"God Almighty, Ron," he hissed. "Learn how to set up voicemail!"

He shut the phone off and tossed it on the seat.

"I have to get some on Walter Johnson. I have to get a little on Walter Junior. I need some on Charlie Garr…tie Tescovitz in through 2nd Rangers…wind up with a little on Sophia and then the finish with her last comment."

He was talking aloud, as if he was selling the idea to Ron Faber in his office. But there was still something missing. He didn't want to just report some dry facts. He wanted to get into the meat, as Faber said it. No sawdust.

"How should we remember Hav Tescovitz?" he mused. Then he was struck by a thought that showed up arm in arm with a not too distant memory. Quickly he grabbed his phone and hit a speed dial.

"He's not home, is he?!" he cried out as he hit the speed dial for the Globe. The one for Faber's office. It rang once.

"Hello Jon," Faber blurted out. "Tell me good things…!"

"Ron! I need a favor!"

"What is it?"

"I need you to reach out to the Army. I need some background on a guy that's dead!"

"Tesco…vitz?"

"No. Walter Johnson!"

"The story is about Hav…Tescovitz. Tescovitz, or some other. What's with, or who the hell is Walter Johnson?"

"It all goes together, Ron! Look, you wanted the real stuff. This is it. These guys were like…like…the Four Horsemen…or something."

"Four? There are others?"

"Yeah, Ron! There's three others! But one is dead. Well, two are dead, actually. One is…worn out…and one is still pretty bitter…about something. I need some background on Walter Johnson. 2nd Rangers. Fox Company. June 6, 1944…Pointe—"

"I know when D-Day was, Jon!" Faber snapped.

"Okay! Okay! Can you run that search for me?"

"I'll run it. Where do you want the results?"

"Email. Send it to my personal email account. I have a wireless joint up here that I just found. By the way…I may be a day later than planned. Okay?"

"Just don't book a room at the Hilton."

"Ron, there isn't a Hilton for at least a hundred miles from this place."

"Alright. Take the time you need. Give me the good stuff and we'll call it even."

"Got it."

He hung up the phone. It's good when the senior editor cooperates.

The Carriage House is a motel of sorts that also serves food. Like the Howard Johnsons of yesteryear. There wasn't much of a tourist industry here and there was no main highway running east-west. Route 953 was little more than a secondary road but it brought the bulk of the traffic to the area.

But Morris didn't care about food. He wasn't even interested in the Hotel portion. Surprisingly he was content to stay at the Marple in the middle of Tescovitz's world. No, none of this interested Jonny Morris. He was wanting the wireless.

"Coffee?" the waitress asked.

"Yeah, thanks. Black. Nothing in it."

"Menu?"

"You bet."

He popped his computer open as the waitress disappeared. When it came up he started to research D-Day, especially the Pointe du Hoc battle. The waitress showed up with the coffee just as he was typing his search: *what went wrong at Pointe du Hoc?*

The list that came up was more extensive than he had even hoped for. There were pages discussing failures, mistakes, conspiracies and what have you. He was going to have to read a good bit. Whenever a pdf or other document was cited he opened it, copied it off and stored it on his main drive. Some docs couldn't be copied so he took screen captures and saved them off. All this would be something to read and make notes on at the Marple... where it would be quiet as the grave. The coffee arrived and he ordered the breakfast special of two eggs, straight up, two pancakes with sausage and toast. Everything he needed to start cracking a great article.

Breakfast came and went. Endless refills of coffee followed.

The article was beginning to take shape. He had several unresolved questions still, though he felt he could run them down. When he could take no more food or drink he sat back and rubbed his eyes, trying to chase the strain away for a little while. Looking around he noticed that time had raced on ahead. It was now 1245.

"Oh, geez," he sighed. He looked around, psyching himself up for the drive back to town. He thought it might be a good idea to catch a nap. Tomorrow would be a big day. The Memorial Service was at one o'clock but he was planning on showing up at Sophia's house one more time. He still wasn't sure if it should be before or after the service. He'd figure that out tonight.

As he began the slow process of packing up his gear he noticed an elderly woman take a seat at a table not far from him. There was something familiar about her but he hesitated to believe what he thought he saw. But there she was, sitting and speaking with a waitress. It looked like she was going to order. Morris checked his watch for the time again. It was a little past one o'clock.

Must have just returned from Williamsport, he thought.

It seemed like a gift from above. His reporter instincts all went to high alert. The food he ate and the coffee he had been drinking all day seemed to vanish. His heart quickened and suddenly he was very aware of everything and everyone that was around him. It was Connie Provenzano.

"Hello. Connie Provenzano?"

She looked up, a bit startled.

"Hello…?"

"Jonny Morris," he said extending his hand. "I was out to the Tescovitz home yesterday. Do you remember me?"

Connie gazed at him a moment, focusing her eyes.

"Oh! You're the…reporter! You came to see Sophia about Hav, right?"

"That's right. I was getting some background for my newspaper. The Atlas Globe? Have you heard of it?"

Connie shook her head sadly.

"No, I don't…read too much in the…newspaper."

Morris chuckled.

"That's okay. I was wondering if I could join you? Would that be alright?"

"Oh! Of course!" she said, extending her little hand across the table as an invite.

Morris sat down and adjusted his chair in as tight as he could so he could be as close to Connie as possible. When he looked up he saw that she was looking right at him with a smile on her face. It was a good start.

"Missus Provenzano can I—"

"Connie."

Morris stopped.

"Oh…okay. Connie. I was hoping that I could…ask you some more questions about Hav and the men he served with like Sonny, Charlie Garr and Walter Johnson?"

"Me?" she said with a small blush of embarrassment. "I'm not sure I know much…but you can ask."

Morris ripped his notepad out and readied his pen.

"First, can I ask, where do you and Sonny live nowadays?"

"Well," she began. "Sonny and I moved to a little place that's…north, I think…no, northeast…of Athens."

"Athens…?"

"That's right," she added happily.

"Where's that?"

"Athens?"

"Yeah. I mean, yes! Where's Athens?"

"Athens is in Ohio, dear."

Morris made a quick note in his notepad.

"So you are…not too far away from Smicksville?"

"Well, I'm not too good with distance but…we had a driver get us here in a little less than four hours."

"Okay…," Morris muttered as he wrote.

"Been there long?"

"What, dear?"

"Have you been there long?"

"Oh, no. We just moved there about a year ago."

Morris made the note.

"And Charlie Garr…? And his wife? Is he married?"

"Ahhh, well Charlie…his Margaret passed just recently too."

"Oh, sorry. How old, may I ask?"

"Oh, she's like the rest of us. Late eighties. The men are starting to touch the nineties. Charlie is ninety one. My Sonny is ninety in a few months."

"I see. Where's Charlie from?"

"Charlie is," she said thoughtfully. "…Charley is from… Michigan. Yes. Michigan."

"Okay. So he lives in Michigan."

"No."

Morris stopped writing.

"No?"

"No dear."

"Where does he—"

"Charlie left Michigan and moved to…oh…he moved to… Maryland."

"Maryland?" Morris repeated, somehow intrigued by the answer. "Where in Maryland, do you know?"

"Yes. It has a funny name. I think it's like the cartoon? You remember? Oh, you don't remember. You're too young. But it was a very funny cartoon…about the…the…prehistoric people? You know, from the dinosaur time?"

"The Flintstones?"

"That's it!" she cried out with a laugh. "I can never remember that name but I always remember the cartoon. Let's see…it was Fred Flintstone and Barney…Rubble. And the wives were… oh…"

"Betty Rubble and Wilma Flintstone?"

"Yes!" Connie cried out laughing. "Sonny always said I reminded him of Bonnie Rubble!"

"Betty Rubble…"

"Yes!" Connie said laughing. "Bonnie Rubble had the same hair as I did!

Morris smiled as he scribbled.

"Where is Flintstone, I wonder?" He said this aloud but he was really talking to himself. Unfortunately or not, Connie took it as a question for her.

"Not far."

"No?"

"No. I think it's in western Maryland in the…panhandle, as Charlie calls it. But it's just south of the Pennsylvania border."

Morris sat back.

"When did he move there?"

Connie glanced upwards, as if to stimulate her memory.

"Charlie moved there right after…no…just before Sonny and I moved to Athens."

Morris was surprised but he tried his best not to show it.

"So…all of you are in pretty close proximity, right?"

"Yes, we are," Connie said smiling. "Oh, it made Sonny and I so happy to be able to see Charlie and Margaret and Sophia and Hav…"

"Oh…so Margaret was alive when she and Charley moved to Flintstone?"

"Yes," Connie answered sadly. But it wasn't long after…right after Sonny and I moved to Athens. She was very ill then."

Her voice trailed off, chased by what Morris thought was the memory of another funeral.

"And Walter Johnson, do you know him very well?"

"Walter? Yes, I know Walter very well…"

"Oh good! Did you know him when he was in the Army?"

"Army…?" Connie struggled. "Oh, you mean Walter that served with Sonny…"

"Yes, Walter…senior, I guess."

Connie hesitated, struggling with a thinning memory Morris thought.

"No, not as much. I thought you were talking about Walter junior. Walter died years ago. I forget exactly when."

"Do you know what high school he went to or where he was born? Or anything like that?" Morris asked a little desperately.

"Oh goodness, no," she said flatly. "You should talk to Walter junior for that."

"Do you recall anything about Walter Johnson, the Ranger? Anything at all?"

Connie thought a moment and then her face lit up with her best recollection.

"Yes…yes I do remember Sonny telling me…Sonny told me

that he seemed to be…what's the word…immune? Immune to bee stings when he was younger! Yes! Sonny told me that Walter could get, as he put it, 'wacked' by a hundred bees and not feel a thing! But…he developed a serious allergy to bee stings when he got older. I always wondered if it was a bee sting that killed him."

There was a short gap in the interview while Morris scribbled. Then Connie spoke up again, her voice lighting up a little.

"You know, they called him 'Hall,' which was short for Hall of Fame because he had the same name as a Hall of Fame Pitcher?"

Morris looked up.

"Right," he said. "Walter Johnson."

"Yes! That pitcher's name was Walter Johnson! Just like our Walter Johnson!"

Morris smiled inwardly.

"Connie, do you remember when Walter passed?" He felt a little ugly asking twice. But it was the only sure way to test the memory of an elderly person.

All's fair in love and journalism, he thought.

Connie smiled but it looked to Morris like she was embarrassed more than anything. He knew he was pushing too hard but there was something driving him on and he couldn't resist it. So long as Charley Garr didn't show up.

"Ten…? Twenty years ago? Oh, that sounds horrible," she muttered in disappointment. She turned away, apparently looking for the waitress to arrive.

The atmosphere had thinned after this remark. Morris sensed that Connie's body language was sending the 'kill' warning, as Morris called it. The interview was over. Luckily the waitress returned with Connie's tea and toast, which she had ordered before Morris sat down. This enabled him to exit under honorable conditions.

"Well, let me leave you to your tea," Morris said as politely as he could. "Hopefully I will see you again!"

"That would be nice," she said weakly.

Morris left the table. Suddenly he was convinced that Charlie Garr was staying here as well. He wasn't ready for him. It would be best if he escaped without having to talk to him. Later he would formulate a plan and make that approach under the best conditions he could. Driving back to Smicksville he was bothered by something Connie said.

"She remembers his nickname and the name of the pitcher being a member of the Hall of Fame," he said aloud. "But she can't remember when he passed? Is that what it's like to get old?"

Morris's reporter instincts were going off. He was used to things just coming together and this story wasn't cooperating. It could be that it was due to his interviewing people who were in their eighties and nineties. Or maybe Faber was right and he was looking for a story that didn't exist. But it wasn't logical to him that Connie could remember Walter Johnson's nickname but not the year of his death. So Morris had to reconcile himself with the notion that there was, in fact, a story to tell. It just had to be found.

5

Plan Of Attack

Back at the Marple Hotel Morris threw his laptop onto the bed and collapsed right next to it. He stared at the ceiling for a good while. For whatever reason he was becoming engulfed in a story that seemed to make less and less sense as time went on, even though certain things had logical explanations. Charlie Garr was bitter because of any number of things having to do with the war and the death of his wife just recently. That could make anyone bitter. Walter Johnson was a descendant of one of the Four Horseman. So his presence is easily explained. Except, of course, the part about a nineteen year old showing up at this time in this town for a funeral of a guy that his great uncle served with? And spending, what…? Three days here? Does that work?

In Morris's mind it did not.

Then Connie Provenzano's revelation that she and Sonny moved to Athens, Ohio just a year ago. Charlie Garr moved to Flintstone just before that.

They like to spend time together? Ninety something year olds like to spend hours and hours in a car just to sit around and talk flowers? War memories? Go to funerals? They would move closer for that? Nobody wanted to move to Florida? What's up with that?

All of a sudden he realized something. It made him slap his forehead in disgust.

"I never asked Connie about Walter Junior!" he cried aloud.

Immediately he rose from the bed and started to pace. There just seemed to be too many things confronting him for what was supposed to be a simple piece about old men recalling the Second World War and saying farewell to one of their own. Morris had to find a way to bring this all together so that it made sense. Of course, it would be easy enough just to write the facts, show respect, insert some pathos, some philosophy, a dash of sweet recollections from wives and such. But suddenly that wasn't enough. Even for him. This story had grabbed ahold of him and wasn't letting go. Just two days ago he didn't want to come here. Yesterday he couldn't wait to leave. Now he didn't want to be anywhere else. He was stuck.

Ron, he thought. *I want a raise…*

Irritated he opened his laptop and started his mail app. One thing he had managed to do was load his mail at the Carriage House. He had a wild hope that Ron had found a friend that could work magic on a Sunday. But when his mail opened it was the usual. Except for one from Betts. And one just beneath it from Lorraine.

He opened the one from Betts.

It was a short note. A one liner. It read: *Lorraine is going to send you email.*

"Well, she was right about that," he muttered. Then he looked at the one from Lorraine. He didn't open it. He just stared at the Subject. It read *Please Read.* Then the name in the 'From' line, which was simply *Lorraine R.* Instantly he saw her face and imagined things the way they used to be just a few weeks ago. Before that night at Green's bar when she ran into what's-his-name.

He dragged it to a folder called 'Unopened.' Then he logged off and shut the machine down. He was headed out. That meant Tally's Tavern.

"He's back!"

Morris strode in and sat down at the same table as yesterday. Glancing up he saw Joe Rake's photo taken in his dress uniform. Joe Rake, the man that dropped everything and enlisted to fight in a war that would free millions of other people. Joe Rake that was killed fighting on an obscure beach in Italy. He never returned to Smicksville.

"The usual Lou!" he called out.

While Lou poured the first beer Morris readied his notepad. There was only a handful of people here and the television wasn't on. That was good. Then he was struck by a thought.

Are the Pirates playing today? Now?

He shrugged it off and readied his pen and notepad. He didn't bring the laptop. This was a one man meeting to get his attack plan together as well as define his objectives. When he looked at it that way it made him chuckle to himself.

Define my objectives, he thought. *Listen to me…Sergeant Morris…*

The first beer arrived.

"How late are you open today?"

"Short day on Sunday, Mister Morris. Five o'clock."

Morris checked his watch. It was three thirty.

"Just enough time to solve all my problems!"

"There ya' go," Lou cracked and he walked away.

His pen in hand and his head held in his free hand, Morris went at it. He started scribbling short ideas and thoughts, re-writing some, crossing others out. In between he would slug some beer down then scribble something else. It was a frenzied repetition of slug and scribble. He was getting a little but it was still not enough. Eventually the pen became warm in his hand, his eyes started to ache, he was running out of pages in his notebook and his stomach was growling.

"Kitchen open?" he called out.

"Another thirty minutes," Lou answered.

"Ham and cheese, on rye, lettuce, tomato and onion."

"Got it."

"Chips?"

"Extra."

"Okay."

"Chips too."

"And another beer."

"Already pouring…"

Morris smiled and laughed. If there was any respite from the current bog of frustration it was here at Tally's. Morris went back to work trying to settle on how he was going to start again with Charlie Garr. The mere thought of it unsettled him. Garr seemed to be always on the border of overheating. It was a kind of subtle thing but you could sense it. If you got his blood pressure up you would find it out. Morris was convinced of that.

He racked his brain again and again, slugging the rest of his beer down. Without thinking he pushed the glass to the edge of the table for Lou to grab.

Garr is like…a hand grenade with the pin pulled, he thought. *I need to keep the pin in the grenade…so how to start an unscheduled interview with him? Maybe the move to Flintstone, Maryland? Maybe. The convenience of being so close to the Provenzanos? Maybe. Does he come visit Sophia and Sarah often? Maybe not. Did the four of you make some kind of pact during the war? Nah. That's corny. What then?*

"Here ya' go," Lou said, arriving with the sandwich, chips and the next beer.

"Ahhh, that's the one," Morris cooed. He dug in and made the sandwich go away. The chips followed right after and the beer, and then another beer after that. And it still wasn't coming in clear enough to satisfy him. His story was too much sawdust.

"I'm tired," he muttered. He paid the bill and left. Now he just wanted to sleep.

Back at the Marple Hotel he threw himself on the bed. His phone already in hand, he reached for his earbuds on the nightstand and put them on. He started his music as he laid back, closing his eyes and pulling his mind away from his problems. He needed to separate himself from everything, try to get another look at everything from a little further away. The right music can do that…

…the firing had subsided but the smell of powder was still heavy. It hung in the air like a lid on a stew, a stew of blood, of the dead and dying. Morris looked to see a line of men in the shape of a semi-circle, dug in and peering over the tops of their foxholes. Every now and then more firing would erupt, sending distorted lumps of lead whizzing by, streaking across the Pointe

on their way to an unknown end. Morris ducked each time. But he continued to make his way to the front. Instinctively he headed towards the right. Across a field he saw a smoking AA gun, its barrels bent and twisted, black smoke curling up from the position like a flag of black.

"What the hell are you doing?!" someone yelled. Morris crouched again, thinking it was meant for him. But then he saw another man walking away from his position. A second man was yelling at him. Morris watched, transfixed, until the man walked close enough for him to make out. It was Hav Tescovitz. Even though the shooting had started again Hav acted like there was nothing to it. He casually walked over to a small patch of grass that wasn't bombed on, or shot up or covered in blood or body parts and knelt down like he was examining the grass.

Just then the second man came storming out of his foxhole and made a bee line for Hav. Morris watched it all, being as no one was paying any attention to him.

"Hav!" he screamed as he came up on his side. "Get your ass back in the hole! You wanna' become a permanent fixture on this shitty piece of rock?!" Morris knew the man. It was Charlie Garr. Sergeant Charlie Garr.

"You see these little flowers here?" Hav said, picking small pieces of petals from the grass.

"What? What flowers!?" Garr screamed.

"I'm talking to this guy here," Hav answered, then he looked at Morris. "Do you see these little flowers here?"

Morris looked and nodded. He really didn't, though.

"These flowers used to grow all over this place. It's perfect for them. But these are dead."

"How can you tell?" Garr asked.

Hav only stared at them as he held them in his hand.

"I can tell."

"Hav, we gotta' get back! The Germans are comin' at us again!"

"There's no guns here, Sarge."

"I know. So?"

"And these flowers are dead."

Morris looked to see the other two Rangers arrive. Sonny Provenzano was gesturing towards the front where a hundred Germans were milling about and complaining to the other Americans. Morris recognized him. But the second man had his helmet down low over his forehead. His face was darkened with camouflage and he was looking downwards. Then he spoke to Sergeant Garr.

"Hey Skip, the Germans are saying they can't continue until we all get back in our foxholes."

"I'm trying, Johnson!"

"Yeah but they say they can't wait forever."

"Yeah? What if they have to?"

"Well, they say that if they have to wait forever, then they want the same consideration when the inland fighting starts."

Garr thought for a moment.

"Okay. Tell them they have a deal if we can't get back to our holes in five minutes!"

"Roger that, Sarge..." Johnson said as he grabbed Provenzano. The two men started back. Then Provenzano turned back and called to Garr.

"When you come back...? When you come back, ya know... you're supposed to come back firing!"

Garr waved acknowledgement.

"Hav, it's time to go."

Hav paused a second while he gazed at remnants of dead flowers in his hand.

"Okay, Sarge. I'm right behind you."

Garr started back.

"Right behind me, right?" he called out as he started to fire his weapon.

Hav waved him on.

"You see, these flowers can grow here. But not now. You follow? They'll get another chance."

Morris nodded.

Hav stood up and started back. He slammed a new clip into his weapon and started firing as he began to leave.

"Remember," he called back. "There were no guns here, either!"

Morris woke with a twitch in his heart, his breathing coming in gasps. He wasn't certain where he was. And where did this sweat on his forehead come from? It took a moment for him to collect his thoughts, to calm his breathing. Suddenly all the reading about the battle, his meeting with the Tescovitzs and the others yesterday and his thoughts on the story behind the story came roaring back like a silent landslide in his mind.

He sat up and checked the time. Four thirty AM. He thought he could go back to sleep. He was wrong. Defeated, he turned on a light and opened his window, letting a gush of Fall air tumble in. Then he dug out his notes. As he started to read he was confronted by all the old cul-de-sacs that he ran into yesterday. And he still felt tentative about going back to Charlie Garr. Then he was certain he didn't want to.

Lying in bed, growing angry and stressed with each shifting shadow in his room, he resolved that since he had decided not to seek Garr, he would see if young Walter would speak with him. He would go around the hard case and see if he could get the right information without looking like he was trying. And maybe Ron would have something for him on Walter Johnson. Maybe. Either way, there was a change in plans.

He didn't sleep the rest of the night.

The memorial service was well attended. Morris put on his best clothes, which, surprisingly, included a tie. Ida Wolley was there. The gas station attendant was there. Even Lou was there. And, of course, he was able to spot Sophia Tescovitz who was standing next to Sarah. Sonny and Connie Provenzano stood nearby as did Charlie Garr. Right next to Garr was Walter Junior. Morris snapped some photos with his phone, thinking some may be good enough to be included with the article.

There was an Honor Guard of eight men in Army dress uniforms. They had rifles and shiny shoes, service caps pulled tight down over the brow.

Like Walter Johnson in my dream, Morris thought. Unconsciously he keyed on the Guard, taking more pictures than he would ever need, snapping shots of them holding their rifles this way and that, executing short, tight marching routines, saluting then lowering the flag. There was a loudspeaker system going as well. It was playing a hymn Morris had never heard but that was no test. Morris wasn't a hymn type of guy.

"They're going to add Hav's name to the granite memorial stone," a woman standing next to him said.

"Oh? How many names are on it now?"

"Oh, my gosh. I don't think I know. Quite a few," she said. "Too many."

Someone started to speak to the gathering.

"That's Ed Rogers," the woman said.

"He's the mayor?"

"Well, head of the Town Council, which is like a mayor, I suppose."

Ed Rogers' speech was a solemn one. Of course he talked about the sacrifice, sometimes the ultimate sacrifice that these men had made. The speech that was heard all too often even now with no World War. No one spoke. Morris didn't remember even hearing a cough or a sneeze. Probably due to the fact that most attendees were elderly, Rogers' remarks were brief.

"...and in that age of men who took up arms to fight against evil and subjugation, to free those in chains...would they not also, were they alive this day, be willing and able to offer their lives up, again, and wage the struggle against tyranny once more? We all know the answer to that."

There was some scattered applause. Then the Honor Guard snapped to attention while an unseen bugle sounded, the lonely strains of Taps drifting across the air like an odorless smoke. Morris glanced around to see if he could find it but then gave up. This wasn't anything to photograph. You just listened.

When it was over the Honor Guard marched off and people started to converse. By chance the military formation came right by him. Soldiers with rifles, their sparkling shoes moving in unison, hats pulled tightly down across their face. That's when something jumped out at him.

That's it, Morris thought. It jolted him to the point where he straightened up as his mind finalized an idea. *I'll go at it through*

Walter Johnson. The guy with no face. Something tells me they'll want to talk about him. He milled about for a short while, attempting to appear as if he was just another person from Smicksville. But all the while he watched as Sophia slowly made her way to a waiting car, stopping now and then to speak with one neighbor after another, Sarah waiting patiently beside her. At the same time the Provenzanos would be speaking with each other while Garr walked Walter all the way to a second car, his arm around Walter's shoulder.

When he thought the socializing was over and Sophia was headed to her car, Morris started off. He quickly cut through the thinning crowd, making his way without uttering a word.

"Hello! Sophia Tescovitz?"

Sophia turned, taking Sarah with her.

"Oh! Hello. Mister…"

"Morris. From the Atlas Globe! I was out to your house the other day…"

"Yes…yes, I remember! Sarah, this is—"

"Mister Morris, mama. I remember too!" she said lightly.

Sophia started to say something but Morris started first.

"I just wanted to say, that the service was excellent. I'm glad I could be here. And…I am sorry for your loss. I know he was a great guy."

Sophia smiled politely.

"Yes. He was…"

"I take it you all are heading home now?"

"Yes," Sarah answered. We're going back to mama's house."

"Right, I was wondering—"

"Mister Morris, would you like to visit us this afternoon?" Sophia asked.

He was struck briefly, not expecting to be asked.

"Well, I just have a few more things to get ironed out. Do you think I could talk to Walter? Would that be okay?"

Sophia glanced at Sarah who shrugged innocently.

"Well, that settles it then! You come out to the house in an hour. We'll have refreshments ready by then."

"Great." He started off then turned around as he walked away. "And thanks! Thanks very much!"

"More ice tea, Mister Morris?" Sophia asked.

"Yes ma'am, and please, call me Jonny."

"Jonny? But that's a little boy's name! You're too old for that!"

Morris laughed as Sophia poured the ice tea.

"Well, I suppose it is. Something that stuck to me when I was growing up."

Morris glanced around the table set up outside in the back yard. The Tescovitz home had a small patio with a grill set up and Sophia and Sarah frequently entertained there, especially on nice days like this one. He risked a glance at Garr but got nothing. He just seemed to be here, tolerating everyone else. He wasn't drinking ice tea either. Sonny and Connie were quiet. She would say something to him that Morris couldn't hear every now and then but then they would go back to listening to everything. Then there was Walter, sitting next to Garr he nursed his ice tea like a man with the last glass of water in a vast desert. Staring at it, he would stir it with a plastic knife in a thoughtful kind of way. Maybe even a distant way. Maybe he wasn't really here. Maybe he was thinking of being two states away playing baseball…or something. Anything.

Then without warning, Sarah left with Sophia saying something about cheese and crackers, some fruit and other assorted items to go with the ice tea. That's when Morris decided to make his move.

Jesus, he thought. *Why do I feel like I am getting ready to scale the Pointe?*

He sat down next to Walter, on the opposite side of Garr.

Here goes…

"Walter! I didn't get a chance to speak to you the other day. Do you think we could chat a little now?"

Walter gazed back, a pair of lonely eyes pretending to find a hidden meaning behind the question.

"Something for your article?"

"Yep. I thought it was very interesting how you have remained close to the Tescovitzs over the years. How old were you when you first met them?"

Walter shifted a little in his seat. So did Garr.

"Geez, I can't remember. Been a while, though."

"Well, do you see them often? Or Mister Garr here? Or the Provenzanos?"

"We don't see him enough, ya know?" Sonny said, interrupting. "This one here we could see every day, ya know?"

"Right," Garr echoed.

"Okay," Morris answered. He was defeated but he hadn't given up yet.

"Can you tell me how it is that you know Charlie and Sonny and Hav Tescovitz?"

Morris readied his notebook, anticipating the answer.

"I looked them up, years ago. When I was reading about… Uncle Walt."

"Your great uncle Walt, right?"

"Yeah."

"Can you tell me, where are you from, or, your uncle Walt?"

"Uh…Uncle Walt lived in Iowa, if I remember right. I think he moved around, though."

"Okay. Okay. What did he do?"

Walter gazed back at Morris. It almost seemed he was surrendering something he had vowed never to surrender.

"He was playing some semi pro baseball. Then the war hit… and that ended."

"Baseball?!" Morris said excitedly. "I play some baseball as well!" Morris went back to scribbling in his notebook.

"How about you?"

"What?" Walter answered.

"You. Do you play baseball? You look like a baseball player."

Garr and Sonny both started to talk. Sonny won out mostly because he didn't hear Garr trying to talk.

"Yeah…ya know? He plays baseball…just like—"

"Just like his Uncle Walt," Garr said as he sloshed the rest of his drink down. Then, grunting as he got up from the table, he said something about needing to take a walk and slowly left. Sonny chatted with Connie while at the same time Sarah returned with a tray of cheeses and whatnot. Then she left again.

"You probably already know," Morris began. "That the name Walter Johnson is already famous in baseball."

Walter continued to stir his ice tea.

"Yeah, I know. That's what they told Uncle Walt too, back in the day."

"Back in the day," Morris repeated. Unfortunately Walter took it as if Morris didn't understand the answer.

"Right. Yesteryear…right?"

Morris thought for a second. Taking a moment to catch up to the confusion.

"Oh, right. Yesteryear." Then Morris went on with his interview. "I see that the other guys have all moved pretty close to Smicksville. Well, fairly close. A couple of hours. Are you close by as well?"

"I'm staying with Charlie. At least for now. He's all alone since Margaret died."

"Oh…yeah…wait," Morris said, struggling with his notes. "Margaret was his wife, right?"

"That's right."

"She moved with Charlie to…Flintstone, Maryland?"

"That's right. But she didn't last but a few months. Hit him pretty hard."

Both men were quiet for a moment or two. Then Walter spoke.

"She was the only woman he ever loved."

"I see," Morris said.

"And Walter Johnson? Your great uncle? Was he married?"

"Yeah," he said quietly. "He was married."

"What was her name?"

"Celia."

Then another stony silence ensued. Even the Provenzanos were quiet.

"Cancer," Walter answered without being asked. "She died of cancer."

He took a hit from the ice tea.

"Margaret. Hav. And Celia. Everyone dies from cancer."

Morris watched as the young man grew distant. It seemed they all did when he was talking to them for any length of time. Was it his reporting style? Or maybe these people were just very private types.

"Uhh, is that what Hav Tescovitz died of? Cancer?"

"Yeah. Leukemia," Walter replied.

"Walter?"

"What?"

"Can you tell me, where your uncle was from in Iowa?"

"He was from," Walter began with a sigh. "a little town just north of Des Moines called Ankeny."

"Ankeny. Got it."

But just as Morris was about to ask another question Walter just upped and left the table. And as if they were in the on deck circle, Sarah and Sophia came back with the rest of the treats and drinks. Garr came back with another glass of something else.

"Are you going to ask us more questions, Mister Morris?" Sarah asked.

"If it isn't too much of an imposition."

"Well," Sophia said faintly. "Maybe just a few more."

Morris went to his notes, looking at all the questions he had. Most were already crossed off. But there was a few still hanging loose.

"Can you tell me a little about your husband's work with flowers, Missus Tescovitz?"

Sophia was acting as if she hadn't heard the question when Sarah leaned over and repeated it.

"Oh! Hav's flowers! Well, it wasn't just flowers you know."

"Really? He worked with…other plants?"

"Oh my! Yes! He worked with shrubs, trees, uhh…vines and

creepers, like Virginia Creeper…and flowers. He won awards, my Hav did."

"Yes. I seem to recall he was awarded a prize of some sort for his work by the Horticultural Society?"

"He did. Oh he was wonderful with growing things. He made them last. Even when they weren't supposed to!"

"Someone at Tally's Tavern said he grew an annual…plant, that's a plant that lives for one year, right?"

"Yes, that's right."

"But his annual grew back? The next year?"

"No," Sophia replied, shaking her head.

"No. What was it then? Was it—"

"It was a biennial that grew back."

"Biennial. What's that?"

"A biennial plant lives for two years, blooming in the second year. Then it dies."

"So he grew a…biennial that lasted how long?"

"Nine years."

"Nine…years…?"

"Yes. It bloomed every other year after the second year. But the ninth year it was unable to keep it up…so it died."

"Nine years!? That's amazing! Did he win more awards for other work?"

"Oh, some…over the years. He grew these tomatoes one year that were out of this world!" Sophia said with a frail chuckle. Morris glanced around the table. Everyone was nodding as if they remembered it. Everyone except Walter, who hadn't returned yet.

"So, he was like…an inventor?"

Sophia laughed again.

"Oh, Hav would love to hear someone call him that! He was

always a scientific type! But no, I think he would be better described as a researcher. A…a…oh, what did the Horticultural Society say, Sarah?"

"Scientific researcher, mama."

"That's it! Yes. Hav was not so much the inventor. More like a…scientific researcher."

"Okay. That's all very interesting. I see you have plenty of growing things now."

"Yes we do. But you should come back in the spring and see the blooms!"

"I'd like that. Thank you."

"We should show him…father's greenhouse mama," Sarah said a little excitedly.

"Oh…I never thought…why yes! He should see the greenhouse…but not now, Sarah. In the spring. When the blooms come out."

Sarah glanced at Morris with a *Better Luck Next Time!* expression on her face.

"Sure. Spring works for me," he said. Though as a rule he wasn't much for flowers and things that grew in greenhouses. But accommodating Sophia Tescovitz would work well for him in the long run. The only thing that remained was his speaking with Garr. And now that he thought of it, when was Garr leaving? Maybe speaking to Sophia would be easier. Maybe for Walter as well. At any rate he knew he wasn't coming back in the spring.

Everyone stayed for a bit longer enjoying the cheese and refreshments. Charlie Garr was drinking again. Sonny spoke quietly with Connie, his characteristic *'ya know'* jutting out routinely. Both appeared indifferent to what Morris observed to be Garr's heavy drinking. Or maybe they had just learned to accept it by this time. Provenzano might be having nightmares as far as he knew. Maybe Garr's fallback was alcohol.

"We're going back inside," Sarah said as she and Sophia rose from the table. "It's getting a little chilly for us!"

"Me too," Connie said as she rose with them. Sonny followed. Morris waited a moment to see what Garr would do. Slowly, the old sergeant rose with a grunt, dragging his half empty glass with him. Morris followed without saying anything. But inwardly he was popping with anticipation. Maybe he would get to talk to Walter again. Hopefully that would bring Garr into the conversation since the two seemed personally linked. And maybe Morris would have a drink with the Sergeant as well. The ice tea was good but at this hour, it was getting a little stale for his tastes.

"Coffee anyone?" Sarah asked.

The Provenzanos accepted. Garr declined. Walter appeared at last. Apparently he had found a book that he had taken an interest in and was reading it by the large window in the living room. Morris declined the coffee but accepted another offer for a real drink. So Sarah made off for the kitchen while Sophia, Connie and Sonny chatted in the living room. Walter took a seat next to Garr and they spoke between themselves. Their talk was low, maybe deliberately so. Morris couldn't hear a word.

While Sarah worked in the kitchen Morris took the opportunity to glance around the living room. Seeing old photos mounted on tables and makeshift wall mantles, he made his way along the wall and took to scrutinizing each photo as he went along. There were some marriage photos and others of family gatherings before the war. And then there were some of Hav in the Army. Morris studied them carefully. Most were of his time after boot camp, returned home, razor thin, grinning, his uniform painting him handsome. Then there were two that were taken during the war when he was in France. A third frame stood next to the other two. It was sitting in a landscape setting except for the fact that the photo was missing.

"That's odd," Morris muttered.

He turned around to see Sarah sitting across the room with Sophia. He was able to get her attention by making an awkward eye contact. When she looked Morris held the empty frame up for her to see. That's when she came over.

"Oh, I remember…I think that's one that…" but her words trailed off to nothing. She glanced back at Sophia who was unexpectedly concerned. She rose slowly and made her way across the room. When she got there Garr and Walter had come over as well.

"Mama, this is the photo that we…didn't we try to get this one…restored?"

Sophia nodded weakly, taking ahold of the frame as she did so.

"That's the photo of…," Garr began but he didn't finish.

"It's the snapshot of Hav's squad," Walter added. "Or, I mean….it was."

"Right," Garr said.

"What happened to it?" Morris asked. The question was obvious but also, he thought, in danger of being neglected.

"We sent it away," Sophia began. "We sent it away for…. restoration. It was getting very worn. I guess we left the frame up anyway!"

Sophia nodded.

"Walter, you knew what this photo showed. I guess you'd seen it before?" Morris asked.

"Yeah. I get interested in all this. Books, photos, people's memories…"

"We all have them," Garr added, his voice a bit disconnected from everything going on around him. "…memories of people we knew, loved, people we depended on—"

"And people that depended on us," Walter added. There was a very awkward gap in the impromptu meeting on the far side of the living room. No one knew what to say next. That's when Sonny showed up.

"That's the photo of all of us, right?" he said taking a quick glance at the empty frame. "Where is it?"

Sarah began the very difficult explanation of what fate had befallen the missing photo. Luckily Garr broke in and drove everything like a cattle rancher driving his herd to market in Dodge City

"It's at the developers, Sonny! Remember? Sophia had it restored, or, is having it restored." Garr's voice was a bit elevated, no doubt from his heavy drinking. Morris became fearful that things were coming too close to being an embarrassing incident.

"Yeah?" Sonny answered. "Ya know, that's the one that had all of us, ya know? All of us in France." Then he turned to Walter as if looking for support. "Right? Wasn't that the one?"

"That's the one," Walter answered.

Another gap in the conversation exploded in the room.

"Well," Morris added in an obvious attempt at levity. "I don't think Walter here was in that photo!"

"Huh?" Sonny blurted out.

"Walter wasn't in that photo, Sonny!" Garr shot back. "That Walter is dead! Dead and gone!" Garr lingered for a heartbeat before taking to the kitchen. He could be heard refilling his drink and going out the backdoor.

"Oh dear," Sophia said softly.

"Sorry if I said something," Morris replied.

"Charlie will be okay," Sonny echoed.

"Yeah. I'll go talk to him," Walter said as he left the room.

Jesus! Morris thought. *Why did he have to crack wise?*

"I'm sorry mama," Sarah said. Morris could hear her apologies to Sophia. It all seemed a bit overdone but he wasn't going to say anything about it. He was already kicking himself over his ill-timed joke.

War vets...memories...alcohol....when are you going to learn Jonny Morris?

His thoughts angrily condemned him. He thought about going out back and apologizing but thought better of it. Maybe it was time to call it a night.

"I think I'll say good night," he said to the remaining people in the living room.

Sophia looked sad. Sarah was obviously embarrassed but he didn't know why. The Provenzanos were speaking to themselves again and Walter was out back tackling a former Sergeant in the Second Rangers. That's where the story was as far as he was concerned but he felt he was the last person in the world that should go out there.

He set his unfinished drink on a table and left.

6

Home Field Advantage

The ride home was long and irritating. Morris was angry at himself for not getting the real story, or the one that he thought was real, about Garr and Walter. And then there was his wise crack in front of an inebriated Charlie Garr that broke everything up. He cursed himself for that. Then he cursed again when he missed his turn. By the time he made it back to Atlas Town it was late afternoon. His drive lasted at least an hour and a half longer than it should have. His article was nearly complete. He just didn't like it.

"I missed the real story," he muttered. He turned the radio up, thinking it would get his mind off of everything. Soon he would be home. His softball team played while he was gone. They might have made the playoffs. That would help.

"Speak of the devil!" Betts called out as Morris strode through the front door. He smiled and waved at her and some others that had gathered around her desk, mostly guys, but inside he was a brooding, drizzly rain just waiting to happen.

"Ron wants to see you!" Betts called out behind him. He raised his hand in response.

Arriving at his desk he threw his shoulder bag on the top and started for the coffee.

"Morris! Say man! Long time no see!"

"Hello Sammy," he replied, his monotone voice matching his mood. After all, he hadn't had his coffee yet.

"Say," Sammy said following him to the coffee station. "Your team made the playoffs! Extra innings! Scary stuff…"

Morris glanced at Sammy and nodded.

"Cool. Maybe they'll let me play in a game now."

"Are you kidding!? The guy leading in all the offensive stats except one? You are so there!" Sammy put this last little boost with a pose and a finger point that quickly became a request for a fist bump. Morris granted the request but he really wasn't in the mood.

"Thanks Sammy…I gotta' go see the man now."

"You got it…see you at the game!"

Morris turned to leave, taking his bad mood with him. He made his way directly to the Senior Editor's office and knocked on the door. He barely waited for the invite to be heard before he was opening the door and coming in, sucking down coffee all the way.

"Jonny Morris," Faber monotoned. "Have a seat."

Morris took a chair, slouched back, his eyes gazing towards the ceiling. He crossed his legs at a wide angle, his one foot barely reaching the other leg to rest on. It was his best effort at displaying attitude when in Faber's office.

"Any news from the Army on Walter Johnson?" Morris asked immediately. Faber only stared back at him, his eyes doing the death scare again.

"Jonny. It's the Army. Not McDonalds Drive-Thru," he snapped.

Morris grinned.

"That's fine. Because I need you to run the other names as well."

"What other names?" Faber snapped.

"Here. I wrote them all down. It's the Four Horsemen that I'm trying to write about. You can lump them all in together."

He handed the piece of paper over and sank back into his chair. His main concern now was breaking something loose in all this. He needed an angle. Even if it pissed the editor off.

"Read your article," Faber said evenly as he scanned the names on the list. "Is this the finished product?"

"No."

"No…" Faber echoed.

"No, Ron. That's why I still need the names!"

"So this weekend piece has become a…labor of love, or what?"

"Well, it certainly is labor.""

Faber eyed the moody reporter who just told him the article that was promised, and was needed, was not available.

"What's wrong?" Faber asked impatiently. He put his glasses down and leaned back. That was his I'm-The-Senior-Editor-Who-Fought-In-Viet-Nam-So-Don't-Try-Me pose to go with Morris's I'm-A-Moody-Reporter pose.

Morris sat up and leaned towards Faber.

"There's more to this story. You said you didn't want sawdust. You wanted the real story, right?"

Faber listened but he gave no answer to Morris's question.

"I know there's a huge story there. Somewhere. I'm close but I can't break through!"

"What story? You have to have some idea what you're even thinking you might be after. What is it?"

Morris stared back. Truth was, he didn't know.

"Ron, you would have had to have been there. I don't know exactly how to explain it other than that."

Faber sat and studied his reporter a second or two before speaking.

"I don't want dirt, Jonny. I don't do tabloid."

"I don't do tabloid either."

"Well what, then? Are they in some dirty business, or something?"

"Naaahhhh…."

"Well, what the hell?! These are eighty and ninety year olds that fought in the war! What's the holdup? Write the story! What you sent in is good enough. Not great but good enough!"

"I want great."

"I want a story."

"I want more time."

"I want to win the lottery!" Faber cracked. "'Want' and 'get' are going to be different items on the menu this time!"

"Ron, give me just…a little. A little more time! When have I ever stonewalled you about the time to produce?"

"Never. That I know of. So?"

"So give me more time. Give me the chance, one more chance to get what I think is lying just under the surface. Aren't I worth that?"

Faber took a breath and glanced at the ceiling.

"How much more time?"

"A week."

"Oh, shit."

"One week. And..." Morris began but was unwilling to finish.

"And what?"

"And...I might need to go back to Smicksville."

"Oh bullshit! I should have sent you to Three Rivers Stadium so you could write about baseball. If you go back to Smicksville you go on your dime!"

"My dime?!"

"Yeah! Your dime! Don't you have any dimes?!"

"That's not right, Ron."

"What's not right is me sending you somewhere for three days and nights to cover the death of a World War Two vet and you can't get it done!"

A smoky silence fell over the office, like the aftermath of a fire fight. That was probably why Faber won all these. He was actually in fire fights.

"Your dime," he repeated flatly.

"Okay. Okay. My dime. But what if I write the article of the century?"

"You write the article of the century first and then we'll talk!"

Another uneasy silence fell across the battleground.

"Okay," Faber said with a sigh. "Today is Tuesday. I'll give you to next Monday. That gives you six days to get this article. God made the whole world in that time so don't tell me later that you didn't have the time. Got it?"

"Okay."

"Did you get pictures too?"

"Yes."

"Good. Now, why are you still in my office?"

"I'm leaving."

When Morris opened Faber's door to leave he was stopped again.

"Morris!"

"Yeah…" he rasped as he turned halfway toward the voice from behind.

"What paper do you work for?"

Morris stood a moment, looking for the hidden meaning of Faber's question. He couldn't find it. The battleground had more fireworks coming.

"The Atlas Globe…"

"No."

"No?" Morris said, turning the rest of the way to face Faber.

"No. You work for the Atlas Town Globe. Get that in your articles when you sign off from now on. Not Atlas Globe. Atlas Town Globe." This final remark was made with the emphasis on 'Town' so Morris would remember.

Morris nodded and turned to leave.

"Jonny!"

Disgusted, Morris turned around again with the familiar *what now?* look on his face.

"Remember. These people are old fashioned. They have old values. Ones that you aren't familiar with. As soon as you enter the room they are closing ranks even if they are smiling and pouring ice tea and chicken dinner down your throat. You go easy with them. Show respect. Got it??"

Morris thought a moment.

"Oo-Rah," he said, turning to leave. Closing the door behind him he made straight for his desk.

"Atlas Globe just sounds better than Atlas Town Globe," he said aloud.

But who could argue with the Senior Editor on the name of the town that you worked in?

"He's back!" someone called out as Morris walked into Green's Bar.

Green's Bar was the classic working man's bar. The jukebox had what the radios would say is the hottest music around, a pool table, dart boards, six different varieties of beer on tap, at least another six available in bottles, three large flat screens mounted in strategic locations above the patrons' heads, a waitress in hot pants and a young athletic guy behind the bar that everyone knew as 'Bash.' It catered to working men making a quick stop after work before going home. But it was usually loaded with revelers every night from Thursday through Sunday evening when it closed at 10 PM. Food on the menu consisted of burgers, a hundred different sandwiches, nachos, fried this and fried that, and finally, their signature flat iron steak that came with a baked potato and corn. The steak order came with one free pitcher of beer as well, which no doubt added to the popularity of steak at Greens. The screens had baseball games on when baseball was in season and football after that. No one watched soccer at Greens. The music was always loud.

Morris strode over to Jack Crawford and shook his hand.

"Hello Jack! I see you all managed to get into the playoffs!"

"A close one! Hey Jimmy! Look who's here!"

Jimmy Wilkes, a former member of the team, had come home on leave from the Marines. He had been the golden glove on the team, lighting up the infield at shortstop and batting a ton as well.

"Hello Jimmy!" Morris said as Crawford slid a beer in front of him.

"Jonny Morris! Still writing for the Globe?"

"Still."

"And the Editor that works there…what? J. Jonah Jameson, right?"

Morris laughed.

"Wrong Spider Man episode, Jimmy! What's next for you?"

"Shipping out, man…"

"Shit. Shipping out where?"

"Headed to Turkey first then, I think, I'm headed to Afghanistan."

"Af-what-a-land?" Crawford cracked.

Wilkes laughed, nearly spilling his beer that was already at his mouth.

"Yeah…Af-what-a-land."

"How's your folks taking it?" Morris asked.

"You know how…Dad is…reassuring me…talking about the future. Mom's real quiet."

"She ain't happy…" Morris mused aloud.

"No. She ain't."

"How long's the duty over there?"

"I think I'll be there most of a year for starters."

"Shit," Crawford added. "A year in Afghanistan. Is that first prize?"

"Yeah," Wilkes said laughing. "Second prize is two years!"

Morris raised his glass in response and the three men drank.

Crawford called for the bartender and ordered three more beers.

"So when do you leave? Morris asked as he killed the last of his beer.

"Gotta go Thursday night. Flying out of JFK on Friday morning."

"Shit. Say, Jack, when do we play next?"

"We?!" Jack echoed in mock cynicism. "What's this 'we' stuff?"

'Oh what?! You're not going to let me play?!"

"You missed two games! You missed a crucial practice last night! I can't reward that kind of behavior!"

"What was so crucial about it?" Morris took hold of his fresh beer that had just arrived. He put the accusatory eye on Crawford while Wilkes took to watching the theater.

"We had beer afterwards!"

The three broke out in a soaked laughter that went on a little longer than it should have.

"But Jonny has what? The highest average?" Wilkes asked.

"Yes," Crawford replied with a groan.

"On Base Percentage?"

"Yes."

"Extra Base Hits?"

"Yes."

"Home Runs are…second…in the league? Highest…on the team?"

"Awright! Awright! You can play! But you're on probation!"

The three slugged some more beer down.

"We play tomorrow night, Jimmy. You can play. You're still on the roster. You're still one of us!"

Wilkes smiled but shook his head.

"Sorry guys. I'm spending time with the family tomorrow. I leave the day after that, ya know?"

"Yeah…" Crawford said.

"But," Wilkes started to say to Crawford. "You'll let Jonny play? Right?"

Crawford finished slamming down more of his beer.

"Yeah, we'll let him play! He missed games and practices!"

There ya' go!" Wilkes cracked.

They must have talked for an hour or more, everything from the military to baseball, from the food at Green's to Morris's job at the Globe. All the while Morris gazing at every opportunity, every chance he had when he thought he wouldn't be noticed, for a glimpse of Lorraine. She wouldn't be hard to spot so he didn't need a long inspection to see if she had come in and gotten mixed up in the crowd.

"Shall we start a round of toasts?" Crawford asked.

"Hell yeah!" they echoed.

"The Bucs!" Crawford called out to anyone who could hear him above the music. "The greatest team in the Allegheny League! Because it has us on it!"

"The Bucs!" Morris and Wilkes responded.

And so the three men toasted the evening away, one after the other until the beer was gone and the refills as well. They toasted the league, the national pastime, Bill Mazeroski. They toasted themselves. Then they toasted Jonny's return to the team. And then Jimmy's all too soon departure. It was the Home Field. The place where all your fans knew you and everyone had your back.

Lorraine was a no-show and Morris never said a word about his assignment.

He spent the next day in his apartment struggling with his article, trying to pry an angle that would provide an escape from the sawdust he hated so much. It was a torturous expenditure of daylight seeing as he knew there was a real story underneath that was not revealing itself. As the hours wore on, bringing him closer to Faber's deadline he became so agitated that he started to turn ugly. He just couldn't figure why, all of a sudden, he cared so much for this article. Was it some affection for the veterans or something more mundane? He began to wonder if the reason for the strain was due to his inability to dig the story out. It had never happened to him before. Writing was always a snap. His feelings flowed, like the article he wrote about the tax foreclosures. Everything practically tumbled out on their own. Now, there was nothing above ground. Nothing that could be seen. It could only be sensed. And that wasn't good enough.

"Maybe there is no goddam story!" he shouted to his empty apartment.

He was drinking alone in the apartment this night.

The game was tonight. Earlier Morris had struggled with writing but gave it up after a short while. He just wasn't in the mood for the hassle. He left the apartment and took a short trip over to see Jimmy Wilkes and his family before Jimmy flew out that evening. It was already getting tense in the Wilkes' home. There was no sound, except for an occasional remark by Morris or Mr. Wilkes. The television was off. No music played. The air itself hung like a heavy tarp over everyone. Morris made a few courageous attempts to reignite the old days when they all would end up sitting in the living room and chatting the hours away but it was no use. Mister Wilkes was almost translucent. Polite, seemingly interested in what you were saying, yet the echo in his words betrayed a detachment, a heavy resignation in his demeanor. Mrs. Wilkes was a withered presence. Coiled inside a breaking heart, her sleepless mind had become shackled by silence, her eyes pocked with tears. Morris didn't stay long.

The playoffs would all be played locally at Memorial Park. And, to add to the excitement, all games would be under the lights. That made Morris's day. It made everything sizzle just a little more, even under the cooler night air, where a long fly ball sailing across the outfield always got a rise from the fans. Morris liked chasing them, too. Tonight he was in more of a game mood than normal. Fast pitch softball was as intense as it got without going to hardball as far as Morris was concerned. All the baseball rules were there even if slightly modified. Stealing, bunting, hit and run, nine innings of play, were all included. And it suited him this night. His frustration over a story that promised great things but eluded capture had driven him to a smoldering foul mood. He had delved in deeper than he had ever done before on a storyline and had come up with nothing. Now he wanted, he needed, to blow it all out, to sweat and bleed, if necessary so as to release the bitterness that had begun to accumulate ever since Lorraine had been caught in the back of Greg Jack's Ford after closing Green's bar. Now he needed competition. He needed to go up against someone. Something. A fly ball, stretching a single into a double, squaring off with another player. Anything. And he didn't care if Lorraine showed up or not.

The first series was a best of three between the Chargers and Bucs. Tonight would be a double header with Morris playing center field and batting third. The third game would be tomorrow night if necessary. He almost wished it so. The Bucs were the Home Team in Game one. So Morris darted out to Center Field like he was lit with rockets. It was time for some head to head, some hard hitting, hard throwing and brutal base running. What he affectionately referred to as 'Smash-Mouth Baseball.'

"Play Ball!"

The first batter for the Chargers was known as a base hit kind of guy. Not a long ball threat. So he was a good leadoff batter. When he drilled one up the middle Morris chased it down like a rabid dog going for a rabbit. When he picked it up he glared at the baserunner just rounding first as if to dare him to try. But the play ended there. The second batter came to the plate. He was a lefty. Morris studied him from center field, checking his batting stance and his grip. When he noticed that he had actually choked up a bit Morris struck on an idea. He would tempt him by playing straight away and a little too far out. Then he would make his move as the pitch went in and let the luck of the diamond have its way.

The batter took a ball and a called strike. Morris jumped a little each time. He didn't want to give his play away but right field was looking a little lonely right now as the Bucs Phil Grayson was playing him to pull. The next pitch went in and there was a shot to left. The fans rose with excitement but died quickly as it was called foul.

He'll play it straight now, Morris thought. *With two strikes... he won't try to drag one to Left.*

Morris committed to executing his trap on the next pitch. Playing back and straightaway as before, he broke the moment the pitcher was in his windup, streaking for the grass behind the second baseman. He was already mostly there when the batter smacked a line drive to center-right, just above the outstretched glove of the second baseman. The stands reacted at once. And so did the runner on first. But then Morris arrived, his legs driving him like a runaway train, his hat flying off and a snarl on his lips. He closed the grass off and nabbed that line drive at the shoe laces. When he came up he automatically locked onto the first baseman and drilled a line drive of his own that didn't stop until it smacked into Jack Crawford's glove at first. It was the first double play of the game and the stands ate it up.

The third batter flied out to Grayson to end the inning.

The Bucs came to bat in the bottom half of the inning. The tension seemed to buzz though the field like a downed high tension wire. But Crawford ground out for the first out and Grayson popped up to the third baseman. That brought Morris to the plate.

"Okay Masher! Let's start it off!"

"Jonny Morris, affectionately known as 'Masher Morris' for that baseball he ripped apart with his bat in college, took his place in the box and got ready. No tricks or fakes. He was setting up to hit. Hit hard. Hit it wherever it would go but hit it hard. Maybe so hard they would never find it.

He took ball one.

The next pitch had a wicked drop at the end of its ride to the plate. Morris unleashed a monster swing but caught nothing but air. The Chargers sang it up. Their fans sang it up as well. But Morris was still smoldering. Still focusing. Still wanting. He took ball two. Then a change-up caught him flat footed. He ripped a foul into the fence on the right sidelines.

Memorial Park came alive with expectation. Someone would be the winner, the pitcher with a strikeout or a putout, or the batter with a hit. As the stands got noisier and benches more belligerent,

Morris decided it was going to be a fast ball. And that's what he got. And that's what he drove into the power alley in left-center, leaving no doubt from the moment it was struck. It raced through the air, high above the grass, as if competing with the stars. It left the field and disappeared over the wall with the Gasoline Service Station advertisement. Masher had drawn first blood.

He came to bat again in the third inning with the Bucs leading three to one. This time he drove that change-up so hard down the third base line that it actually looked like the ball had changed shape. The ball broke into foul territory and Morris broke for second. When the throw arrived there was a massive collision at second as Morris came in under the second baseman, between his legs and bowling him over from underneath. He nearly slid completely off the base. But he was safe.

The second baseman didn't take it well, though.

"What's your problem?!" he screamed as he took hold of Morris's jersey.

Morris flew right into a rage.

"Do you want to know what my problem is?! Do you?!"

The two men grappled with each other, grabbing and punching, spitting death threats. The benches emptied and the umpires all raced to second base. It took players from both teams to pry their respective teammate from the other.

"You come into second like that again Jonny and I will rip your head off and piss down your neck!"

"I'll do it the very next time! I'll run right the hell through your ass Phil! I'll leave you in ashes!"

The home plate umpire stepped between them.

"Stop! Goddammit! One more word out of any one of you and I'm throwing you out! C'mon! Try me! You'll be out! Understand!"

Both players went silent then slowly backed off. Phil Grier retreated to second base, stopping to pick his hat up, dust it off and retrieve his glove. Morris picked his hat up and put it on his head. Dirt and all. He didn't knock anything off his pants either.

He scored two batters later increasing the score to four to one.

After the Chargers rallied in the fifth Morris came to bat for the third time as the Bucs held on to a four to three lead. With two out and a man on first, the Chargers held a timeout to discuss their strategy with Morris. The third base coach took the opportunity to chat Morris up.

"They might walk you but that puts Carter on second and Carter's fast. That's what they're talking about."

"They won't walk me, I don't think. But they won't give me anything to hit."

"Right. So be patient. Don't get too much in a hurry…until you're rounding the bases, got it?"

"Got it." Though the coach had made an attempt to keep it light Morris hadn't picked up on it. He was too far into this game.

Morris took his place back in the box. When he dug in, though, he set himself a touch closer to the plate. Just because he was in a mood.

When the first pitch came it was just a touch outside, which went well with his tight to the plate stance in the box. He rocked it to right-center and took off. The stands erupted as Carter raced along, heading to third. He got the 'go-ahead' from the third base coach as Morris glanced at the outfielders vainly trying to catch a liner that had nobody's name on it. It crashed into the wall and ricocheted off towards center. Morris made second and immediately began a scorching run to third. He was hoping the third baseman would take a throw because he wanted to knock him over anyway. But the throw never came. The signal to stop by the coach did, however. That made no difference to Morris. He knew the fielders were just getting to the ball. He didn't care how good their arms were. They were going to have to prove it. He broke for home, racing through the upheld arms of the coach. Everyone rose to their feet. Everyone was screaming but nothing could be heard. Words were mangled and blurred over the chaos the play caused. Morris knew Mazeroski heard the same noise when he smashed that home run at the 1960 World Series. Now he was hearing it.

"Slide! Slide!"

"Get down!"

Morris took a head first slide into home, cheating on the in-field side after he noticed the catcher sliding just a little towards foul territory to take the throw. He hit the ground and let his legs angle out towards the mound and he held his right arm back. When the catcher tried to bring the tag to the plate Morris was reaching for the other side of the plate with his left hand. Both catcher and base runner met at the plate, covered in a smoke-screen of dust and dirt and a tangle of arms and legs that pre-vented anyone from knowing who was where. Morris ended up on his back while the catcher finished sprawled across Morris thighs. Both turned to the umpire for the call.

"Safe!"

The Bucs bench emptied. Like a mob of hornets they raced for home plate and picked their center fielder up and dragged him back to the nest. The fans were cheering and groaning. Pictures were snapped and others were recording everything on their phones. Fans settled back in their seats and umpires anxiously returned to their positions, waiting to restart the game. The noise never subsided. But as the dust settled the Bucs were leading six to three. And that's how it ended.

The second game contained none of the drama of the first. The Chargers appeared beaten from the outset. It ended seven to one. Morris hit another home run and went three for four as well. The Bucs tumbled into Green's Bar and spent the rest of the night raising the noise level. Morris was voted MVP, which brought a white capped river of beer and pizza slices. But after the initial wave of revelry had been soaked by foamy pitchers and greasy slices, Morris's emotional high found itself running on empty. He tried to compensate with more alcohol and all the toasts that went with it but it didn't work. Thoughts of the still incomplete article wormed their way back into his mind's front store, chasing the revelry right out of him. He got quieter with each raucous minute. The drinks slowed. The music became more distant and so did he. And just like that, through the beer, the music, the toasts and even the women who had showed up, Morris felt the fire in him subside. He was no longer on top of a world he had just conquered. Softball was far away. And he felt real bad about his altercation with Phil Grier.

7

No Plan Survives First Contact

"Jonny Morris!"

He glanced up as he came rolling in to the Globe. It was Betts calling out from her desk. He waved but he didn't change course as he normally would have. He didn't want to hear another round about Lorraine calling and crying, wanting another chance and so on. Instead he made his way to his desk and then the coffee and donuts. When he made his way back he sank down into his chair and started a morning ritual practiced thousands of times: login, check mail, delete it all, send an email or two and then go see Ron Faber.

"You thought I was going to talk you to death about Lorraine, didn't you?"

Morris looked up and saw Betts standing by the side of his desk. But he already knew she was there before he looked up. Her perfume always gave it away.

"Hello Betts. And 'yes' I thought you were going to bring her up again. Was I wrong?"

"Mostly. She did call again last night. We went into town together. And yes, she did ask about you."

Morris stared back.

"She told me that she wasn't going to go to any of the games, so she wanted you to know that."

"So…you had a good time in Pittsburg?" he asked plainly.

Betts stared back. She wasn't really a small talk type of person. There was almost always an underlying reason for her to stop and chat you up.

"You aren't reconsidering, are you?" Betts dryly asked.

"Wasn't thinking of it…"

"She has literally lost weight, Jonny. About ten pounds…"

Morris sighed.

"I can't have this conversation right now, Betts. I am neck deep in Ron Faber. This is Friday and the deadline is Monday. He is really on me this time. So…"

"I know. I heard. We both think you are putting too much on yourself. Driving yourself too hard…or something."

"Yeah," he echoed. "Or something."

Betts began to move away but spoke once more before turning away.

"Any messages that you need delivered to…anyone?"

Morris only shook his head as he got up from his desk.

"Headed to Ron's office?"

"Yep."

"That's a good idea."

She turned and walked away.

"Jonny Morris! The man with the looming deadline!"

Morris made his way to his customary chair opposite Faber and slumped into it.

"Morning Ron."

"Tell me you have an article ready to go and I will be a very happy senior editor…"

"Sorry to disappoint…but it's slowly cracking."

"Slowly cracking," Faber answered. "As in, cracking the mystery of why you can't spit this out during a lunch break?"

"Yeah. Something like that."

Faber gazed a moment at his reporter. It was like a coach gazing at a star player to see if he is telling the truth about being able to play.

"I heard you had a big night at Memorial."

"Yeah. It went real well."

"Yeah. Frank wrote a piece on it. He showed it to me because he thought I would be interested. He was right. You got into it with Phil Grier?"

"It was…a moment of passion."

"Moment of passion."

"Yeah."

"Moment of passion that quickly became a fist fight?"

"Yeah."

"A fist fight with Phil Grier, the guy who does all the volunteer work at the—"

"Yeah! I know who Phil Grier is!"

Morris wrestled his way out of the chair and paced over to the window. Staring out the glass, his eyes resting on the hum drum goings on of Atlas Town, Morris tried to explain himself without looking like he was trying to do just that.

"This article is beating me. I don't like to admit it but it is."

"Is it all that bad? Or are you letting your personal life get in the way?"

"Nah. Lorraine has nothing to do with this. It doesn't help any…but it's not that."

Morris heard Faber's glasses topple onto his desk.

"Well…I'm afraid this is past me, then," Faber said. He was irritated. It was in his voice. But Morris knew that already when he heard the glasses hit the desk.

"I don't like telling a man his business," Faber said. "But something in me says that you need to take a step back. Like… you can't see the forest through the trees. You're too close."

Morris turned around.

"Too close…" he repeated.

"Yeah. Looks like it to me. The detail you're looking for might not be as detailed as you think. You're looking in small places. But it's hiding in plain sight. Right in front of you."

"Still no word from the Army…on Walter Johnson?"

"No," Faber answered bluntly. "I'll put a call in to my guy… again. Hopefully he won't hang up on me."

Morris strolled a few steps, taking in Faber's military trinkets.

"I'm going back to Smicksville, Ron."

"That's what I was afraid of."

"And Flintstone."

"Flintstone. Where the hell is Flintstone?"

"It's in the Maryland panhandle. Not far."

"Jonny, aren't you playing in the World Series of Softball… or whatever they call it this weekend?"

"Am I?"

"Well yeah. The Warriors beat the Cardinals two games to one. The World Series is this weekend. You're throwing that away?"

Morris thought a moment.

"I know this guy," Morris began, staring across the room as if no one else was around. "He's a great editor…one of the best that ever lived…a famous guy. He once told me that twenty years from now I wouldn't remember who won a three game series in Pittsburg. But I would always remember a great article. Do you remember the name of that guy?"

Faber reached for his glasses. Putting them on, he leaned back into his work on the computer.

"Enjoy Flintstone."

Nodding, Morris strode out the door and straight to his desk. Grabbing his backpack he made his way through the office to the donut station. Grabbing two, he walked out the front door with a short wave to Betts and made for his car. Soon he would be on the road. He just needed to make a call to Smicksville first. He decided to call on the way.

Flintstone is a small town that lies tight to the Pennsylvania border just a short ride east of Rocky Gap State Park on the old National Highway. It's a town with a smattering of everything from rolling, grassy hills to biker bars, churches, a casino and an ancient Indian trail once used by the Five Nations of New York on their way to the Carolinas. People usually came here to vacation, to relax, to drink beer, camp, dance, gamble and cookout. But that was most people. When Jonny Morris rolled into town he was looking for 12 Perrin Lane, the address Sarah Tescovitz gave him over the phone. He was determined to have his long sought after conversation with Charlie Garr…without the whiskey.

"Here we go," he said aloud as he turned onto Perrin Lane. Morris was calculating that he would get a great interview with Walter, maybe even Charley Garr, then he could write his article

Saturday, play in the World Series over the weekend, and still have time on Sunday and Monday morning to tidy up and present his story to Faber. It all put a smile on his face, especially when he came to 12 Perrin Lane. He turned the car sharply onto a gravelly driveway and brought it to a quick stop, the tires skidding a short distance over the stones and the radio blaring *You're Still the Same* by Bob Seeger. He killed the song when he switched the engine off. Then, grabbing a notebook and checking for a pen, he swung the car door open and strode up to the front door. There was a screen door but the main door was open. Peering through he could see all the way through the first floor and out to the backyard. Someone was sitting in a lounge chair facing away. So he knocked. The person didn't move so he knocked again a little harder. That's when the man in the chair turned and saw that he had company. He waved him in and turned back around. It was Walter.

"Hello Walter."

"Hello Jonny Morris."

Jonny took a seat that was nearby and settled in. It was a nice day today. And the sun wasn't in your face. That made it a little nicer. But the large number of beer cans scattered around Walter's chair gave a darker forecast than the immediate surroundings.

"Starting the party early?" Morris thought this was a risky start but Walter seemed a little more people friendly than Garr so he thought it was worth a try. He had to get the interview started some way.

"Not a party without girls," Walter droned. He finished off his can of beer and threw it on the ground. Then he grabbed up another from a little cooler he had under his chair.

"Right," Morris answered. "Say, is Charlie Garr here?"

"Nope."

"Oh. I was hoping to talk to him a little." It was a lie but one he could bear, given the situation.

"Why?"

"Well…oh, I don't know. I'm trying to get to know all of you. You are all very interesting people. And…I am trying to write an article about Tescovitz and…World War Two people in general." Morris studied Walter's face after he said this. It was obvious the man had been drinking for a while. Maybe all day.

"Well, Garr is gone. He went to Smicksville. To Sophia's house."

"Did he drive himself?"

"No," Walter answered nearly choking on his beer. "He doesn't drive anymore. He made a phone call."

"Oh. Damn. When did he leave? Maybe he'll be back soon?"

"He left soon after Sophia called. Which was right after you called Sarah."

Morris stared at the ground.

"So…you knew I was coming?"

"It's only polite to let people know you're coming."

"Yeah…sorry. But…well, I don't think Charlie likes me anyway.

Walter took a big hit off his beer and sat back gazing straight ahead.

"Charlie doesn't like too many people these days," he said hoarsely. "He likes Sophia. And Sarah. He likes Sonny and Connie. He likes me. The rest of the world…not so much."

"Yeah. Yeah that's what I thought. But…I'm only trying to write something that tells the real story about Hav. And the… the…Four Horseman."

Walter sighed heavily.

"Where'd you get that?"

"Oh, I heard it somewhere. Maybe at the house the other night. It fits doesn't it?"

"There were…lots of Four Horseman back in the day. That war seemed to make them…like in a factory."

Morris could tell that Walter was beginning to fade under all the alcohol. He knew the signs well since he had so much experience himself. He decided to try and interview Walter anyway since Garr wasn't around.

"Walter, can you tell me…anything about your great uncle?"

"Oh man…I really can't."

"No?"

Walter shook his head.

"Well, how about his family? His brothers? He must have had brothers and…maybe sisters as well?"

"Look…he was a great uncle…not my brother. I don't know about the family. My only connection is through Garr, Tescovitz and Provenzano. Uncle Walt is dead."

"Where's he buried?"

There was a heavy silence after Morris said this. It was a reflexive response on his part in answer to what looked like stonewalling by Walter Junior. Morris was surprised he actually asked it but he was glad he did.

Slowly, Walter turned to him, a weary eyed, red faced young man with the dread expression on his face.

"In the ground."

"Can you tell me how you got hooked up with Garr and the others?"

Walter hesitated a moment. Then turned back to stare at the backyard.

"Charley found me. He had gone looking for…Walter…and found me instead."

"What was he looking for him for?"

"To…see an old war buddy. To get together and drink."

"So where were you living then?"

Walter sighed. It was obvious he was getting tired or impatient or maybe both. Still, it made Morris wonder why he invited him in.

"I was…living everywhere. Moving around. Living life."

Morris closed his notebook.

"Alright. I've come at a bad time. I'm sorry. Maybe I'll come again some other time…next week…or something."

Morris got up to leave.

"Well hold….on," Walter said weakly. "Sit. Sit…down. Have a beer."

Reluctantly Morris took his seat and waited. He didn't bother to open the notebook. He wasn't that optimistic.

"Have a beer."

Walter held a cold one out for Morris who took it. He felt certain he was going to need it.

"You said you were into baseball. Did you play hardball?" Walter asked.

"In college," Morris answered. He was encouraged by the shift in the conversation. Baseball was a good topic to get the ball rolling.

"So who is your favorite team? The Pirates?"

"Yeah. I'm pretty big on the Pirates. Mazeroski is on my computer screen."

"Computer screen…" Walter echoed.

"Yep. That great shot he had in the Series. 1960. What a series that was."

"Do you have Hal Smith on your…computer too?"

"Who?"

Walter turned in his chair.

"Hal Smith. You don't know about him?"

Morris stared back. He was a little embarrassed but he didn't know why yet.

"Hal Smith came to the plate in the bottom of the eighth inning. The Yankees are up seven to six. Right? And there are two outs. Hal Smith comes to the plate. He's the backup catcher…"

Walter took a moment to finish off the rest of the beer. Throwing his can on the ground as well, he fished another out of the cooler.

"So Hal Smith…Mister backup catcher…comes to the plate. Dick Groat and Roberto Clemente are on base. And Hal Smith knocks one over the left field wall. Now the Pirates are winning nine to seven."

Morris listened, nodding his head as he slowly opened his notebook. Suddenly the interview seemed on…sort of…and he wanted to be ready to start writing.

"…and there's Smith getting mobbed in the dugout…only to be replaced in baseball history by Mazeroski."

A stony silence followed. Morris was waiting for the moment to steer the conversation back to the war and the men who fought it but he was interrupted.

"A good thing, too," Walter continued. "Because the Yankees

come back in the ninth and get two runs to tie. And that's what sets up Mazeroski's solo shot."

Another silence followed. Morris was about to speak when Walter jumped in again.

"So, if Smith hadn't hit his home run, Mazeroski's might only have been a last gasp. Right?"

Morris was intrigued. He made some short notes and then looked over to Walter.

"So…you do know some baseball."

"Sure. Uncle Walt did too."

"So…do you play, Walter?"

There was no answer at first. Morris started to think he might have to ask again, or even ask a different question.

"If the war hadn't come along…" Walter started. "…everything would have turned out different…for him."

"How so?"

"Are you kidding?" Walter answered after a short pause. "Baseball instead of going to war?"

"Well, what if he didn't make it to the pros?"

Walter smiled dismissively.

"He would'a made it."

Walter's voice trailed off and everything got quiet again. Morris took to scribbling a few thoughts on his pad and kept talking.

"But instead he invades France…scales the cliffs at Pointe du Hoc…"

There was no reply so Morris decided to press a bit. He didn't think he would get a chance like this again.

"When did your uncle pass, Walter?"

Walter rubbed his forehead impatiently, as if the question was an annoyance.

"Oh…ahh…about twenty years ago."

"Twenty years…and did he and the others fight in the Bulge, right?"

"What?"

"The Bulge. The Battle of the Bulge? That was a nightmare, right?"

Walter turned in his chair, an expression of mild impatience on his face.

"I read that, too," he said. "But why doesn't anyone know about the Hurtgen Forest just down the road?"

"The what?"

Walter looked away quickly and then turned back. This time he was visibly annoyed.

"Hurtgen Forest. Hurtgen Forest! We dropped over thirty thousand casualties in that chunk of woods! And for what?"

Morris was back on his heels. He made the note on the battle but had no idea what to say next, or even if he had inadvertently ended the interview…again.

"I…don't know."

"No…that's what everyone who was there is asking. First… it was the guns on the Pointe. Or should I say, no guns on the Pointe. How many guys went down for that? And then the Hurtgen Forest. Thirty thousand casualties. Thirty…thousand."

The two men were silent a moment or two while the tension eased. Morris was out of his knowledge on the war so it was an easy thing for him to let Walter talk.

"That's why you don't know anything about Hurtgen. And the Pointe. You only know about Normandy…and Bastogne. Because they were successes. Bloody, but successful. And… they made sense, at least…military-wise. But if General Omar

Bradley had pulled out of Normandy, like he was close to doing…you wouldn't be hearing anything about that either. And the Pointe? Someone is jerking someone's chain. Because they knew beforehand that there were no guns on that bluff!"

Morris waited. It felt like there was more to come.

"It's no surprise it drives some out of their minds. And…and they never come back…they go…they fight…they come back. They're right in front of you…but they're gone."

There was a short pause. A dog started barking off somewhere. A car drove by. Then it was quiet again.

"Sorry," Morris said softly. "I don't know much about the war. I—"

"Let me ask you something," Walter said turning in his chair again. "Let's say you're walking down the sidewalk…on your way somewhere…and you come across something… blocking your way…taking up the entire sidewalk. What do you do?"

Morris paused, attempting to assimilate the real purpose of the question.

"Uhh…go over it?"

"It's too tall."

"Pick it up…move it out of the—"

"It's too heavy. And it's sharp. Lot of edges. You're looking at bleeding…a lot…if you try that."

Morris stared back at Walter. Suddenly he was getting the feeling that this kid knew more than Morris did about this. A whole lot more.

"Go around?"

Walter stared back. Slowly he started to nod his head.

"You go around."

"So why didn't they go around?"

Walter leaned back in his chair and gazed skywards, as if he was retrieving the answer from the heavens.

"Because lots of generals love that straight ahead shit. They think it's hard-nosed…or something. They start looking ahead at history…and how it will remember them. A tough, hard fighting general! But the truth is less glamorous. The truth is, many… most even…are not very good generals. They are scared out of their wits at the prospect of maneuver…they don't understand... or they are too afraid of being caught while maneuvering. So they play it safe. They go straight ahead. They completely forget or reject what Napoleon already proved! When was that? Over two hundred years ago!? But they aren't up to it. So…the hell with everybody! At least I'll go down as a hard fighting general!"

Morris sat back, struggling a little to take this all in, suddenly realizing how much more there was to all this. It would have been enough to understand that war can make a man bitter. But the underlying reasons had been teeming unseen just below. It was a certainty that Walter was getting this from Garr in one of their very private conversations. But Walter had taken it to heart, maybe too much so since it seemed to have made him bitter as well. Morris wondered what, if anything, could be causing that. His great uncle was dead. He apparently had no other blood relative that was in a war, then or since, or it would have come up by now. Morris wanted to know how this teenager could know so much about everything from baseball to D-Day. But it all seemed too much of everything he really didn't care about so he dropped it.

The two men sat amidst some street sounds from the front, their beer in their hands and their own thoughts coursing through their brains. It looked like Walter had spent himself on his rant and the beer. Morris decided it was time to go but he didn't want to just get up and leave. He had to say something.

"Well," he said wearily. "I think I need to get on the road. Thanks for the talk. I never knew…well…it was all such a brutal affair."

He let his words trail off. Then he noticed Walter turning to face him, his bloodshot eyes betraying his drunken state and the bags under his eyes, now suddenly so apparent, made Morris realize this all was more than normal source of stress. He almost hated to leave.

"Brutal…" Walter droned. Morris didn't reply as he was halfway out of his seat.

"Let me tell you about brutal, Jonny Morris. Let me tell you about…Hill 400."

As Morris stood he realized that Walter wasn't done spilling. He really wanted to go but his reporter instincts sounded the alarm. The story he was certain was lurking somewhere behind the smoke of old histories and the tortured memories of ninety year old veterans seemed to dart in and out of the shadows, lingering only long enough to tease the eye and haunt the imagination. Somehow he suspected that Walter Jr. might be the key to unlock some of the mystery. Slowly, almost against his will, he sat back down and took his notepad out again. His schedule had suddenly changed. And he couldn't blame Faber's deadline for all of that. He wanted to know. It was as simple as that. Morris' insides were screaming at him, telling him that this was the story of a lifetime.

"...and everyone stay here until we get the order to go forward!"

Morris scrunched up against the earthen wall that hemmed in the sunken road that ran along the base of hill 400. Him and the rest of Dog and Fox companies. His heart was pounding. His breaths came in short gasps. There was mud on the end of his rifle barrel. German machine guns were peppered just inside the wood line about a hundred yards away. Erratic machine gun fire was streaking over their heads and into the ground just in front of the line of men doing their best to flatten out against the side of the sunken road.

"Why don't we just call in the artillery?!" someone shouted.

Just then mortar fire erupted to the front of the men. The explosions sent mounds of earth and smoke into the air and shrapnel in all directions.

"We can't charge through that shit!" someone shouted.

Morris wanted to look over the small berm that concealed him from the machine guns but he couldn't work up the nerve. Chunks of steel would come streaking by on a hissing ride through the air. He was sure he would catch one in the head if he dared to glance over the top.

Just then more explosions came, bigger ones, this time to the rear. They seemed to grow and grow, working their way towards the road. At the same time the mortar fire was working its way towards the road from the other side. Everyone hunkering down knew how this would end.

"Lieutenant!"

No one answered. The artillery from the rear and the mortar fire from the forward area continued to grow together, threatening to kill everyone on the road. Suddenly the line of men cowering under ordinance arriving from both sides of the battle line came to life.

"Lieutenant!"

"Shut up!"

"What the hell..."

"We gotta move soon!"

"Shut up! Shut the hell up! Send the scout out!"

"What?!"

"The scout! Send the scout out!"

"No! Fuck you!"

"Send the scout out now! I mean now, goddammit!"

Slowly, jerking with each impact of mortar and artillery fire, a man crawled out from the berm and attempted to make his way forward. After a few feet he stood up to move at a run. He was wiped out almost immediately, turned to mist inside an exploding mortar burst.

Just then Corporal Walter Johnson showed up at Morris's position.

"Remember this part? You'll never forget it from now on!"

He grabbed Morris by his pack and, pulling him to his feet the two men started over the berm. The entire line, both companies, rose up in a rage and swarmed over the berm like a solitary beast from the shadows. Driven by a rage brought to life by the death of the scout, they scorched a wide-eyed, curse spitting charge across the smoke choked field that lay between them and the German lines.

"They...don't know we're coming!" Johnson gasped on the run.

"How...what?" It was all Morris could muster at the moment. He was short on breath and he was sure he would be blown away like the scout any second now.

"They don't know we're coming! Because all the bombs are

drowning us out! The smoke and dirt in the air is hiding us…until it'll be too late for them!"

Morris raced along with Johnson until they hit the tree line. Then he could hear rifle and machine gun fire from Dog and Fox.

"There's Garr now!" Johnson shouted. Morris looked to see Sergeant Garr destroying a machine gun nest and the two man crew manning it. All up and down the line the Rangers hit the German machine gun nests simultaneously. The German crews never knew what hit them.

"Let's go!"

Into the woods they went, Morris following Johnson every step of the way. No one knew what they were about to run into until it couldn't be avoided. German resistance reacted sluggishly, their lines beginning to hunker down as the allied bombardment began to move across the field in their direction. But just like that the charge by Dog and Fox companies descended on them like an avalanche of brown and steel. They wiped out one machine gun nest after another as they came across them before rolling on. When they had reached the German rear they could practically run up on them before dropping them, the bombardment following just a short distance away. Smoke was everywhere. It covered the ground and ten or fifteen feet in the air. It was as if God himself had pulled a shroud over the dead and living alike.

The Rangers halted to regroup, reorganize and catch a breath or two. While Morris leaned up against a rocky patch of ground that jutted out to form a natural wall, Johnson reloaded.

"Didn't you get a shot off?"

Morris glanced at his weapon.

"No…no I don't think so…"

"Geez," Johnson replied. "You must be the only SOB on this hill that can say that."

Morris glanced back down the hill.

"How many...how many do you think got hit?"

Johnson slammed a new clip into his carbine and then stared right at Morris.

"Never...never ask that while the battle is still on. Got it?"

Morris stared numbly back at the Corporal.

"Got it."

Just then Garr rolled up with Provenzano and Tescovitz.

"Fox Company goes left," Garr rasped. "Move out."

"Bombardment stopped?" Johnson asked. Everyone looked to the rear, finally noticing that the explosions that seemed to be hunting their very souls had given up the chase. That was a good thing.

"Yeah," Garr answered while looking further up the hill. "We radioed in. Now we move up the hill. Let's go!"

Everyone rose up and took off in Garr's wake. Fanning out they met and destroyed more German resistance frantically attempting to regroup and form a battle line. But Fox mowed them down as they came upon them, killing them and moving on... and not looking back. Morris gasped a prayer to himself that he wouldn't meet up with anyone in the German army. He was locked and loaded and he wanted to stay that way. He was gasping for air as the hill got steeper and steeper. But his prayer went unanswered. Or perhaps the answer was 'no.' Regardless, Morris emptied his carbine at the first sign of a German soldier. Teeth gritted, eyes closed, he squeezed one round off after another until they were all gone.

'Cling!'

His clip leapt from the carbine.

Gasping, he stood frozen for a moment, expecting that he would be shot as well. But when he wasn't he forced his eyes open. That's when he saw the German lying still in the brush, his jacket smoking from the effect of Morris' shots.

He ran on, desperate to keep up with the others. Garr and the others were back at it, running up on disorganized units and wiping them out. In his effort to catch up, Morris remembered that he had spent the last clip on a now very dead German soldier. He stopped to reload, frantically looking up the hill as the others raced on. But suddenly he couldn't function. Soldiering abandoned him. He was losing sight of his company and he was convinced that he would run into another German at any moment. He needed to reload. But he couldn't remember how. He needed to get caught up but he didn't know what direction they took. He couldn't even hear them. His breaths were coming in short, choking gasps. It seemed his lungs were filling up with smoke. He called out for Johnson but that was useless. Johnson was far gone now and the sound of sporadic combat drowned everything out anyway. He started to panic. Why was he here? He didn't know a damn thing about soldiering, let alone killing people...

That's when he came up on a machine gun crew desperately trying to ready an MG 42 in a hidden position on the hill.

"Jesus!" he cried out. The crew answered something in German. Morris couldn't make it out but it didn't matter. Mindlessly he leveled his carbine and unloaded into the nest, his mind exploding with the thought of death, his death. Wildly he screamed though it all, releasing his own inner terror as he killed. He didn't stop until he ran out of bullets and air.

'cling!'

His empty clip jumped from his rifle, singing its merry little sound that more belonged to an ice cream truck then a rifle. Morris, frozen in the moment, his first kills lying quietly on the upslope of Hill 400, was suddenly parted from the raging carnage that was unfolding only yards away. The men in the nest were dead, their eyes wide with terror, their mouths open, their faces contorted and misshapen with bullet holes and exit wounds, their minds slowly releasing the last thought before death struck.

"Good. Reload."

Morris turned to see Walter Johnson standing next to him, smoke coming off his jacket.

"Reload Morris."

Morris grabbed another clip and jammed it into position.

"Up the hill," Johnson said, pointing the way.

They started up together but soon Morris found himself moving alone again. Then Garr called everyone to a stop.

"Regroup! Find your people! Check ammo! We dig in here!"

"Dig in!!!" Morris gasped. As his eyes scanned left and right, he could see nothing. He could hear nothing. Even the smell of death was missing. But he was breathing hard again. And he was sitting up in bed.

Uneasily he threw off his covers and paced across to the other side of his room. Slowly, he re-oriented himself, his mind trekking slowly back to Smicksville and the Marple Hotel. He looked out the window onto Main Street just to make sure. There it was. Smicksville in all its silent glory. A lone streetlight marking the way.

Morris wiped the sweat from his face. The memory of the tortured conversation he had with Walter Johnson in Flintstone tumbled back into his brain. Then the ride back to Smicksville, seeing Ida Wolley again and getting his old room back. He had started to write his article but was stalled again. His laptop was still open but shutdown due to low power. Sleep for Morris had become as elusive as the story he was so convinced lay just below the surface.

Morris showed up at the Tescovitz home around 11 AM. Officially, he was there to get the final touch on his article, tie up some loose ends and write the article of a lifetime for Ron Faber. Then to hurry back for the start of the World Series between his Bucs and the Warriors. But he knew how troubled all that was, how unlikely he felt it was that he would be able to finish this to his satisfaction. So, he fell back on hoping for a miracle, like a revelation from Garr or an admission from Johnson or even Sophia Tescovitz herself. Failing that, an invite to lunch would suffice.

Sophia and Sarah seemed delighted to have him back. Garr was not there nor was Johnson. So it was going to be a throw of the dice with the widow and daughter. It wasn't his first choice but he had to put an end to this torment. So it was small talk and chicken dinner, some old music and tall tales that Sophia recalled. But then Morris decided to take his shot.

"I hear around town that Hav was an expert gardener."

He said this matter of factly, to no one in particular. After it had hung in the air a moment or two Sarah spoke up.

"Oh, goodness…father worked magic with all things green!"

"So I've heard…"

Sophia smiled thinly, nodding her head as if she was wandering down a memory of her husband and his growing things.

"You have to remember, Mister Morris," Sophia began suddenly "that my Hav had seen so much death, endured so much hurt with the others, that he felt so much more at ease growing things, growing rather than destroying, creating rather than killing…"

Morris stared back. Then he noticed that Sarah was silent as well. So he sat back with his notebook in hand, waiting for Sophia to finish.

"When Hav was in Germany, they were fighting on some hill…somewhere…and they all had to endure bombing by the Germans…and the Americans. After one particular time, Hav told me that he crawled out of his…foxhole…and came across another soldier…one that he knew…who was dead…he was killed instantly…by one of those…incendiary bombs, I think, and this poor man, he was burned to death instantly…while digging his foxhole. And that's how my Hav found him. He was still posed like he was digging a hole, on his knees…and burned to death."

The room was overrun with a raw silence. Morris wrote what he heard, thinking all the while how much it reminded him of the interview with Walter Johnson. Sophia had begun to wipe tears away while Sarah reached over and tried to comfort her. Morris was uncertain if he should proceed. Without looking at Sarah for some guidance he decided to move the conversation to a calmer subject and keep the interview going.

"What was the man's name?"

"Hav would never tell me!" she answered sharply. Then she sat back, shaking her head and starting to cry all over again. "I don't think he wanted to run the risk…of me getting too close to what haunted him, see?"

"If he told you the name it would make him more familiar to you?"

"Yes."

"So, that transformed him…"

"Yes. That a man could die in such a way, while digging a hole…in Germany. Digging a hole in Germany."

Morris struggled with his notes, attempting to fend off the uneasiness he had encountered with his nightmare, one that came without him ever being near a combat zone. He didn't even go hunting.

"So gardening came natural?"

"Like magic," Sarah said, interjecting, as Sophia was still recovering from her revelation.

"Magic…"

"Oh yes," Sarah added eagerly. "He bred plants to grow longer than they were ever supposed to. He could grow them in winter. He even brought dead plants back to life. He won awards, competitions, people wrote about him—"

"The Pennsylvania Horticultural Society—"

"Uh-huh. Exactly."

"And…was Charley Garr and…Walter Johnson also interested…in Hav's gardening?"

No one answered.

"I mean, they visit here often, don't they?"

"Well," Sarah began. "I suppose they were interested… mother?"

Sophia stared deep into Morris's eyes. It was a knowing stare. Or maybe she was just tired and her eyes had changed somehow. Either way, it wasn't the glance you get when you are about to be offered ice tea.

"That was before," Sophia said shakily. "Before Charley Garr's Margaret passed away."

Morris didn't understand the answer but he jotted it down anyway, thinking he would work it out later.

"And Walter Johnson's wife—"

"Celia."

"Yes. Celia. Was she interested—"

"Long gone. Soon after the war. Nothing to be done."

Sophia sat back abruptly and looked away. Sarah got quiet as well.

Suddenly Morris felt unwelcome. The interview was over. He knew it. And he still had almost no idea what to write in his article.

"Okay, well—" he began.

"I'm sorry Mister Morris," Sophia interjected. But I have become…very tired just now. Thank you for coming."

With that Sophia rose and quietly made her way out of the room and up the stairs. Morris stood as she left, nodding in gratitude for the afternoon. Sarah smiled weakly as she passed by.

"Sorry," she whispered. "She gets like this every now and then."

"Sarah," Morris said quickly. "What does your father's gardening have to do with Charley and the others?"

It was a raw question, one that he normally wouldn't have asked. But this entire episode in his life had become too odd. Mysterious even. He was beginning to stress over it. God knew he was already losing sleep over it. So it just came out.

"Oh, Mister Morris," Sarah said wistfully. Then she took a step closer, as if afraid that her mother would be listening in at any moment. "That's really something for mother to speak about. Sorry."

She turned to leave, eventually disappearing upstairs. Left

alone, Morris gathered his things and walked slowly to the door. He had a final glance at a small table filled with old photos of war vets: Hav and the others returning home, meeting later, hoisting beers and triumphantly holding forks with barbecue speared on it, and again years later when they did the same thing as old men.

Just before Morris reached the front door he noticed a glass case he had seen before. It held a familiar picture frame perched inside that contained several items of memorabilia. Stopping, he saw it was the frame he had seen earlier that had no picture in it. It still had no picture in it.

Would love to see this photo, he thought.

Quietly he tried the glass door. It opened. Carefully he pulled the frame out to examine it. Not having anything to look at on the front, he turned the frame around to view the back. Then he saw it. At the bottom. There was an engraving with three words and a name. Morris read the words to himself.

"All the best. Walter Johnson," he whispered.

Morris drove back to the Marple, his mind buried beneath a swirl of doubts and suspicion. When he arrived he couldn't remember any turns he had made, or any stretches of road he had travelled. But he knew he didn't want to drive back to Atlas Town with all that hanging over his head. He retreated to his room and broke open the laptop. He had to put this story out of its misery. Part of him was yelling and screaming about the softball games tonight but he found himself resisting. He knew that if he drove to the game he would just be haunted by the story. So it had to be resolved.

But that didn't happen. Every time he got started, throwing his best thoughts and ideas into the mix, he became stymied as before. It happened over and over again until the frustration drove him to the point of anger. There were just too many questions and angles that had no answer or end. He slammed his laptop closed and began to pace across the room, interrogating himself, his hands cradling his head as if he had been wounded.

"Why do these guys stay so close together? Why did they move closer to each other? Why isn't Walter Johnson off in school somewhere, or working a job somewhere? Why didn't he even know what high school he went to? And why display a picture frame with no picture? Was it simply a memento from a wartime friend who was deceased?"

His words echoed off the walls and came back to him in ripples. Unable to defend against the onslaught of unanswered questions, his mind reached out to happier times, times when baseball and writing, cruising in his Chevy and being in love with Lorraine made up a perfect life for Jonny Morris. It felt like a million years ago.

It was at that moment when he felt the surrender. The story was just too deep, too far away or maybe too close and too small to see. At any rate it eluded him and he knew he couldn't, or he wouldn't write something second rate just to put an end to a deadline. Not this story. Like the tax story before it, this one was an all-or-nothing story. Something that would make Faber's eyes light up again.

He decided he needed a drink.

Arriving at Tallys he quickly took a seat at the bar and set his laptop up. It was all for show, though. Deep inside he knew he wasn't going to get anywhere with his writing here at the bar. He needed, or thought he needed, to take the edge off and there was nothing like a dozen drafts or so to do just that. He made a vain attempt to find out more about Hav Tescovitz by chatting up

Lou. But there was nothing he could say that Morris hadn't already heard. That's when the frustrations spilled over and killed the rest of his instincts. The soon to be missed deadline, the very real possibility that he would be fired, the fact that he was missing the world series, the breakup with Lorraine and fighting with Phil Grier, not to mention the lack of sleep and now nightmares of combat starting to invade his sleep, all coursing over him like the mother of all psychological tsunamis.

Morris responded with a soul soaking binge of beer drinking. It was almost self-defense. He had to shut his mind down and force sleep even if it was right here at the bar. When that sleep actually arrived Lou put him in a cab and sent him back to the Marple. He started a tab for him and sent a note to the Marple. That would go over real well later. Because Ron Faber wasn't paying for any of this.

8

Counterattacks And Rally Points

Morris woke up late Sunday morning and stood in a daze, trying to recall what had happened to him. When his mind finally cleared he knew he had turned a corner and it wasn't pleasant. Painfully, like a man headed for the scaffold, he packed his things and paid his bill with Ida Wolley. Then he stopped at Tallys and left money for Lou who hadn't shown up yet. He let the car run while he was inside. And the music was rolling along a little too loudly. When he came out he backed away from the Tavern and hit the road for home like he was starring in a James Bond film.

"Hey," he said aloud. "You only live twice!"

When he arrived in Atlas Town he was feeling much better even though all the problems that had overwhelmed him earlier started to return as his head cleared. Morris always got a little cocky when things were going against him. It was his way. He knew his story was due tomorrow morning and it wasn't even started. The looming meeting with Faber would be gruesome. But there was more. Now he wasn't only bothered with a story that wouldn't tell, he was suddenly not liking what he was doing.

Pressuring Connie Provenzano? What was that all about? She was eighty something and he was trying to dig a story out of her? What kind of human being does that? Then the fight with Phil Grier. If Lorraine had been caught with Grier Morris could have handled that. But Greg Jacks? That wouldn't do. Jacks was just one of those boys that used to push smaller kids around in high school. When he got older he just couldn't get it in his head that high school was over. Lorraine couldn't be with him. And now, he was not only suddenly hating his writing and hating going in to the Globe, he was shucking off softball, including the championship series. He started to think that his life choices were telling him something. Maybe he needed to change course. Not worry about the Atlas Town Globe, Ron Faber, softball, writing about sports and sweating hard memories over Lorraine. Or World War Two vets and Story Road in Smicksville, Ida Wolley and Lou and the whole goddam mess with his story for that matter. His world had suddenly grown small and uninteresting. Even annoying. Like working in an assembly line. Maybe…just maybe he needed to go back to basics, take his degree and look for a job with a bigger future. With bigger money. In a big city. Leave Atlas Town. Leave Lorraine.

"Jonny Morris!"

Morris looked up as he strode into Green's Bar. Bash was working and he was waving Morris over to the far corner.

"You guys lost! Where were you, man?"

He pulled himself up close to the bar, trying to be discreet. But what he really wanted was a big frosty beer and a sandwich.

"My life…it's getting complicated, Bash," he sighed.

"Oh man! The guys are kinda' sore, Jonny! Crawford especially!"

"A cold one, Bash. Turkey club…with chips."

"You got it. Man, the guys are so gonna' want to talk to you!"

Bash set a foamy headed beer in front of Morris and disappeared with the food order. That suited Morris. He didn't want to talk about the series or much of anything else. When the food came he kept his head down and didn't look up until it was gone. Then he ordered another beer. Then another. And then another.

Three hours later…

"Jonny Morris…"

Morris didn't look up. His mood had worsened considerably. And he had been drinking ever since he came in for a beer and a sandwich. He recognized the voice. He just didn't want to hear it.

"Jonny Morris," the voice came again. "The man who can't remember when the championship games are. Or maybe, he can't remember where they are."

Morris set his mug down.

"Greg Jacks," Morris said turning in his chair. "The ass-hat with two first names."

Jacks stiffened.

"I'm getting word that you have something to say to me," Jacks said as he began to square up.

"Yeah. I do."

Morris got up from the barstool and faced off with Jacks.

"Why oh why…do you have two first names? Why don't you just settle on one, like…ass-hat. Yeah…ass-hat. That should work."

It was right around then that the fists started to fly. It was no boxing match. More like a simple slugfest between two men who couldn't stand the sight or sound of one another. After chairs had been sent flying, tables overturned with food and drinks hitting the floor like the bar had been hit with a deli downpour, the entire matter became just one of who could throw the most right handed knockout punches. They both threw a lot of those. Each man was holding the shirt of the other, trying to rip it to shreds and throwing heaviest punches they could generate. It was straight out of a brawler's guide to a hockey fight. In the end Jacks was sitting down on a chair with his hand over one eye and Morris was sitting on the floor holding his jaw. They were both spent, cradling sore knuckles, bleeding from the mouth and nose with torn shirts sporting fresh bloodstains. And that's how the police found them.

"My God, Jonny," Betts said in a hushed voice. "You look horrible!"

Morris sat back in Betts' SUV with a grunt. In one hand was his jaw and the other gripped two citations.

"You 'chud see da' udder guy…"

Betts revved the engine and drove off from the police station. She couldn't resist looking over at Morris constantly, which caused her to drift over the center line a few times.

"What the hell happened? You were in a fight? On Sunday afternoon?"

Morris said nothing at first. It hurt his mouth to speak, a fact that Betts was apparently not aware of or indifferent to.

"Do you want to go to the hospital?"

"No."

"Are you sure?"

"No."

"No, you're not sure you don't want to go, or—"

"No I doh wanna go to da…hospi—dal…ow!"

He jerked back in pain as his mouth had gone in a direction it shouldn't have.

"I 'dink I have…looz' teeth."

He was really talking to himself but Betts heard anyway. She was eyeing him for serious bodily injury and determined to get him to the hospital.

"We're going to Memorial. You're a wreck."

"No!" Morris groaned. It hurt his mouth to do it but it was that serious to him.

"Ta' me to da' Globe first."

"I already called Ron, Jonny."

"Bess. Don't make me talg. Jus'…taig' me to da' Globe."

"Jesus," Faber said. "I've seen casualties of war that looked better than you!" He held his office door open for his reporter to totter through.

"'Tanks," Morris murmured.

Faber waved to Betts out front and closed the door.

Morris sat down in the now familiar chair in front of Faber's desk. In dark times he referred to it as the Executioner's Chair. And this was a dark time.

Faber sat down and leaned back in his chair.

"Well," Faber began. "at least you're wacking Greg Jacks instead of Phil Grier. That's an improvement."

Morris nodded.

Faber took a breath and started the part of the meeting that he dreaded.

"Jonny, I'm looking at you and I see…I see that you have… no article for me."

Morris shook his head.

Faber sighed. After glancing at his reporter for a second he took his glasses off and tossed them on the desk.

Incoming, Morris thought.

"Look Jonny. I think I have gone about as far as I can with this. I'm not a shrink. I don't believe in that crap anyway. But you are clearly off the rails and you are costing me."

Morris said nothing. It was what he expected.

"I am turning over all your assignments to Frank and I am releasing you. You can drop the story on the vets. You can forget about all the deadlines and just get yourself together. You're due one more paycheck next week. I'll even pay you a $250 bonus for your effort here at the Globe. But that's it. You'll need to clear your desk out by the end of this week."

"Id's 'shtill…my 'shtory," Morris droned.

Morris looked up and caught Faber's eyes. He knew he looked like a train wreck but he had to look the man in the eye for this.

"There won't be any story."

"My…'shtory."

"Not in the Globe."

"'Den 'shumwhere…'elsh"

Faber sighed and took out his checkbook.

"What did the hospital say?"

Morris said nothing. When no response appeared Faber looked up again.

"You didn't go to the hospital. You didn't go to the hospital?"

Morris said nothing.

"You know, Morris, I have seen self-destructive behavior before but you…too much drinking…fighting…missing work…travelling all over the place…you take the brass ring."

"'Shmicksville…is travelling?" Morris protested.

"I was paying for it! Yeah! That's travelling! Travelling and not giving me anything for it!"

Morris went quiet. Faber was right, of course but Morris was backed into a corner. He had to be expected to fight back, at least a little. When Faber didn't speak right away he tried again.

"I 'shtill 'wunt to…hear 'fum…'da Army. Walter… Johnson."

Faber glanced at him as he tore a check from his checkbook.

"Here's your bonus. $250. I suggest you use it at the hospital, which is where Betts is taking you next."

"Walter…Johnson," Morris groaned.

"Walter Johnson, yeah. I got it. But only if I get word from Betts in the next thirty minutes that your ass is at the hospital."

Morris stared back at Faber as their professional relationship came to an end.

"'Ogay."

Morris got up and slowly walked over to the door. He went through it and closed it quietly behind him. He didn't look back and he didn't take the check.

One month later...

"All rise!"

Morris rose from his chair and waited while Judge Berks made his way to the Bench. District Court 39-03 was about to begin its first session of the day. Judge Berks was the picture of a Norman Rockwell judge. His hair was grey, his face chiseled and his mood a little more than a touch on the impatient side.

The courtroom was a modern affair with drop ceilings, recessed lighting and uncomfortable chairs. Contemporary prints adorned the walls and the courtroom also boasted a sound system that enabled the spectators to hear the goings on as if they themselves were on trial. Though it was missing a lot of the old style charm in turn of the century courtrooms, it did retain one important factor in Jonny's eyes, though. The judge still used a gavel.

He glanced across the aisle quickly. Jacks was there, standing stone-like except for the slight slouch that betrayed a rebellious spirit. There were usually two deputies from the Sheriff's Office that maintained order but this day there were four. No doubt due to all the sizzle the Globe and other newspapers had given this story. There was no jury, however. Both had waived that in lieu of a hearing. As far as Morris was concerned there was nothing to fight so why bother twelve people who had better things to do?

The judge took his seat while speaking briefly to the Bailiff. Then he turned his full attention to the court.

"First of all, let me say that the two of you made a very wise decision NOT to have a jury trial. I firmly believe you would have been roasted and eaten by a jury. However, that was, apparently, the only smart decision you two made recently. Now I am getting information on this fight and the possible reasons behind it, I find that the two of you are simply not in control of your lives. I will fix that."

Morris took a breath and glanced behind him. He saw Betts sitting in the audience, no doubt reporting on the outcome to Ron Faber. She glanced back at him, a Mona Lisa class smile on her face. She couldn't help his case but she could help him deal with the outcome.

"Mister Jacks. You are charged with Disorderly, Assault and Destruction of Property. How do you plead?"

"Guilty," Jacks droned.

"Mister Jacks. This is the second incident with you in the last six months," Judge Berks said as he leaned back in his chair. "If I remember it was at a barbecue at a friend's house…strike that… at a former friend's house, that ended up with the police having to be called. You were fined for that, too, correct?"

"Yes."

"Yes. Therefore, I am fining you $1,250 for the Assault charge, plus costs, a further $1,000 for the Disorderly charge, plus costs, and further assess your liability in the destruction of property contained within Green's Bar, located at 285 Carillion East, Atlas Town, Pennsylvania to be 50% of the total claimed damages by said establishment, which neither of you contested."

Judge Berks glanced up from his pronouncement to confirm that both parties were still in agreement with the court. When both remained silent Berks went on.

"Said damages totaling $2,650, which you would be responsible for half, which comes to...$1,325. That comes to a total liability on your part to be $3,575, plus costs of $250, which shall equal…a total liability of $3,825."

The judge looked up, adjusting his glasses so as to focus on Jacks.

"That or ninety days in County. What say you?"

"I'll pay the fine judge."

"Let the record show that defendant has plead guilty and elected to pay the fine. Mister Jacks, you have thirty days to make restitution to Greens bar of $1,325, but the fine for the Assault charge is due in ten days or I will have a warrant for your arrest and you will go to jail for the ninety days plus whatever else this court adds to that for your contempt. Do you understand?"

"Yeah, I—"

"What? What, I didn't hear clearly…I thought you said—"

"I understand, Judge."

Berks slammed his gavel down.

"Done. And Mister Jacks…one more time in front of me… and I will start out with sixty days at county. And no doubt save the eating establishments of Atlas Town any further concern. Understand?"

"Yes, Judge. I understand."

As Jacks was led out of the courtroom Morris readied for his.

"Jonny Morris…"

"Yes Judge," he blurted out without thinking. The judge stopped and looked up. It was not a pleasant look.

"Jonny Morris…as this is the first time I have seen you in court for any reason, I am inclined to be more lenient. The testimony given by some who have come forward has Jacks as the aggressor so I will deal with you a little differently. First, whatever happened to taking it outside?"

Morris glanced up at the Judge. He wasn't expecting a question but thought that was a good thing. At least it was better than the look the judge had just given him.

"It happened so fast Judge, an opportunity didn't present itself."

Berks nodded cynically. Looking over at the Bailiff, who had all the appearances of a man with some experience in most things, Berks threw a hypothetical at him.

"I don't know…in my day there always seemed to be an opportunity to take it outside. What say you Bailiff?"

"I was always able to take it outside, your honor," the Bailiff gruffed. "It always worked for me."

"Yes…me too," Berks replied. Then he turned back to Morris.

"Jonny Morris. I hereby fine you $795, plus costs of $100 for the Disorderly charge and assess you $1,325 for reparations to Greens Bar. What say you to that?"

"I'll pay Judge."

"Mister Morris. You know what happens if you fail to follow through with this. Thirty days to pay Greens and ten days to pay the court?"

"Ninety days at County and a contempt charge."

"Don't disappoint me."

"No sir."

Berks slammed the gavel down once more.

"Done. Next case!"

Later, at the Boulevard Café

"Well, I might as well get to the point."

Jonny looked up from his sandwich and coke. Betts wouldn't

allow any alcohol and Jonny was feeling very cooperative right about now.

"First, here is your bonus check. Take it and don't give me any crap."

She slid the check sharply across the table, pushing it into his hand. Morris took it, knowing that his money was going to run low soon enough. He needed the help. So he swallowed his pride and stuffed it into his breast pocket.

"Don't be so down about it!" Betts cracked. "You earned it. Take it and be happy."

He nodded. He was going to say something but Betts cut him off.

"Ron asked me to come and see how things went today. He…feels that you and he have had a rough go of it lately so, he thought maybe I would have better luck."

"Okay," Morris sighed. "I have my seatbelt on…"

"Well, looking at this from everyone else's point of view, and I mean…everybody else…Ron and I talked it over and we agree…you're missing assignments, you're gone for long stretches, you miss work, you miss deadlines, you're fighting too much…you're drinking too much…"

The two stared at each other a moment. Morris thought there might be more but he wasn't sure he wanted to hear it. He loved Betts, and somewhere deep down he loved Ron Faber, but facts were facts. He couldn't be contained in Atlas Town and the Globe any longer and he didn't know why.

"…you're not even making it to your softball games," Betts added, killing the silence with her soft echo. "So…we are worried. Worried about you self-destructing. And…we don't think it's all about Lorraine but certainly she's a large part of it."

Morris sighed and leaned back in his chair.

"Betts, I don't know how to say this…but all of a sudden… it was like everything was closing in on me. Nothing worked in my mind anymore. The paper was too small, the town was too small, softball...was too small. Lorraine…she was, apparently, the thread that was holding me together. But I lost that. So, I just wanted out. I still want out, I think. Sometimes it seems like there's something in me that has never seen the light of day and now it wants to. There's something in me that hasn't worked but wants to. Or something…"

"Jonny," Betts began. Her voice a little final, maybe unbelieving, like an impatient sigh. "I might be able to write this off as a reaction to losing Lorraine. But all the rest about 'something trying to get out' and so on, I'm not buying any of that."

A stony silence erupted between them. It was uncomfortable for Morris to hear that his strongest ally didn't believe him. But it was just as uncomfortable for Betts to say it outright. The real sting for him, though, was knowing deep down that he didn't feel that way at all.

"What's this story you're writing about?" Betts continued. She was going to drive this conversation in a positive direction despite his best efforts to the contrary. "You know, the one that you told Ron was yours and yours alone. What's that have to do with all of this?"

He fiddled with his fork a moment, slowly pushing food scraps around on his empty plate.

"I'm not writing about it. I'm…trying to write about it. I can't bring it to the surface."

"This is the story about the world war two vets?"

"Yeah."

"You interviewed them, right? I saw the pictures. They looked pretty good. So—"

"But there's something else there that I can't let go of. Something they aren't telling me. Something I don't get. Something..."

Betts had a strained expression on her face.

"Jonny, do you know what Einstein said about insanity?"

"Uhh...no," he said impatiently. "What did Einstein say about insanity?"

"He said that people who try to do something, and go about it time after time using the same methods and practices, only to fail every time, are the true definition of insane."

He stared back at her as if waiting for the punchline.

"What that means is, whatever approach you are using to get to the bottom of this...you need to change. The approach, that is. You need to change your approach."

He thought for a moment, thinking that he had already done that, maybe a couple of times.

"You're thinking you've already done that, right?"

He smiled broadly, the first time in a long time.

"Yeah, yeah I am."

"Well they didn't work either. Maybe your problem is that there is only one approach that will work to get what you want, whatever that is. Nothing else works."

"Betts, you're starting to sound like Mister Spock."

"I hate Star Wars," she replied flatly.

"Star Trek."

"I hate that too. Especially the robot guy who wants to be human."

"Star Trek...Next Generation."

"Star Trek you said."

"Next Generation."

"Next Generation? What's that?"

"It's Star Trek but—"

"I hate Star Trek, Jonny. Let's talk about something else."

"Right…yeah. Something else," he said scratching his head.

They didn't speak for a few minutes. Betts finished her lunch and had coffee. He ordered another coke. When the waitress offered to bring the check Betts said she would take it. That suited him. He wasn't feeling chivalrous at the moment. Especially now that she had dismantled his own cover story, the one he was telling himself, over burgers and fries.

"You should go into psychiatry, Betts," he said when the waitress was a safe distance away.

She didn't answer. She just sat there staring back at him.

"Change you approach, Jonny."

"I wouldn't know where to start."

"I do."

"Where then?"

"Stop drinking so much. Start with that."

Now it was his turn to go silent.

"Stop drinking so much," she continued. "Change your approach to get your story. Get your story. Send it to Ron, because I know that's what you intend to do anyway. Send it to Ron and then take a moment to scan the horizon."

He looked up.

"What am I scanning for?"

She grabbed her purse and laid out cash for the bill.

"The next adventure for Jonny Morris."

Morris was making plans for one last trip to Smicksville when an unexpected email hit his laptop. There was that familiar *ding-dong* sound his computer made when mail arrived. He paid no attention at first. He was in the middle of writing a checklist of things to say, questions to ask, all things that still lingered in his mind. There were plenty of them.

But then he noticed the little blue message that popped up on the upper right hand corner of his screen. It stopped him dead in his tracks. It was the long overdue email from Faber about Walter Johnson. He tore into it like it was an actual letter.

Let's see, he thought as he started to read. *Walter Johnson... hometown...Baltimore...okay. Infantry...2nd Rangers...World War 2...okay...Battle Stars Pointe du Hoc...Hurtgens Forest...*

"Hurtgens Forest," Morris said stiffening. "That's the battle Walter Junior mentioned." All the heart breaking details of that battle came flooding back to him, Walter's voice echoing in his head. The Scout, the charge up the hill, Morris' first kill that came in a nightmare. Slowly he shook it off and read the rest of the email. He found Johnson's father and mother but it made no mention of brothers or sisters. That didn't make sense.

Ding-Dong.

This was from Faber as well.

Morris tore into that one. Faber had gone through the trouble of soliciting the American Legion. They had records that detailed Johnson's family as well as his battle record. Again, there was no mention of brothers or sisters. And neither document contained a death reference. That had to be wrong. It had to be.

He shot an email back to Faber thanking him for his work and asking if these documents show death records as a matter of routine.

Ding-Dong.

"Yes. They should."

Morris was set back on his heels.

"What in the hell is this now?" he growled to the ceiling. "Everyone says he's dead! Everyone except the government!"

Ding-Dong.

Faber again.

"I know you are screaming at the ceiling right about now so I am looking into this. Get back to you later. Ron."

Morris slunk back into his chair.

"Jesus," he murmured. "I didn't get this much attention from him when I worked for him."

He started to pack. That evening he was back in his room at the Marple Hotel, Ida Wolley Proprietor.

"Hello Sarah. Yes, it's me again. Jonny Morris…from the Globe."

Of course this was a lie. He no longer worked for the Globe but he decided to take Betts' advice and try a new tact. Besides, he was just a little desperate.

"Oh…yes. Hello Mister Morris. How may I help you?"

"Yeah, well, the photos I took last…they didn't fit with my editor's requirements, so—"

"Really? What was wrong with them?"

He almost choked on the question. Suddenly it seemed that Sarah was getting suspicious.

"Oh," he said with a dry laugh. "Who can tell with an editor?! Too much this…not enough that…ya' know?"

"Well," she answered with an uncertain laugh. "Not really, but—"

"I was wondering if it were at all possible…at all possible… could I come out one more time and meet…with whoever is there…?"

"I…dunno…you see…"

"I promise it won't take long. I—"

Suddenly Morris sensed that Sarah wasn't talking to him at the moment. He could hear discussion going on in the background. It was a little tense. He could make out Sophia's voice, her thick accent slicing through the background noise like a rifle shot through evening prayers. Then he heard others. It was voices of men. Sometimes they were all talking at once.

They're there, he thought. *They're all there*.

Just then Sarah came back on.

"I'm sorry Mister Morris. But we are entertaining tonight and would rather not be interrupted. Let's make it some other time."

"Oh…okay. Listen, I'm very sorry to interrupt your evening."

"That's alright, Mister Morris."

"Please pass on my greetings to the Provenzanos, Charley Garr—"

"Alright now. Goodnight!"

Sarah hung up the phone and left Morris holding his cell phone to his ear as if he might hear something. In the back of his mind he feared that one of them, like Charley Garr, might call the Globe to complain. Then the door would be shut in his face for sure. He had to dismiss it, though. He was in the breach, so to speak. There was no going back.

But what were the odds of all of them being at the Tescovitz's home? Morris hadn't been in Smicksville for over a month. He comes back one day and they are all there? It didn't seem likely. He tried to think of all sorts of reasons for the ongoing reunion but what intrigued him more than anything else was Walter. What was a young guy doing hanging out with World War Two vets and their wives and widows? Why wasn't he out chasing girls and driving fast cars? Deep down he knew he only heard Sophia and Charley Garr for certain. But if Charley Garr was there Walter had to be with him, right?

He wasn't with Garr when you visited Flintstone, Jonny, he thought. The admission was annoying but that was par for the course for this entire episode in his life. But he succeeded in turning the assumption into fact, if only in his mind. Walter had to be there. He had to be there because it would be consistent with every other screwball thing about this story. Not to mention the last two months of his life.

Reluctantly he opened a webpage that had his personal banking. He had to keep a watch on the money because the Globe wasn't paying. He was running off his savings and the bonus check that Betts delivered. Satisfied that he had enough to survive a little longer he decided to skip going out to dinner and just crash. Maybe tomorrow he would feel differently. At least he wouldn't be hung over.

"You alright?"

Morris looked up to see Walter Johnson standing over him, his M1 rifle in hand.

"Uhh…yeah. I'm good." Morris looked but was still unable to get a close look at Walter Johnson's face. There was always a shadow, or his helmet was pulled too far down or there was too much dirt on his face. Or it was night time.

"Good. Okay…listen up! We're being reinforced. Fox is being sent down the line to the Rally Point."

"Rally Point…" Morris repeated. He didn't know how but suddenly he knew what a Rally Point was and why they were heading there.

"Yeah. Rally Point. We get some hot chow. Maybe a shower. Good night's rest. It's heaven on earth. Gear up and get ready to move out!"

Morris pulled himself out of his foxhole, which he didn't remember digging, and started pulling himself together. When he straightened up he saw Garr, who was barking something at Provenzano, and there was Hav Tescovitz standing there saying something to Walter Johnson. There were others, too. But they just ambled by, heading down the hill. At the same time there were other men coming up.

"Hey!" one of them called out.

"What?" Sergeant Garr answered.

"You guys taking him?"

"Taking who?"

"Him!" the soldier said, pointing off up the hill. When they looked they saw it was the guy killed while digging a foxhole. He was still there. Burnt to a cinder. And he was still holding what was left of his shovel, digging on his knees, trying to dig a hole in the ground for him to crawl into.

"Would it do him any good?" Garr snapped as he ordered his men down the hill.

Morris fell in line with the others and started trudging downhill. He looked back once at the dead soldier with the shovel remnant in his hands.

"It wouldn't have made any difference!" he called out to Morris.

Stunned but afraid to stop marching, Morris turned his head to see where he was going and then back again to the burned soldier.

"What!? What wouldn't make any difference?!"

"The foxhole! It wouldn't have made any difference if I had finished! Direct hit, okay? I wasn't going to make it to the Rally Point no how! Okay?!"

Morris nodded twice at the guy.

"And don't tell anyone how you found me!"

Morris turned around and plastered his eyes on the back of the man marching in front of him.

"I won't," he gasped to himself.

He was shaking in terror and he couldn't make his body work at anything or think anything except marching down Hill 400 and making it to the Rally Point. That's where they were supposed to get hot chow, more ammo and a short breather. Maybe even a hot shower. He didn't say a word to anyone all the way down, past the dead scout who had a tarp over him by now and then a mile or so down the sunken road that a short time ago was Fox Company's community foxhole against two opposing bombardments. He closed his eyes, relying on the sound of the man in front of him to tell him where to march. Because he didn't want to see what was looming up ahead. It was the long row of men lying still and dead, covered in tarps or their field jackets until it appeared to be one large muddy green hump running along the side of the road. He couldn't look. He didn't want to be one of them. He wanted to make it to the Rally Point.

But then he knew who these guys were. He didn't know how he knew but he knew all the same. They were the guys the dead soldier with the shovel was talking about. Morris lowered his head and shut his eyes hard. He didn't say a word to any of them about what happened to their buddy. He was terrified they might answer. Might ask questions. So Morris buried his fears in the same pit he buried his thoughts and trudged along with the rest. It was deathly quiet. Not a single voice. Just the occasional cough, some clinking of cold gear against itself and the never changing droning on of boots on the ground echoing beneath a misty fog rising above with each man's breath. It was like that all the way to the Rally Point, where all the military strategists planned to refresh and refit the men and get them ready for another charge up a hill. Jesus, could that be done with hot chow and a shower?

Morris snapped to, coming to a sitting position. He was drenched in sweat just like the last nightmare he had. His breathing was heavy and he was disoriented. Then his thoughts short circuited. The waking reality he had sprung into so suddenly overwhelmed him. Instantly he was confronted with visions of the reality that he had left, possibly for good, just a few short weeks ago. The Globe, Ron Faber, Betts, his championship softball run and all the glories he had experienced only to be replaced by World War Two vets, horrifying battles, faces that didn't show themselves and stories that wouldn't write. Then, when he thought the worst was over, she came back. Lorraine reappeared in his life in all the good times they had shared, promises they had made, dreams they had dared to dream.

He struggled to his feet and staggered to a chair that rested by a window. There he collapsed, exhausted by the lack of sleep and all the rest that had gone wrong in his life. Everything began to melt together, like an enemy massing for an attack and it was finally coming at his most vital parts, the ones he had worked so hard to conceal. He begged for sleep but none came. And then he was overrun. His eyes shut hard, creasing his face and his hands reinforced the last effort to stem the final breakthrough. But it all failed. The tears came in irresistible spasms, broken only by the sobbing that rode with them.

And that's where he was when daybreak found him, the sun reluctantly climbing into the sky, offering a lonely pale light that drifted across the horizon in search of a home.

"I didn't tell them," he whispered to himself, his thoughts suddenly returning to the dead soldier still kneeling by an unfinished foxhole. Morris' face was stained with the remains of countless tears, his face ached and his eyes were half closed with oncoming sleep. He didn't try to stop it.

"I…didn't tell them."

9

Home Fronts

The coffee at *Don's Dive* is the best in Atlas Town. Everyone says so. And there's free refills. They also serve up the tried and true steak and eggs, hash browns and even scrapple. Or you can have pancakes or waffles. Add a hundred different brands of toast, muffins and bagels and you have the universal breakfast place. There's no music.

Morris sat alone in a booth overlooking the parking lot. He was scanning the classifieds in the Globe, occasionally looking up to watch the traffic through the window roll by, the world going about its business. Everyone had somewhere to go. Everyone had a job. A reason to get up in the morning. But here he was, at a dead end with the writing and out of work. Now that the real world had burst to the fore his primary worry was money. Even with the bonus Faber paid him it wasn't going to last long. Maybe another three weeks. Four if he scrimped. He needed to find work. Either that or he had to consider the real possibility that he would have to move back east to his parents' house.

Anything but that.

He returned to scrutinizing the Globe. It had a fairly large classified section. But there was nothing that suited him. Feeling a little desperate he made a few calls in an attempt to convince prospective employers that they needed something more than what they were advertising. But they didn't. Or, at least they weren't convinced they did. It was getting to be a little scary, though he wouldn't admit it. He even considered going back to Faber and asking for one more shot. One more chance to be a reporter. Maybe if he went back on his hands and knees.

Crap on that, he thought.

Then his phone rang. He grabbed it like an alligator snaps on a human leg, not bothering to check the calling number. Maybe someone changed their mind, wanted to give him a shot. Maybe it was Faber calling to bring him back.

"Hello."

"Hello to you. You back in town?"

It was Betts. Her voice was like a glass of water in the desert. Like the better part of his past reaching out. Maybe something would happen. Maybe Faber really did want him back. Maybe he wouldn't have to go back on his hands and knees after all.

"Uhhh…yeah! Back in town."

"How long?"

"Oh…uh…I dunno. I'm still looking for a new job and…I…"

"You're still working on that article," Betts said flatly.

He paused. Then he thought, *what the hell* and confessed.

"That's right. I can't let go. If it takes the rest of my life. If it kills me—"

"Let's hope it doesn't come to that," Betts cut in dramatically.

"Right. Okay."

"Ron said you would still be working it."

There it was! His heart started to beat again.

"Yeah. He's right. The voice of reason."

"He wanted me to tell you two things."

"Okay. I can handle two things right now."

"First, he will work this…Walter Johnson thing, and those other names. At least until he gets a solid answer from the..."

"Army," Morris added.

"Right. Until he gets an answer from the Army."

"Oh. Good," Morris answered. "Tell him thank you for that. And?"

"And…for you to remember that he will give you a top recommendation for any new position you apply for. Use his name with the office number."

Morris didn't speak. He was too busy trying to keep his heart from hitting the floor. He should have expected it, though. In fact, deep down he did expect it. But it still stung to know that the Globe was gone. The morning ritual by the coffee and donut stand. Talking to Betts. The little head butts with Ron Faber. It was all more desirable now than before. Much more. But the voices and faces were relegated to memory now. Memory and whatever he could imagine in an email.

"Jonny?"

He folded the newspaper and pushed it away.

"Yeah. Still here Betts."

"You okay?"

"Never better."

"Well, okay then. I…uh…well, where to next?"

He knew Betts was asking for the next significant change in his location but he just didn't want to oblige. Truth was, he didn't really know and he didn't want to speculate on the phone.

"I'm headed…Oh, I dunno. Somewhere to do some thinking."

There was a short silence.

"Jonny?"

"Yeah."

"Remember who your friends are. Okay? Remember who they are…and where they are. Okay?"

"Sure thing. And…Betts—"

"Yes?"

"Whatever you do…don't change the perfume."

She laughed briefly.

"Take care of yourself, Jonny Morris."

"Bye Betts."

Since time began for Jonny Morris there had been one place where he could go to think, to get away and reset his mind. Starting with the Little League years when he quickly became a ten year old obsessed with baseball, perfecting his game constantly whether he was at practice or home. Then, when he started to fight with his teammates after a loss he would end up here often, driving his parents into a frenzy when he failed to come home after school. Then came senior high school where he made All State two years in a row and MVP from his sophomore year on. But still it was the troubled teen struggling with who he was, where he was going and how well he played the game.

Then came college. Stormy romances dominated the lineup as he found it impossible to make room in his life for love or anything else not connected to baseball. Through it all he would pressure himself and often take it out on friends and family when plans and expectations failed to materialize. When he struck out in a key situation. When he muffed a ground ball or his throw to first sailed high over the head of the first baseman. When his team lost. It would all bring the dark cloud that would hang over him for days. No one wanted to be around him. Girls steered clear.

Then his college days ended. Despite the accolades, the awards, the famous incident where his bat tore a piece of the baseball from his stitching, the much anticipated invite to the pros never arrived. Desperate, he wrote to several clubs asking for a chance to try out as a walk-on. But that avenue had long ago closed in professional baseball. And so the path that he would finally end up on would be much different than what he expected.

Even as he hung up the phone with Betts he knew where he was going. Thirty minutes later when he sat down and leaned back against the metal backrest he finally felt like he was the home team again. Here he could reawaken old threads of memories that tasted sweeter. Winning games. Making great plays. Seeing Lorraine. Kissing Lorraine for the first time. Here he was always able to get deep inside himself and think things through, going back to the days when he had freckles. At the ballpark.

He leaned back and let his head gaze skywards. His fight with Jacks sprang into his mind like the proverbial visit from the in-laws. He struggled with his lack of success at ending the fight decisively the way he had intended. Namely, leaving Jacks in a pool of his own blood. The memory of that drove his blood pressure up. His teeth started to gnash together and his face became flushed. Even now, the thought of Jacks fooling around with his girlfriend then holding him off in a fist fight drove him to a smoldering rage.

Maybe I had too much to drink, he thought. Any excuse for not beating Jacks to death would do now.

Frustrated, he let his head fall forward until he was gazing out across the ballfield. Then, as always, the sound of the ballpark crept back into his head. The fans, the vendors, the smell of hot dogs on bright sunny days came to him in his own brand of virtual reality, slowly evaporating the memory of the Jacks' fight.

As he surveyed the diamond, noting little defects in the line, or the unevenness of the ground at home plate, his eye focused on the gap between first and second base. Then another memory fought its way to the front. His fight with Phil Grier.

He leaned forward, his gaze dropping to his feet and his thoughts scurrying to find refuge. He didn't feel good about that fight either. Phil Grier was about as straight laced as they came. He was the first to show up when a family suffered a calamity like a house fire or a death of a family member. He could also be seen out on the roads working a plow when the heavy snows came and everyone else was inside drinking hot toddies and watching movies.

Oh man, why did I do that? He thought, serving as his own tormentor. *What was I thinking?! It would have been better if I was a hundred miles away on assignment...*

But it was too late for that kind of hind sight. His fight with Grier would end up sticking in his craw more than the Jacks' fight. It was the one he won, but wished he hadn't.

So he got quiet. The sounds of the ballpark drifted through again but they became thinner, shorter, and didn't bring the same good feeling he was used to until he found himself staring ahead to the outfield and beyond, his mind a complete blank.

"Hello Jonny..."

The voice jolted him to his senses. It was familiar as it was unexpected. He turned in a flash, his eyes searching out a person that his instincts told him shouldn't be here, the person who left the huge hole in his heart.

Hello…Lorraine," he said haltingly.

She came around the side of the bleachers keeping her eyes averted. At first it looked like she might climb up a few rows to sit with him but she halted. Then she looked up and stared at him.

"Betts said you would be here."

He nodded. Suddenly there was a battle raging in his brain. He was still angry. Hurt. Still wanting vengeance. But Lorraine wasn't here to fight. That didn't soften him any, though.

"Yeah," he muttered. "It's a go-to place."

She smiled thinly and turned to look out across the field. Then she turned to face him and, striking up what courage she had, she attempted to start a dialogue. It would be the first in many months.

"Betts told me you were into a really tough article that you were writing for the Globe."

"I don't work for the Globe anymore."

"Yeah…I heard…Betts told me that, too."

He nodded impatiently.

"So…what's up with this one? You usually run through an article pretty quick? Is it—"

"I don't know Lorraine!" He snapped. "Why don't you ask Betts? She's told you everything else!"

"Sorry…I…I just wanted to know what was going on with you—"

"Oh! That's rich! So you want to know what's going on with me? Well I'll tell you! First, there is a story that won't be told and I'm trying to tell it! No one believes me when I say that! But there it is! It won't be told! When I get close it jumps away! And when

I am far away it cruises by me in the dark! Second, let's see… well second is…I lost my job! I lost it because no one believes what I say about this story! But I just told you that! Third…not long ago I stopped in to see you when I came home early from an assignment and found you in Jacks' pickup truck…in a very compromising position! So there's that! There's that going on in my life right now!"

His blood up he glared at Lorraine who was still several rows below him. She tried but couldn't look at him. Defeated, she made her best attempt to withdraw.

"I'm sorry Jonny…" she said softly. "I don't know why…I can't…explain…I just…wanted to know what was going on with you. I can't think of what else to say—"

"And neither can I Lorraine! If this is all you were interested in you should have saved it. I have too much shit on my mind right now!"

"Okay Jonny!" she cracked. "Okay! I won't ever again take an interest in anything you do! And I'll tell you something else! I won't ask anyone else, either!"

"Fine!" he shot back. "That will save Betts a ton of headaches, won't it! She won't have to listen to your bullshit! Over and over again!"

Lorraine gazed back at him, her eyes welling up in tears. Her lips trembled as she tried to say something but her shattered feelings failed her.

"You know what your problem is Lorraine?" he cracked. "You have never wanted something, been close to something, but couldn't have it even though you needed it! And there it was! Right in front of you! That's your problem!"

He sat back, satisfied that he had laid a truth on her that could not be refuted. He knew she would go running to Jacks anyway so why should he send her off with sweet, rosy words with some deep philosophical relevance?

"Yes I have," she sobbed. And she turned and left.

Jonny listened to the sound of her quickening footsteps growing fainter until he heard a car door opening. After it slammed shut the engine started and the car began the slow exit down a gravel lane. He didn't know why he hadn't heard it coming. But that didn't matter now. When the sound died away completely he knew she was gone. He never once looked back.

He stayed there on that bleacher for another hour. His thoughts slowly drifted away from baseball, great plays, heroic wins and the losses sprinkled in between. Quickly his mind travelled forward in time to the assignment in Smicksville and the interviews that followed. The suspicions that grew inside him and the fight with Faber. Then finally, inevitably, he reached the still raw memory of the conversation with Lorraine Reynolds. Her voice was jammed into his head like a hard fastball coming in at the wrists. But it only made him all the more determined that everything he said needed to be said and it couldn't be unsaid. He picked himself up and strode down the bleachers until he was able to jump over the last two. Landing on the ground he walked quickly to his car and got in, slamming the door just as she had. He started the engine and peeled out, leaving a trail of gravel and dust in his wake. His radio sprang to life, the music coming on extra loud. Morris was running out of options and out of time as far as he was concerned. Something was going to have to break, even if it went down more brutal than he would like. Everything that had gone wrong in his life, as well as the lack of sleep and spending his days grinding his teeth over all of it had finally pushed him to the edge. Maybe journalism wasn't for him. Maybe he should break free and do something else.

Like what, he thought. *Be the next Sean Hannity?*

He shook it off. There was no way to go but forward on this. The story had to be broken or he wouldn't be able to hold a job delivering newspapers. Suddenly the music broke through his mental barrier. It was Juice Newton singing *Break It To Me Gently*. It was too loud. Even for him. Without a glance he reached for the radio and spun it to a new station.

The Next Day

"Is she coming down?" Garr asked.

Sarah only shook her head as she made her way into the living room where everyone else was sitting. Charley Garr was standing across the room, drink in hand. Sonny and Connie Provenzano were seated on the couch but they still turned their head to see Sarah come into the living room. Walter sat across from them, near a table that had several of the photos of the Four Horsemen posing in various parts of Europe. He was looking at one when Sarah arrived from upstairs.

"It wasn't supposed to be like this, Sarah," Garr said sadly. "She shouldn't be going through this."

"That's right, Sarah," Sonny added. "Did you ask her to come down? Ask her to come down, ya know?"

"She will, Sonny. She'll come down but she just wants to be alone for a little.

Garr set his drink down.

"She's too old for this! We all are! Sarah, go back and tell her to do what she has to do! Life's too short…for any…of us! Tell her to come down!"

Sarah glanced at Garr impatiently.

"I will…Charley. I will. But we are going to give her some time and leave her to her own thoughts. Now…everyone… please…have a drink. There's still food in the kitchen. But we are going to let mama be for now."

With that Sarah strode into the kitchen, either to bring food that no one asked for or to give herself some space. The others were left in total silence, slaves to their thoughts, faking interest in old photos or some activity seen through a window. It was only a few minutes, but then Connie got up and walked the short distance to the kitchen and sat down with Sarah. At first the two women didn't look at each other. They didn't even acknowledge each other. But that didn't matter. They both knew the other was there and why. And they both knew what the other was going to say.

"She's worried about the others…about…all of us, isn't she Sarah?" Connie said softly.

Sarah looked up slowly. Her eyes stained with tears and her words uncertain.

"Y-yes. She has so many…things…in front of her and she doesn't know what's b-best."

"But…I thought she had already decided that it—"

"Yes but not for all of you! It's the part about all of you that is breaking her heart!"

Connie sat back. Her face betrayed a sudden realization. She had never considered it, thinking Sophia was straining over something that she had already made up her mind about.

"Oh. I…didn't realize…"

"No…I know!" Sarah said taking her hand. The two women took comfort in each other for a few moments, squeezing their hands together and wiping their eyes every now and then. The only sound was the murmur from the men in the other room. The words were unintelligible. Finally, when the silence in the kitchen seemed more like an explosion, Connie spoke.

"You know, we are getting too old for this."

Then they looked at each other again, thin smiles spreading across their faces until Connie was reminded that Sarah was more than forty years younger than she.

"Well, I'm getting too old for this!"

In the next room Sonny Provenzano pulled himself off the couch with a soft grunt and made his way across the room in Garrs direction.

"Hey, Charley…"

Garr drained the last out of his glass and turned to face Sonny.

"Yeah."

"Look, I think…maybe the best thing to do is for everyone to leave, ya' know?"

Garr stared back, his face unmoving, giving no clue as to what effect Sonny's suggestion had on him.

"You mean, just walk away?" he gruffed. "Leave…Sophia and Sarah?"

"Look…Walter over there," Sonny said motioning with a nod of his head. Walter Johnson Jr. was holding a photo in his lap but staring out the window that opened up to the approach to the house from Story Road.

"He's gettin' depressed, too, ya' know?" Sonny continued.

"I can see it in him. And Sophia…she don't need this. She's lost enough. It's making her life hard…and Sarah's life too. You said so yourself."

"I don't want nothin' from Sophia," Garr rasped.

"I know, I know," Sonny rasped. "But it's all too much for Sophia, I think. It's too much. Nobody has any regrets. And nobody wants anything here. But we don't want to ruin anyone's life either, ya' know?"

Garr nodded slowly. There was no getting around Sonny this time.

"Oh hell, Sonny. Maybe you're right. Maybe we all should pack it in and go home. I just…I think I don't like the thought of…leaving them with the wrong impression."

"Yeah. Yeah," Sonny whispered. "That won't happen…that won't happen."

"Maybe when she comes down," Garr said softly. "We'll say 'goodbye' and leave then. We'll just say it's time for us to go home. How does that sound?"

"Okay Charley. Okay. I'll tell Connie when she's done in the kitchen.

Garr nodded.

A stony silence settled in, pinning both men together. After a few restless moments Sonny turned to head back to his seat on the couch, leaving Garr with a brotherly squeeze on the arm. Garr nodded again and started to pour himself another drink.

"Somebody's here," said Walter.

"What? Who?" Garr cracked.

"I think it's that guy from the newspaper," Walter said as he studied the figure emerging from a car. Garr came over to look but his eyes were of no use.

"Yep. It's him," Walter sighed. Then he turned to the others in the room.

"Jesus Christ," Garr said in disgust. "Doesn't this guy have a job?"

Just then there was a sound at the bottom of the steps. Everyone looked to see Sophia coming down the last two steps and beginning to make her way to the living room. Garr put his drink down and motioned for Sonny.

"Did you call the driver?"

"What?" Sonny answered.

"The driver, dear. He wants you to call the driver," Connie said, holding herself close to Sonny's ear so he could hear.

"The driver?"

"I'll do it," Connie said to Garr who was making his way towards Sophia. He met her just as she was about to enter the living room.

"Sophia," Garr said softly. "We thought it was time for us to go."

"Oh?" Sophia glanced at Garr and then Sonny who was now up again and walking towards her.

"Sonny? Why are you all leaving?" Sophia pleaded.

"Well, we thought there was…enough going on, ya' know?"

"Right," Garr echoed. We can come back in a few days, maybe after the weekend."

"But you've only been here a few hours!" Sophia answered, her face souring.

Garr and Sonny glanced at each other, each waiting for the other to speak. After an awkward moment Garr spoke up.

"That newspaper guy is here again. We thought it best if we weren't here, that's all."

"The newspaper man," Sophia answered softly as she tried to view him through a window next to the front door. "He's a nice man—"

"He asks too many questions," Garr answered quickly.

Then Sarah arrived in a rush.

"What? Mama…are you okay?"

Sophia nodded briefly and put her hand on Sarah's arm to reassure her. Then she glanced back at the two men.

"Yeah, Sophia," Sonny continued. "It's not good. Better if we leave, ya' know?"

Sophia stared back, not looking directly at either man. Then slowly started to shake her head.

"No. No, Sonny…I don't know. We are all friends. For many, many years now. You can't go running off because of…someone at the door!"

She looked back and forth at the two men. When she got no response she tried her best to keep them at her house.

"What looks worse, you staying and acting like you all do every day…or leaving just as he knocks on the door?"

Neither man could answer. And there was no more time.

"Who's here?" Sarah asked, desperate to get caught up.

"I…guess not," Garr sighed.

Sarah took a few steps so she could see through a window.

"It's him," she whispered. "The man from the newspaper!"

The doorbell rang.

Everyone near the door simply froze, not knowing what to do. Finally Sophia spoke up, her soft voice taking command and shooing all the uncertainty.

"Now…wouldn't it be best if we were all seated in the living room?"

"What? You want us to stay?" Sonny asked, his hearing failing him again.

"Yes, Sonny. Please. Go sit with Connie."

Sonny turned and walked uneasily back to the couch and his waiting wife.

"Did you call the driver, Charley?"

"Connie did."

"Then cancel the driver."

The doorbell rang again.

Garr sighed.

"Okay, Sophia," he muttered as he walked away.

Alone with Sarah, Sophia started for the door.

"Refreshments," she said with a turn of her head, sending Sarah back to the kitchen.

Sophia opened the heavy door as best she could. It creaked and groaned as if reluctant to let the visitor in.

"Oh. Mister Morris. What an unexpected surprise."

10

Spies And Lies

Morris took a seat across the room from Garr. Walter Johnson Jr. sat nearby on another chair to his immediate left while the Provenzanos were on the couch towards his front. Everyone seemed cheery enough. Sophia Tescovitz was her usual sweet self, the Provenzanos smiled and waved. Walter smiled thinly and nodded his head and Sarah arrived with a tray of refreshments and snacks. Charley Garr wasn't scowling this time.

"So, Mister Morris," Sophia began, taking another seat on the couch. "What brings you to our home?"

Morris thought a second. While he was driving he was running all his thoughts through his head, what he was going to say, how forceful he was going to be and how he was going to flush out the misdirection, which he had convinced himself was there. But he hadn't expected the house to be full. He was banking on the Tescovitzs being the only ones at home. He hadn't seen extra cars but then he reminded himself that the Garrs and Provenzanos hired a driver. So, already he was on the defensive and nowhere to go but forward.

"Well, we were about to go to print on the article, with all the pictures and…well…my editor got on me about some holes in the story. So I took some heat for that."

"Holes?" Sophia asked.

Morris gazed back. He wasn't sure how to explain this but the word had just jumped out of him.

"Uhhh…parts of the story that don't…run smoothly."

Sophia nodded slowly.

"Well, I don't know about these 'holes' as you say…"

"Maybe…maybe if I just ran over the basics one more time…get a starting point…they might all iron out on their own."

No one spoke. Morris took that to mean he had a green light. Now the trick was to be firm but not arrogant.

Don't be pushy, he told himself.

"Now, Sonny. Can you tell me where you were born…what year, then tell me when you joined the Army?"

Sonny gazed back a moment then, with a quick glance towards Garr he stumbled on with his answer.

"Well, I was born in Brooklyn, ya' know? Brooklyn, in 1923. I guess I signed up after Pearl. They sent me to the Rangers and…the next thing I know, I'm climbing up this muddy caved in cliff and fighting my ass off in France!"

Morris noticed Garr's short smile after Sonny's remark. Walter Johnson Jr. chuckled. So far so good. Of course, Morris had all this info but it was the only safe way to start this visit.

"Now, Mister Walter Johnson. Your uncle—"

"Great uncle."

Morris stared back.

"Oh. Right. Great uncle. Do you recall where he was born and when?"

"Man, I thought we went through all this when you came to Flintstone."

"You came to Flintstone?!" Garr blurted out.

Morris could only stare back as Garr's eyes were trained on Walter Johnson. It felt good not to be the target of Garr's anger.

"Yeah. He came a while back."

The old sergeant only glared back.

"You could have told me. You should have told me!"

Walter Johnson didn't answer right away. He looked straight back at Garr, though. No doubt there was a message in that but Morris couldn't read it.

"Alright. I shoulda' told ya'. I'm tellin' ya' now."

There was a tense, almost electric silence that settled in, like the aftermath of a bombardment. Morris held his tongue, hoping that the interview wasn't already over.

"I was drinking. Wasn't myself," Walter added.

Still no response from Garr.

"And…I thought it would just upset you." He added this last bit almost as a conciliatory remark. It had the initial effect of a peace offering without losing too much of the defiance.

Garr tossed the rest of his drink down and slammed the glass on the side table he was standing next to. Then he left the room, heading for the back door and leaving a wake of fire and smoke in his path.

Shit, Morris thought.

After the sound of the back door slamming shut alerted everyone as to Garr's disposition and location, Walter Johnson went on.

"So…where were we?"

Morris attempted to kick start the interview.

"I…uh…I was asking about your great uncle . Where and when he was born. When he joined the Army. And…uh… well, that's as far as we went."

Morris watched as Walter Jr. took some drinks from the refreshment tray Sarah had brought in. Then he looked around and found the bottle Garr had been drinking from on the side table across the room. He headed that way.

Morris knew Walter Jr. was not twenty one years old. He was sure Sophia would not like his drinking the hard stuff. But, surprisingly, Sophia said nothing. She and Sarah just sat and gazed ahead, like they were waiting for a train. Sonny and Connie were quiet as well. He had his arm around her and the both of them were just a bit huddled together, staring off into space.

"Yeah, that's right," Walter replied. "Great uncle Walter was born in…I think Michigan. I don't remember the year. But I do know he joined before Pearl. I guess he just liked the military thing. So he ends up in the Rangers. Second Rangers. He storms up the Pointe, fights his way across France with Garr, Provenzano and Tescovitz. Lots of stand up gunfights with the Krauts. Then he ends up at Hurtgens Forest, which I already told you about. But there we were, digging holes, crawling around, lying around, the dead ones, that is."

Walter stopped there as he refilled his glass. Morris was stunned even though he had almost all this information already. But no one was interrupting. No one was trying to get the kid to calm down. Ashamed of himself deep down, Morris didn't try to stop him either.

"But," Morris interjected, attempting to segue into calmer waters. "wasn't the battle of Hurtgens a victory for us?"

Walter Jr. only stared at the wall as he took a big hit from his glass. Then Morris heard Sonny's voice.

"It didn't have to be fought, ya' know?" Connie said something to Sonny that only he could hear but he reassured her with a nod of his head.

"It cost a lot of guys their lives, ya' know? And it didn't have to be fought. It was…somethin' like climbing up the Pointe to get the guns and finding no guns for miles."

Morris stared back at Sonny who seemed to be waiting for an answer. But Morris had none.

"Ya' know?" Sonny said before settling back on the couch.

Yeah. Morris was starting to figure this out. There was a lot of pain marching along with the Four Horsemen, or the Two Horsemen, though Walter Jr. seemed to be carrying some for his great uncle.

There was a sound in the kitchen like a door opening before it slammed closed. Then a figure and a voice arrived in the entranceway that joined the living room and kitchen.

"What newspaper do you work for?" he rasped.

Charley Garr was back.

Morris stared back for a heartbeat or two. It was obvious Garr was spoiling for a fight. It would be all he could do to keep the interview alive.

"Uh…the article was for the Atlas Town Globe…"

"The Atlas Town Globe? So they sent you here again…to do another interview?"

Morris shifted in his seat. He was going to have to be very careful how he answered this time.

"Do you want to call them?" Morris said evenly.

There was a tense stare down between Morris and Garr. One man calling another's bluff. Then the second man returning the favor.

"Yeah. I think I do," Garr cracked.

Morris fished out his cell phone and held it out as an offer to Garr, who didn't move.

"I have the office number on my cell."

"Why don't I just call from here?" Garr snapped, pointing to the telephone in the living room.

"Well, you can do that. But—"

"But what?"

"But…it'll be a long distance call charged to the house."

Morris wasn't sure that the call was long distance but he had to throw everything in front of Garr that he could. The last thing he wanted was for Garr to get hold of Ron Faber. Two combat veterans talking about a go nowhere former reporter did not hold a bright future for Morris.

The old vet stared Morris down a few moments, cell phone extended, the tension crackling with each heartbeat. In the end Garr waved him off in disgust and instead strode over to the table with the liquor on it. Pouring himself another drink he mumbled something to himself that no one needed an interpretation of.

"I'm tired of talking about this!" he gruffed. "This had better be the last! D'ya hear!? The last!!"

In the short silence that followed, Morris felt himself shrinking in his seat. He had no right to be asking these people anything. He had no right to simply show up here and gain access to an interview by these underhanded means. This was all a lie and he was the liar. Then another thought appeared in his mind, one borne of countless sleepless nights and the nightmares that rode with them. The heavy drinking and fighting and a broken heart had all added to his desperation to slay the ghosts that had taken up residence in his soul, all dancing around a shadow that was the real story behind the lives of the Four Horsemen, their wives and family.

"I'm sorry," Morris said softly. His words drifting through the thick air like the first snow flurry of winter. "But you're story, the story of World War Two, and the people who fought it, is being forgotten. And that ain't right. I…just wanted to get it right. Tell the story. No mistakes…"

His words trailed off to nothing. But Sonny was nodding slowly while Connie dabbed a tissue at her eyes. Sophia, Sarah holding her by the arm, gazed straight ahead, slowly rocking forward and back, her face concealing all emotion. Walter Johnson Jr. was leaning forward with his head in his hands and Garr said nothing. He stood frozen, staring at the wall directly in front of him, his chest moving with each agitated breath.

"They always forget," Sonny said at last. "Everyone always forgets, ya' know? I think that's how people are able to move on. They forget. Ya' know?"

Another unsteady quiet followed. Sophia, Sarah and the rest were deep in their own thoughts while Morris was praying that the interview wouldn't end. He couldn't escape the truth staring him right in the eyes, though. That behind the pleasant smiles, the hospitality, the sheer will that permeated their personas, there was a constant tension, like a spring that was never fully unwound. It would show itself in short bursts, like an occasional quick temper or a period of quiet reclusiveness. One would suddenly become moody. Drunk. Violent. It was a hurt that wound its way through the heart with a stitching of images of lost friends and dead men, woman and children, animals, all the sights and smells that silently burned its brand upon the soul itself. It could be hidden, even resisted but it would eventually burst through into the waking world. It would never heal.

Morris glanced up suddenly, his cell phone still in his hand. Sophia and Sarah were still on the couch. Connie too. But Charley Garr and Sonny had left, presumably to go out back. Walter Johnson Jr. was still in his seat. He was looking straight at Morris, a look of distant emptiness in his eyes. It seemed that there were no more words to say in the whole world for him, like tomorrow didn't matter anymore.

Morris stood up. As much as he wanted to interview Garr he knew there was no chance of that tonight. Maybe never. But there was Walter Johnson Jr. He was staring right at him almost as if inviting him to take the plunge. To push just a little harder tonight. But Morris was not up for it. The more he spoke with these people who fought the last World War the more intimidated he felt. They were the generation that left their youthful and carefree days behind to fight in some far off chunk of the world. The ones that came back never came back fully. As Morris was discovering that so was he also finding it more difficult to approach. In fact he was suddenly shocked that he had made this trip. He felt unwanted. He didn't belong. Not like the others, even Walter seemed to fit.

Morris stuffed his phone in his pocket and rose up from his chair. He returned the stare to Walter Johnson briefly then turned to Sophia.

"Thank you for having me Missus Tescovitz," Morris said softly as he gathered his things. It seemed the interview was over after all.

The Marple Hotel. Ida Wolley proprietor. Morris had almost forgotten the musty odor that seems to permeate old buildings. The creaky door that opened to the foyer with a chandelier that cast a dingy light in all directions. The creaky steps with the faded runner. And the second floor hallway and its wide floorboards that were not quite level. It was all ghostly familiar.

His old room was exactly the same. The same chair in the corner pointed towards the center of the room. The bed. The linen. The quilt that lay on top. All that and the same window that could only be opened by brute strength, looked out over the same timeless road that ran through the middle of Smicksville. It was almost a second home.

He threw his bag on the bed and himself right after. His interest in the story had faded somehow. It reminded him of a certain type of burnout. Maybe he should just let everything go. Let these people lead the rest of their lives in the peace they had earned. He thought it would be a good idea to fire up the laptop and check his finances. But then he thought it was no use. He knew what his finances were. They were bad. He was down to his last few hundred dollars and the only thing that would make that go away this night, even if only temporarily, was sleep. Sleep. That was a good idea.

Sitting in a muddy foxhole, surrounded by a nightfall that was being reinforced with every passing second, he was suddenly aware that there was someone standing over him. He looked up and, straining his eyes through the darkening sky and the soft drizzle that was falling, he saw it was a soldier standing at the edge of his hole. He was apparently lost and had stumbled onto Morris' position. He was ragged, like he had just been in a fight.

Maybe that was the firing Morris heard an hour ago. The soldier was muddy down to his boots, his slumping shoulders haggard with fatigue. His face was a sullen and dark shape in the shadow that lived just under the brim of his helmet. He wavered a little, his large form teetering left and right as he tried to maintain his balance.

"Say man," Morris whispered. "You lost?"

"Yeah," the soldier rasped. He then looked around briefly, as if trying to find a familiar landmark.

"I...don't know where to go from here."

"Corporal Johnson?" Morris asked. "Man, you're hit!"

Corporal Johnson glanced down at this forearm noticing the blood that had soaked through his jacket and the tear in the material that went with it.

"It'll keep."

"Look, get in the hole here. We'll figure out where you gotta' go."

There was no answer.

"Look man," Morris continued. "Get in the hole and maybe you can show me bee stings don't bother you!"

"That...was a long time ago," came the answer. "A long time ago...way over there."

He turned and pointed off in the distance. Then he turned back to face Morris.

"You were just a replacement when you started up the hill," Johnson said.

"Yeah," Morris answered, still desperate to get Johnson in his hole. "C'mon. Jump in..."

Johnson scrutinized Morris huddled in his foxhole.

"You saw the guy that got burned up trying to build his foxhole," he said evenly.

Morris nodded, remembering the horrific image of the soldier with his shovel, or what was left of it, incinerated on the spot while he knelt to dig his hole.

"I saw him."

"Did you hear what he had to say?"

"Yeah," Morris answered slowly. "He said...that he didn't want me to tell anyone how I found him."

"Right," Johnson whispered.

"I didn't tell anyone," Morris muttered.

"And you won't, either. Right?"

Morris could only nod. He had no idea who the man had been. But somehow he knew that he had left a huge hole in the lives of several people back home.

Then the soldier started to shuffle off, moving around the right side of Morris' foxhole.

"Hey, wait a minute!" Morris hissed. "Where you going?"

Johnson stopped briefly, still scanning in all directions, looking for a way to go, maybe a route home.

"Nah. I've been in that foxhole," he said matter of factly. "I need to find a way to go from here."

"Man, how you gonna' know how to go from here if you don't know where you need to get to?"

The soldier turned around one last time.

"I'll know when I see it. So will you." There was one more pause, a noisy interlude stuck between two soldiers in the middle of a silent battlefield.

"Do me a favor," Johnson asked.

"Yeah. What's that?"

"Don't tell them how you found me, either. Got it?"

Morris stared back, his eyes still searching for the face that eluded him, lurking somewhere behind the unshaven faces, the mud, the pain, the broken hearts and the coming nightfall that would soon overrun their position.

"Yeah," Morris answered softly. "I got it, corporal."

And with that Johnson turned away and trudged off into the growing night. Morris watched until he had been swallowed by the same shadows that clouded his face, until the sound of his boots on the wet ground died in the night...

"Uhh! No!" Morris gasped as he came to with a jolt. He sat up in bed, his legs dangling off the side. His eyes darted about, his mind racing to get oriented. The soldier from Hill 400 was just here. Maybe he was still here. But there was no one. Only the sound of his heavy breathing penetrated the silence. Wiping his face with one hand, he began to collect himself. He had slept in his clothes, his body in the same position he took when he first collapsed last night. Or was it yesterday afternoon? He couldn't remember. He saw that his bag was still laying on the bed next to him. The window was revealing the initial shards of light from an advancing dawn break through. The ceiling light was still on.

He stood up as if on command, trying to clear his mind from the images that had paraded past him. Apparently he had slept better than recent days. His mind was fairly alert for a change. He wasn't hung over. His hands weren't shaking and he was hungry. He sat back down and let himself wake fully. If there was going to be a change in his life then it would, or it should, start today. It would be a fresh start for a new Jonny Morris.

It began with a shower and shave, a clean set of clothes and a coffee from a fast food joint in town. When he finished his coffee he got his free refill and headed towards Tally's Tavern.

It was the best place for him to think about his determinations from last night. Whether or not to drop the entire story and move on with his life. More than one person was advising the same. If he did drop the story then he could concentrate on getting his professional life back together. Return to the sweet distraction of softball. A new girlfriend. He would square things with Phil Grier. And he wouldn't be making a liar out of himself in front of the vets and their wives and family. The shame of that ploy returned sharply, forcing him to decide that dropping the story and moving on was the best course of action after all. The mere thought of that brought relief to his aching conscience. Maybe, in time, he could forget it. Write it off as a personal crisis of sorts, boredom with the job, obsessing over a story that wasn't there. Losing his girlfriend to someone like Jacks. He would sleep better, that's for sure.

He arrived at Tallys before they opened.

"You're back!" Lou said as he continued with his opening ritual. Morris took a seat in a booth that had a window that overlooked the parking lot.

"I am," he said cheerily. "I always try to make time for good food."

"Ohhh, flattery," Lou said sarcastically. When he came around next he dropped a menu off and took a drink order.

"Beer with lunch?"

Morris thought for a moment. Beer at 1130 in the morning would not suit the new Morris very well.

"Nah. How about a soda?"

"Soda. Something new. Cola?"

"Sounds good."

While Lou was getting Morris' drink he took the time to fire up the laptop and open his mail app. There was still mail coming in for him from his Globe days. They would be difficult to look at right now. And there was some junk. But there was one from Ron Faber.

He clicked Faber's email open and went to full screen.

Army says that Hav Tescovitz; Private, served in 2nd Rangers with Charley Garr; Sergeant. Sonny Provenzano; Private First Class and Walter Johnson: Corporal. Unit assaulted Pointe du Hoc; 1944. All survived the war. Hav Tescovitz passed away this last Fall, as you already know. No record existing on any other member's passing.

I found Walter Johnson's record most interesting, of course. So, I asked my contact to dig more into that name. He reveals that Walter Johnson, 2nd Rangers, was originally Walter Benton. Originally from Knoxville, Tennessee. He was a ward of the state of Arkansas briefly. Mother passed away from tuberculosis in 1922. Father dead in a construction accident in 1926, in Arkansas. Walter was four years old. Since there were no relatives that could be found he was eventually sent to a Catholic orphanage that is no longer extant. The Brother's Orphanage of Little Rock. Walter lived there until 1930. Family by the name of Johnson adopted him and took him to Michigan. Joined the Army in September 1941. Volunteered. Walter Benton/Johnson has/had no known siblings in either family. Both step parents have now passed away.

Not sure what else I can find for you. Drop me a line if I missed something. Good luck with the article. Hope all is well. Ron.

Morris slammed his laptop shut. So hard, in fact, that he initially feared he might have cracked the screen. He opened it again and found it sound. But Ron's email was breaking him up inside. He was here to find the last bit of encouragement to support his decision to give this all up. Now this. Uncle Walt? Great Uncle Walt? Morris was swamped with thoughts of Charley Garr and Sonny Provenzano being duped into some scam run by a wise guy from nowhere who just happened to be related to one of their own or so he claimed. But if Walter Johnson had not passed away, where was he? What did the kid know about it? And who was Walter Junior and what was he after?

Christ, Morris thought. He rubbed his forehead hard, trying to chase this new set of doubt and suspicion from his mind. But he couldn't rationalize this away. It stuck to his instincts like bubblegum trapped on the bottom of a shoe. He rethought his decision to have soda instead of beer. But just then Lou showed up with the soda.

"Ready to order?"

"Two of your deluxe burgers, Lou. Lettuce, tomato and onion. Lots of onion. Can you toast the bun?"

"Yep."

"Toasted bun, then. And fries."

"Coming up."

Lou strode off, order in hand.

Now what? Morris thought.

He agonized over Ron's email until the lunch came. But even though he had a good hunger on, the meal lost something with Faber's email. He finished his lunch, ordered another soda and sat back. There he let his thoughts go to the dark corners again. The darkest he could conjure up. Anything that would explain what was going on. But then there was a noise at the door as more people came in. Morris didn't know any of them until the last two came through. He recognized a voice, which caused him to look up. But when he saw the faces he quickly looked down, pretending to be absorbed with his meal. He buried his head in the leftover fries and soda and opened his laptop to conceal his face even further. They walked right by him and settled in the booth behind him. It was Sonny and Connie Provenzano.

As they sat down Morris played it low key. He tried to listen to anything they might say about last night. But their voices were too low. He found himself craning his neck to get his ears into a better position, which made him feel foolish. Once more he was tempted to just let it go. This was all too much. Nothing ever resolved and he wasn't in the mood to chase down one mystery after another. But then he was struck by an uncomfortable idea. It chilled him. But after Ron's email and now this, his resistance had crumbled a good bit. Taking the seat opposite him in the booth so he was facing away from the couple, he fished the microphone out of his computer bag. After he plugged it in, he strung the mic out so that it rested on top of the menu stand, finally ending up on the window sill at the end closest to the Provenzanos. Then he opened up a special app on the computer to manage the mic and set it to its most sensitive settings. Hesitating a little, he clicked the record button. Casually he went back to his fries and ordered another soda. Lou didn't notice. And just like that the old Jonny Morris returned and threw the new Jonny Morris out into the street.

An hour later the Provenzanos finished. They made their way past him just as they had when they came in. Morris waited, watching from his window until they had gotten into their car.

Incredibly, there was a third. The driver had sat at the bar and escaped Morris' notice the entire time. Now they were all leaving. He watched as they turned out of Tallys and headed west.

They're going home, he thought. And so was he.

Back in Atlas Town Morris settled back into his chair that stood in the corner of his living room. Staring straight ahead he was forced to reconcile the events in Smicksville. Now it was less frustration and panic over the elusiveness of writing the real story behind the Four Horsemen but what the entire matter had done to him. He no longer felt like a reporter. He stopped believing that the story, whatever it ended up being, would justify what he had become or what he had done. Spying on elderly people, vets at that, with his computer and microphone. It disgusted him to the point that he was wishing that Phil Grier had beat him bloody a few weeks ago. But that was then and this was now. Here he sat with his recording of Sonny and Connie Provenzano knowing full well he could process the recording and get the information he needed. Or at least that's what he told himself. There was a tense battle of conscience between his old self and what was left of the new Jonny Morris that was tossed back at Tally's Tavern. He tried hard to convince himself that he should just trash the recording and get on with life like he had told himself before. But the new Morris was still out in the street. It never had a chance.

In the end he brought his bag to his dinner table and opened it. He listened to the recording and then started to process it so he could understand all the words. All the while he knew what he was becoming. He didn't like it but he was past the self-pity and the typical frustration that comes with being stymied, the hot shot reporter being beaten by what appeared on the surface to be a simple straight forward assignment that a part time cub reporter could handle. It was beyond his ability to accept that. He was angry now. His blood was up. If he was able to lie to a hero like Charley Garr and tell him he worked for the Globe, then turn around and spy on the Provenzanos then he would have to admit that this all had changed him irrevocably. So he took the last turn in his soul and let the darkness in as much as he dared, promising himself that he wouldn't let it own him outright even if he feared he couldn't stop it from doing just that.

The Next Day...

Morris threw down a coffee as he digested the recording from yesterday. It all became very cryptic after the initial small talk cleared away. The Provenzanos were definitely concerned about young Walter Johnson. What on earth could that be all about? He ran a thousand scenarios through his mind and they all came up broken. It was yet another wrinkle in a rolling sea of wrinkles. But there was a sudden spark, the bolt of lightning from somewhere in the sky that brought a little sense to what had become a hopeless tangle of nonsense. It was when Connie Provenzano uttered what would become the cornerstone of Morris' new theory.

"Did you get the idea that Walter was going to tell last night?" she said in a tense whisper.

"I thought...maybe...maybe..." Sonny answered.

"And that newspaperman was sitting right there! Do you think he knows more than he should?"

"If he does...Charley will go off. He'll go off, ya'know?"

"Oh...poor Charley," Connie echoed.

Then the conversation died. It was as if the recording had failed or maybe the Provenzanos had disappeared from the planet. Morris believed that they were digesting their own words and whatever thoughts were running through their heads at the moment. His heart quickened as he waited for the conversation to pick up again. But when it did it was just more of the usual. Had the couple seen his recording device? It didn't seem likely but then again, there was so much about this that was like that. Morris decided that they hadn't seen him. That was ridiculous. The Provenzanos probably wouldn't know a recording device from a salt shaker. It looked as if it would end with the mundane until Connie made one more remark that would prime Morris' nerves for one more push.

"When was it that Sophia said she would decide?"

"Huh?"

"Sophia, dear. When did she say she'll decide?"

"Oh. This week. Yeah...she said this week."

Morris clicked his email open. His mind was boring down into the last possibility he could think of. If Walter Johnson had simply become infirm there would be no secrecy swirling about. Elderly men and women end up in homes all the time. So Morris ruled that out. That left only one thing. And there was only one person Morris knew that could get to the bottom of it in the shortest time, especially if Morris said he needed it in the shortest amount of time.

He started a new email and addressed it to Ron Faber. He would have preferred going there but decided that it would be too painful for him, not to mention awkward. So he wrote a quick note:

Walter Johnson, Corporal 2nd Rangers. He must be alive. Fellow veterans seem to refer to him in the living. But I was told he had passed. Therefore Walter Johnson must be somewhere they don't want anyone to know about. I believe that leaves one possibility. Walter Johnson is institutionalized for insanity. Somewhere. Can you locate?

He read it once then decided he needed to read it again. Hopefully Faber meant it when he said he was still there for him. He hit send.

11

The False Front

Morris waited for Faber to send him something back while having a late lunch at Green's Bar. He still wasn't drinking, which absolutely floored Bash. Every now and then he would drift by and ask if Morris wanted to try this new draft, or that new bottle but the answer was always no. Morris was totally focused now. He was waiting for the confirmation from Faber that he was certain would come. Nothing else interested him. As they would say in battle and baseball, Morris had his game face on. There was no more mister nice guy. If Walter Jr. was playing an angle Morris would declare war and run him into the ground. Then he would write the best damn article about the men who fought that war and feature Walter Johnson as his main subject. Walter Johnson, Corporal. Driven mad after fighting his heart out. It would be great.

"Say Jonny," Bash gruffed. What's with you? I hear you're not working for the Globe no more?"

"That's right. Things weren't working for me anymore at the Globe."

"You heard about Jimmy Wilkes?"

Morris looked up. The question stunned him. No, he hadn't

heard anything about Jimmy Wilkes. He was too busy getting drunk, getting into fights and losing his job to be concerned about anything or anyone except himself. He was afraid of the answer but he had to ask.

"No. What happened to Jimmy?" His voice pitched high and went to a whisper at the same time.

"Missing in action, man," Bash said softly. "Ain't that a bitch?"

Morris was rocked. He sat back in his chair, staring straight ahead, suddenly confronted with stifling tears.

Bash took to wiping the bar down.

"Man, he's gotta' come home. He's just gotta."

"He is coming home," Morris said defiantly. "He's coming home and he's going to play ball. We're going to be on the same team."

"Yeah!" Bash exclaimed. "Wilkes up to bat. He gets another chance! Man, if he doesn't then no one deserves one!"

Then Bash turned to greet a new customer.

"See you later Jonny!" he said cheerily.

Morris nodded.

"See you—"

But there was no one to talk to. Bash was already out of earshot and waiting on the new customer. So Morris made do with the rest of the bar's amusements: darts, shuffleboard, big screen tv. He even had an intelligent conversation about baseball with some guy who was just passing through. Then it was time to order another burger. More soda and fries. And then the inevitable sitting alone at the bar, a nearly finished soda that he couldn't drink another drop of parked in front of him.

No email from Faber.

Morris was tempted to start drinking. He stared around and assessing the various brands that Bash had to sell. But Betts' voice came back to him just then and he gave it up for the night. Besides, his finances were now getting too thin for alcoholic extravagances and God knows his head couldn't handle another hangover right now. Not with the triumphant return of the old Jonny Morris.

He went home.

The next day he rose early. That felt good. He was awake and alert for once. It was amazing what not drinking a case of beer will do for your senses. Eagerly he opened his mail up thinking that Faber might have written last night or very early this morning. Morris glanced at the clock. It read seven fifteen. When his mail popped up he saw one email for an interview for a job he had applied for last week. It was for an "exciting opportunity" in the world of journalism for WXGI, which was a regional news network. They wanted to talk to him this morning. Nine AM. Could he make it? He replied that he could meet them but he was not interested in anything entry level. He needed to move on and up. They didn't blink. The interview was on. So it was time to hit the shower.

Driving home a few hours later he was mildly encouraged by the interview, though the typical "We'll get in touch with you if we would like to interview you again" didn't do much to raise his spirits. Obviously they had several others to interview. Best keep his expectations in check. The music was playing loud again. Just the way he liked it. It was a song by Sting. *If I Ever Lose My Faith In You.* He thumped the steering wheel as he kept beat to the song.

He eventually ended up at Green's Bar again and having lunch. Amazing Bash and himself as well, Morris ordered club soda. His will was locked and loaded and he wasn't about to stand down before a line of beers that stretched across Bash's bar. While lunch was in the making he opened his email again. Even though it was still early he was convinced that Faber would not abandon him. Morris had begun to think that the old man had actually become interested in the story, whatever it was. Faber would come through. He was like that.

When the mail came up he saw the note from Faber had arrived. His heart jumped. This was it. He clicked Faber's email open, skipping three or four others that were in front of it. Instinctively he went to full screen and leaned forward to read.

Walter Johnson, Corporal. 2nd Rangers. No record existing locating veteran in an institution of any sort. No death record. VA reports wife passed. Last known address was in Arizona. Do you want the address?

Morris slumped back in his barstool. If ever there was a time to consider defeat this was it. He had nowhere else to go. All his ideas were exhausted. He was sure his welcome was worn out in Smicksville. Probably Flintstone as well. His next trip to either could involve the police. So he sat quietly and ate his lunch. Drank his club soda. Cursed under his breath. Jesus, why did he have to say goodbye to the new Jonny Morris?

He contemplated a reply to Faber's note. He had no intention of going to Arizona and looking up another address, interviewing people he didn't know about things he was sure to forget as soon as he left Arizona. Fact of the matter was, Morris couldn't afford to fly to Arizona but he wouldn't tell Faber that. Disgusted and beaten, he tapped out a quick response.

No. Don't need the address. Thanks. Any chance that your contact could be wrong?

The reply came back a minute later.

Not for a mental institution. They are all mostly in hospitals nowadays. If he was being kept in a private home, then maybe. But not in a hospital. There would be records.

"So much for that," he said aloud, catching Bash's attention.

"Need somethin' Jonny?"

Morris waved him off.

No, he thought. *I don't need anything…not here at least.*

An hour later he was on the road. Where to he didn't know. He ran his mind over thousands of possibilities and variations of possibilities. What would Sophia have to decide on that was so crucial to the rest? What was Walter Jr. doing in all this? And since Johnson had no brothers or sisters, just how could Walter Johnson be his great uncle? At best the young Walter Johynson was not blood but still thought of himself as kin somehow. At worst he was trying to scam Sophia and the others but for what? Money? Keep a secret? Or to keep telling a lie? Morris rubbed his aching forehead with one hand. His head filled with all sorts of wild stuff. Was Walter Johnson a coward? Was there a Dishonorable Discharge? None of it seemed to require a possible scammer like Walter Jr. He shook it all from his head. If it was that deep then it needed to be handled by a professional investigative reporter. It was beyond him.

He found himself on the road back to Smicksville anyway. The main reason being that the drive to Smicksville gave him more time to think than driving around Atlas Town. What he was going to do when he got there was more problematic. His money was going razor thin. He had enough for a day or two at Ida Wolley's Marple Hotel but then he would be dry until his last paycheck came in from The Globe. And that would be a small one. What then? He had nothing and he knew it. He had nowhere to go and he knew that too. His mood darkening, he decided that he was going back to Story Road and the Tescovitz home. He would confront Sophia and Sarah with his suspicions, his knowledge that Walter Jr. could not possibly be who he said he was and that he suspected they were being scammed if not extorted. But then he caught himself. Why did he care? Couldn't they handle their own problems? Garr and Provenzano were combat veterans. Neither was a pushover, especially Garr. What did Morris think he could accomplish that they couldn't? He didn't know. He only knew that he was on the road to Smicksville one more time. Probably the last time. And thank God for that.

A few hours later Morris was cruising down Main Street in Smicksville. He had already checked in at the Marple and was now formulating a plan of approach. It was going to be direct. He intended to drive by the Tescovitz home and check to see what automobiles were there. The Provenzanos, Garr and Walter Johnson Jr. all rode in a large dark colored SUV with tinted windows. If that was there he would keep going. But if the driveway was clear he was determined to go forward, confront Sophia and

Sarah with what he knew about young Walter Johnson and use that as cover for his real concern, like why were these people together so much? What was Sophia deciding this week? Since this was Tuesday afternoon, Morris guessed that he had until Friday, Saturday at the latest, to get that part of the story. Then he began struggling with a last nagging question: what if none of this had anything to do with his original story? Wouldn't that mean this had been a terrible waste of time and a job?

He scattered the thoughts from his mind. Not because he didn't want to think on it but because he thought he saw familiar faces on the street. Two women walking down the opposite sidewalk going in the opposite direction of Morris. He glanced at them several times, trying to steer the car through traffic and not go through a red light. But the traffic light gave him the opportunity to confirm that he did recognize these women. It was Connie Provenzano and Sarah Tescovitz strolling down the sidewalk heading away from him. He thumped his steering wheel waiting for the red light to turn. When it did he quickly parked, desperately looking back to see if they turned into a store or crossed the street. Then he jumped out and threw some change in the meter and jogged across the street. Walking briskly down the sidewalk he strained to keep an eye on their direction. Finally he could see them stop in front of a large bay window and chat for a moment before entering. Morris hurried to the same location and saw that they had entered a small bookstore. Morris reached for the door and hesitated.

Now or never, he thought.

He threw the door open and strode inside. Inside he scanned for the two women. When he saw them strolling down one aisle he feigned interest in a display at the front of the store before taking the plunge. When they had stopped to view a certain area in the shelves Morris left his spot near the front and walked directly towards them. He knew that if he delayed his approach or attempted to make it all look like an accident he would not be able to pull this off. Best to do it and get it over with.

"Hello ladies," he said formally.

"Oh! Mister…" Sarah began.

"Morris."

"Yes. Mister Morris. How are you today? Back in Smicksville again?"

"Yes. Briefly," he answered bluntly. "Ladies, I'm sorry to have to say this but…in the writing of my story I have come across some very…troubling things. Things that you all should know about."

"Oh?" Sarah said timidly. Morris noticed that Connie had taken ahold of her arm, as if to be reassured in some way.

"What troubling things?" Sarah added.

"I'm afraid that it has to do with Walter Johnson. Sorry to have to say this but it would appear that he is not who he says he is…nor could he be."

Morris studied the two women for a reaction. Any clue to lead the conversation into an area that would start resolving the questions in his mind would do. Sarah stood transfixed while Connie seemed to hold on to her for dear life. She had a defeated look in her eyes…or was it fear? Morris wasn't sure. But he was sure that he was on to something because they weren't laughing him off and telling him to get lost.

"I'm not sure…I don't know what you are talking about," Sarah muttered. "Walter is…Walter…"

"I'm not sure if that's so anymore Miss Tescovitz." Morris

said flatly. He was putting on his best interrogation style voice and felt that it was having an effect. "Walter, whoever he is, cannot be a nephew or a grand nephew of Walter Johnson, the man who fought with your father in World War Two. It's that simple. I also believe that there might be a scam of sorts being perpetrated on you, your mother as well as Charley Garr and the Provenzanos. Or possibly…"

Morris let his voice trail off in the hopes that it would inspire one of the women to spill something that he could latch onto.

"Possibly what?" Sarah echoed. Her voice had taken a more aggressive tone. She was getting defensive.

"Possibly…extortion. Does this Walter guy have something on the Tescovitz family? Or the others?"

"Certainly not!" Connie lashed out. "We—"

Sarah touched her on her shoulder and whispered something in her ear. Morris couldn't hear but he knew he was getting through.

"Look," he said in his best attempt to reassure both women. "I know there is a lot of affection between all of you. I'm not trying to destroy that. I'm trying to save it. Where did this guy come from? What school did he go to? Where did he live before Flintstone?"

Both ladies were silent. When Morris was convinced there was no answer forthcoming he took the final plunge. The fact that he was finally at this point was enough to give his soul the feeling of being freed even if it ended up putting a very angry Charley Garr at his door.

"Walter Johnson is not who he says he is," he repeated. "It's just that simple. I am not wanting to do this but I cannot just let all this slip by. I am staying at the Marple down on Main. I am leaving tomorrow morning. If I don't hear from either of you I will take it that you don't wish to talk to me about it, which is your right. But you must know that I will go to the police with my suspicion and my research. After that it will be between them and everyone at the Tescovitz house."

Morris stood back for a reaction. There was none. So he smiled thinly, said goodbye and turned to leave. Exiting the front door he retraced his steps all the way back to the car. He revved up the engine, which sprung the radio back to life. Then he made an illegal U-Turn and headed back to the Marple. On the way he breathed a huge sigh of relief. He was finally breaking through. The story would come to the surface. He would write it. Then he would give it to Ron Faber because he deserved it. After that he would get a great job at WXGI and get on with his life.

So why did he hate himself ?

He wasn't back at the Marple for more than an hour when there was a knock at the door. It was Sarah Tescovitz.

"Hello," Morris said awkwardly. "I wasn't expecting you. Come in."

Sarah stepped inside and stood a bit defiantly. Morris' skin was tingling. He always got that way when a big story was coming together. This might be it.

"I stopped by…to tell you that I phoned home and spoke with mother."

Morris nodded.

"Where is Missus Provenzano?" he asked.

Sarah stopped short, her thoughts interrupted by Morris concern over Connie.

"She's downstairs…speaking with Ida," she said haltingly.

Then, her thoughts interrupted, she stood staring at Morris for a moment.

"You were speaking to your mother…"

She glared back at Morris, her mood obviously becoming ugly for the first time that Morris could remember.

"She wants you to come to dinner…tonight. Six sharp."

Morris nodded.

When she turned to leave he noticed that she was carrying a book in a plastic bag.

"Did you get the book you were looking for?" he asked. It was his best attempt to restore civility between him and Sarah.

She stopped a moment, looking down at the bag that she had carried with her up to Morris' room.

"What's it about?" he asked, not expecting an answer.

"It's…it's about General Patton. About his life…and the experiences he had…"

Her voice trailed off to a whisper before she looked up again and turned to leave.

"We'll expect you at six."

When Morris turned onto Story Road his mind began to fill with what he would say to Charley Garr, the Provenzanos and even Walter Johnson himself. Or, as Morris had taken to referring to him as, 'Mister X.' His pulse quickened as he came to the same familiar bends in the road that would slowly reveal the entrance to the Tescovitz driveway. He beat the rhythm of the song on the radio as *Every Day Is A Winding Road* blared away. Then as he was about to make the last bend before the driveway, his insides tightened up as he cleared the now familiar turn onto the Tescovitz driveway. He knew the black SUV would be parked in its usual spot and he knew what that meant.

But it wasn't.

What the hell, he thought. *No one is coming to dinner...but me?*

He parked his Chevy across from where the SUV usually parked. It was almost as if he feared the empty space itself. He shut the engine off, killing the radio as usual and took a deep breath.

"No backing down now," he muttered.

"Good evening Mister Morris," Sarah said coolly as she held the door open. Morris stepped in with a short 'hello' and waited for Sarah to take the lead. She brought the both of them into the living room where Sophia was already sitting in a chair on the far side of the room.

"Mister Morris," she said politely.

"Hello Missus Tescovitz. Thank you for having me."

With everyone seated Morris noticed a new book on the coffee table that sat in front of the couch.

"Oh. Is this the book you bought at the book store?" he asked, straining his eyes to scan the far side of the coffee table.

"Yes," Sarah answered. "General Patton. His Life and Times."

Morris nodded, taking his seat on the couch. No one spoke at first. Morris certainly wasn't sure how this would all play out. He had been pretty direct with Sarah. Did Sophia think she could do better? Morris sat back on the couch, waiting for the assault, however subtle. Maybe Charley Garr would appear out of nowhere and waste this evening in a hurry.

"I understand you have some...concerns about us?" Sophia asked.

Morris fidgeted in his seat a little. He didn't want to bring the same kind of pressure on Sophia that he had brought on Sarah at the bookstore. But he knew immediately that it would be impossible to dodge her questions.

"Well, I…have a concern that this…Walter…kid is not who he says he is. In fact, he couldn't be who he says he is. And I have the research to back that up."

"Oh?"

"Yes. And my concern…is that he is pulling a scam or…he is extorting you all in some way."

Sophia only stared back at him. Then she gave a quick glance to Sarah who was sitting alone.

"Why won't you take our word…that…we are quite safe and not in….need of your protection?"

Morris' skin tingled. Sophia was more aggressive than he had imagined.

"Because I don't believe you appreciate the gravity of someone misrepresenting themselves as this Walter guy has."

There was another stony silence as Sophia searched Morris' eyes, trying to gauge his intent, he thought.

"What could…Walter have to gain? I have no riches."

"Not sure, Missus Tescovitz. A retirement account? Savings? This house? Maybe something you aren't aware of but he is… somehow? Walter Johnson Jr. seems to have no means. He also seems to have no, or very little background. He is also not related to Walter Johnson, Second Rangers in any way shape or form, and yet that is how he is passing himself off. If I ignore all this, it…well, it goes further than me writing a story. If something horrible should happen to either of you I would never be able to forgive myself. Never."

"So…you would simply decide to go the authorities?"

"Look…there may be nothing to all this. I may be chasing shadows. But this kind of thing has happened before…to nice people just like you. It would be best to have the police check all this out. What's the harm?"

Sophia sighed. She glanced in Sarah's direction but there was no response from her either.

"Sarah, is dinner ready to serve?"

Sarah nodded.

Sophia rose from her chair. Morris followed suit and the three moved to the dining room. The places were set. Old style dinnerware, forks, knives and spoons all out of a catalog from yesteryear. The aroma of a roast chicken dinner filled the room. Sophia sat at one end of the table with Sarah on the right side of the table close to her mother. Morris' place was opposite Sarah. Except that he was somewhat further away from Sophia.

As dinner progressed the talk became somewhat tame. So tame, in fact, that he became suspicious that the ladies didn't take him seriously. There was no way around what he was telling them. What was there that was so easy to ignore, even over dinner? It went on a bit too long as far as he was concerned. But just as the apple pie appeared Sophia picked up the conversation again.

"I find it interesting…in a way…that your newspaper…is so interested in us. Why is that, Mister Morris?"

She was still resisting. It irritated him this time. He was talking sense. Giving sage advice. And they were coming up with all sorts of obstructions for him to jump over.

"It…was a piece on your husband's passing. The Globe wanted to do something that was…respectful of the men who fought in general and your husband in particular. If you knew my editor, he's a combat—"

"You don't work for a newspaper anymore, Mister Morris," Sophia said softly. Morris sat transfixed, unable to find a response quick enough.

"I called your…Atlas Town Globe, Mister Morris," Sarah said defiantly. "I asked to speak with you and…a lady said you didn't work there anymore. Her name was…Betts? When I asked what had happened she told me that it was a professional fall-out…between you and your editor. Of course, she asked for my name. I made one up and said goodbye."

"Of course," Morris said nodding.

"So that leaves you. Why is it that you are so interested? What business is any of this of yours?"

Morris pushed his apple pie away. Sarah was right, in a general way, but Morris looked at it all differently now. To him it was the same as being the first to arrive at an accident. You render aid. Period.

"You're right, Sarah. I do not work for the Globe or any other newspaper at present. But I did until recently. During that time I gathered a ton of information about all of you for the story, one that has yet to appear. So…I am still working on the story, though I have no one to sell it to at present. But…what I uncovered, quite innocently I might add, appeared to me to pose a grave threat, or a possible grave threat, to all of you. I had to decide whether or not to walk away and let fate take its course…or I could take action. I chose the latter."

There was quiet around the table. Sophia and Sarah exchanging glances, a passing car going further down Story Road, the ticking of the clock on the small side table, was all that occurred for what seemed like an age.

"I'm looking out for my neighbor," Morris added. When there was still no response he figured the evening was over. He rose to excuse himself.

"Thank you for having me. I am sorry about the trouble and… about the deception. If you called the cops I wouldn't blame you."

"We're not the ones threatening to call the police, Mister Morris," Sarah replied. There was a slight tone to her answer, a bit of irritation mixed in as well.

"Sarah. I am not calling the cops on you. I am calling them to look into Walter Johnson!"

His response surprised him. He would have never thought to answer so sharply to anyone in this house when he first took this assignment. But there it was. It jumped out before he could get a rope around it and now it was out there for anyone to make anything out of it they could. He cursed under his breath as he continued to make his exit.

"Thank you for coming, Mister Morris," Sophia said softly.

Morris turned briefly, interrupting his accelerated exit from the dining room and the Tescovitz house.

"Sorry," he muttered before leaving. It was clumsy but it was all that came to mind. He let himself out. Walking briskly across the front lawn to his waiting Chevy he jumped and revved the engine to life. When he pulled out he had to remind himself not to peel out and leave a bunch of stones hurtling their way towards the Tescovitz front door. So it was all nice and slow. As slow as he could stand it. When he made Story Road he let the engine out and spun the volume knob on the radio up. The Beatles came on. They were singing *Nowhere Man*. The song burned a hole into him even as he started thumping the beat on his steering wheel. He roared down Story Road. One more night at Ida Wolleys and he would be headed home. Now that he had decided that WXGI wasn't interested and would never contact him again, he was determined to get more resumes out and pound the pavement. Start his life over. Never come back to Smicksville again.

After leaving the Tescovitzs Morris made for Tally's Tavern. He could have stopped at the Carriage House but all of a sudden he was convinced that everyone else was there. Charley Garr, the Provenzanos and Walter Jr. He didn't want an interview now. He wanted to stew over what had just happened. Thought it would be best if he did it with a couple of brews in familiar territory.

Tallys was its usual low key self for a week night. A couple of guys at the bar, a few more in booths. Lou was on duty. There was still no waitress. Morris took his first draft quick and ordered another. He opened up his laptop but that was for appearance's sake. He had no intention of doing any work. He ran the visit to Story Road over and over in his mind, looking for a nuance he might have missed, a hidden meaning…something. But there was nothing jumping out at him. He ordered his third beer and then a fourth. After that he lost count. He needed to drain the ugly stress from his mind, cleanse his soul so to speak. He wanted to feel good about himself again but somehow couldn't see how that could ever be again. As the alcohol began to build up in his brain he cast an uncertain eye to the walls that held the photos of the men who died in combat, a faded star hanging just below the frame. The shadows cast by the uneven light in the bar danced from their long dead faces, casting an accusatory eye in his direction. It snared his imagination and held it. All of the men he looked at were condemning him as if he had run from a battle and left them all to die. Morris started to sweat. Then the room started to spin and just like that he realized that no one in this town liked him. Maybe they all hated him, wanted him to go away, to leave them and their own alone forever. And just like that he wanted to oblige. When Lou stepped back Morris paid his tab, leaving himself with just enough money to cover one last night at the Marple and then home. Hopefully his Chevy had enough gas.

...Morris peered over the rim of his foxhole, convinced he had heard something he didn't want to hear. Maybe the Krauts were attempting an infiltration. But when he got a good look he saw one of his own men coming towards him in the fading light of a winter dusk. It had recently rained, leaving a heavy mist hovering throughout Hurtgen Forest. But the silhouette was definitely familiar to Morris.

"Say man!" he hissed. "Get in a hole!"

The soldier walked right up to the leading edge of Morris' foxhole and stopped.

"Didya hear?! Get in a hole!"

The soldier didn't answer. Instead he looked this way and that as if taking in the situation for the first time. His face was covered in mud, he hadn't shaved in days and there was that helmet. It was pulled down hard over his brow so that Morris couldn't see his face clearly.

The soldier stooped down like he was examining Morris' foxhole.

"I wanted to tell you...you're the guy I spoke to before aren't you?"

Then Morris remembered. This was the guy who was lost... looking for where he was supposed to go. It all came back to him.

"Yeah...yeah! I remember you!" Morris hissed. "You were looking for the way home...or something. Did you find it?"

The soldier looked around some more, examining the ground like he had dropped something.

"Yeah. Yeah I think I got a handle on that. Thought I would come by and say 'so long.'"

Morris almost laughed.

"But...aren't you Corporal Johnson? C'mon man...get in the hole! We might get more action!"

The soldier shook his head.

"Nah. This ain't the front. The front is...back there somewhere," Johnson said, pointing to somewhere down the hill, towards the rear.

"Back there? What? No way!"

"Yeah. That's where it is. You'll figure it out."

The two men stared at each other a moment.

"You're leavin' aren't you?" Morris asked.

Johnson nodded.

"Yeah. Seen enough. Done enough. This battle's over. There'll be others, though. But I got another chance. Chance to go somewhere else. Try again..."

Morris raised up in his foxhole.

"Not following, man."

Johnson only gazed off down the hill.

"You want me to go with you?" Morris said, attempting to kepp things in a context he could understand. "I mean, if the front is really back there..."

"Nah," he answered.. "You should stay here. There's stuff you need to do here."

"What stuff? Man, I don't know what you're sayin'!"

Johnson stood up and readjusted his gear with a shrug of his shoulders.

"That's because...you ain't one of us. It can't be helped. But that's the way it is. I go where I have to go and you go where you have to."

As the soldier started to walk away from Morris' foxhole for the second time, Morris suddenly became afraid. What if the Krauts attacked in force? What if they brought Tiger Tanks?

"Don't worry about Tiger Tanks," Johnson echoed as he walked away. "They can't operate in the forest."

"But shouldn't I be going to the front?" Morris called out. He was breaking all the rules on silence but he couldn't help himself.

"Not this one," the soldier answered, his voice becoming faint as his steps crunched their way down the hill. Then, when he was almost completely swallowed up by the growing night Morris heard him call back once more.

"Hey!"

Morris turned his head.

"Yo!"

"Watch the line, Private!"

And with that Corporal Johnson turned away and trudged off into the dark of Hill 400.

Morris slunk back into the belly of his foxhole. There he sat until the forest had grown completely dark. Instantly he was overcome with fear. He couldn't hear anything. No one else was making a sound in their foxholes, no jokes, no cursing, no moving around. There wasn't even a sound from a bird or a bug. Morris needed to touch base with someone, hear a voice or some kind of sound from someone. Feeling desperate enough, he crawled out of his foxhole and stood up. He was expecting all hell to break loose but it didn't.

"Sonny!" he called out as he started to move around. First his steps were careful and quiet. But when Sonny didn't answer he darted to where he thought his foxhole was. When he got there he went down on his knees and peered into the hole.

"Sonny! Corporal Johnson is gone! Sonny!"

But the hole was empty.

Morris raised up. Desperately he scanned the area for the other holes that he knew were there just an hour ago. The holes and the men that were in them.

"Hav! Sergeant Garr! Hey!"

He scurried all around, darting this way and that, looking for someone to confirm he was in the right position but there was no one. No one answered him. No one called out to him. No one told him to shut the hell up. No one made a sound. Because no one was there. Morris was alone on Hill 400 in the Hurtgen Forest. Alone and facing nightfall. Hell, even the Krauts were gone.

He was overcome by a sensation of drowning. He couldn't breathe. Everything started to go strange. He started to run downhill, stumbling over trees and bushes, holes in the ground and anything else that the misty night air could conceal. He tried his best to follow Corporal Johnson but he lost his way. The harder he struggled the more lost he became. Then he started losing his gear. First it was his helmet, making a metallic bumping sound as it rolled away in the night. Then his pack. Finally he lost his footing and went down hard. When he got up again to resume his frantic race down the hill he found himself without his rifle.

"I don't know where I'm going!" he gasped, turning this way and that. "I don't know where I'm going!"

"Where am I going!?" he cried as he sat up in bed. "Where am I!? Where am—"

Morris' eyes opened wide, his chest heaving and his breath coming in short gasps. Frantically he scoured the room, trying to remember where he was. He was covered in sweat. He was half expecting to see Corporal Johnson but no one was there. Catching a glint from the window he raised up in his bed and stared through the glass. There was light gathering outside. Light was good.

"My God Almighty," he wheezed, unable to think for a few moments. At first he had started to look for the Corporal. But then his mind began to clear. Rubbing his forehead to chase the last of the dream from his head, he rose out of bed and stood up. Moving over to the window he gazed out for several minutes, proving to himself that he wasn't on Hill 400 anymore. He was in The Marple. In his favorite room. And it was almost daylight. His last day in Smicksville had begun.

12

Atop Pointe du Hoc

He showered and packed, his thoughts scouring his last two dreams. He had no idea why he would be having them, what with him being a member of one of the storied units in World War Two. He had no military background. He couldn't remember ever thinking that he wanted one. But there he was. In a foxhole on Hill 400 talking to Corporal Walter Johnson, known as 'Hall' to his friends.

He had to wait for Ida to get up before he checked out. That was a difficult hour for him to pace around his room anxious to leave. Money wasn't even his first concern, though maybe it should have been. The rent would clear the last of his loose cash, money that he had held in reserve for emergencies. The fact that he had spent it on The Marple annoyed him some but that didn't last. There was something else growing in the back of his head. It was something that he didn't want to believe, maybe something that he couldn't believe. He kept rejecting it out of hand as he tried, unsuccessfully, to return his thoughts to his imminent money concerns. But it kept coming back. And by the time he had cleared the Marple and was driving away in his Chevy, the fear that took hold of him was that whatever it was that was emerging in his mind was something that he was afraid to believe.

After a sullen and distracted breakfast at a fast food place, Morris revved the Chevy up and was determined to head back to Atlas Town, or, that's what he told himself at any rate. The ghost that had sprung into his mind after the last dream was not going away. Nor was the addition of breakfast mitigating the sharpness of what he had been unwillingly possessed with. When he got back on the road he was quickly confronted with the choice. Go right and go back to Atlas Town. Look for a job. Hang on for the last paycheck. Forget about this story. Try to get his life together. Go left and head out of town to Story Road. Risk running into Charley Garr. He didn't want to go back there. He didn't want to see Sophia and the others. But he was still hating himself for being a crusader. Minding other people's business even if he had the best of intentions was not setting well with him. Now he just felt like he was making everyone miserable, just like he had done at the Globe. No, he didn't want to go back to Story Road but he was tired of hating himself. He was not liking the old Jonny Morris any more. Even if he never solved this story to his liking, his frightful insight that had jumped on him like a thief in an alley would never give him rest. Jonny Morris was becoming tired of Jonny Morris. He was weary of the guy who always gets his story, always gets what he's after, whether it's a baseball game or the girl of his dreams. It wasn't attractive to him anymore. He wanted to try the new Jonny Morris again. He felt he could only do that by starting at Story Road. He would go back and tell Sophia that he was dropping everything. He would never come back. And he would write his story with what he had, though he really thought he wouldn't write it at all. At least then he would have his self respect back, even if the rest of the world hated the sight of him. Maybe then this thing in his head that was lashing his brain like a team of horses would go away and die a quiet death.

Not so fast, Jonny boy. Let's not get too far out in the weeds, he thought.

He revved his engine and turned left, on the way out of town and headed for Story Road, radio blaring. It was Heart playing *These Dreams*.

His pulse was trying to beat itself out of his arm when he pulled in at the Tescovitzs. The black SUV wasn't there so that made it a little better. Still, it was only a little after ten in the morning and he wasn't sure he would be welcome. In fact, he wasn't sure he would be welcome at any time in this house. So, it was better to find that out right away. He killed the engine, letting the car drift to a stop with a short 'crunch' sound on the gravel. Just that fast he walked up the stairs of the front porch, his legs moving reluctantly as if they were crying for him to turn around and go home. But he was past that. Without another thought he opened the screen door and knocked. No answer came. So he knocked again. Still no answer. He was that close to going back to his car and driving away. But then he heard voices. They weren't happy voices, coming from around the side of the house. He crept to the one side of the porch so he could hear. He could clearly make out the voices of Sophia and Sarah.

I have to do this, he thought.

So he jumped the railing on the fence and walked around the side of the house. That's when he heard a sound behind him. He turned sharply, like he was being attacked, and saw the black

SUV entering the driveway. Turning back to the back of the house Morris saw the two ladies go into Hav's greenhouse. There was no going back now, especially with the SUV blocking the retreat. Morris knew that Charley Garr was in that SUV because this was the worst possible time for him to show up. He turned and walked briskly towards the greenhouse. It felt like he was walking to his own execution.

"This'll be my penance," he mumbled to himself as he entered through the still open door of the greenhouse.

"What are you doing here?!" Sarah hissed.

Morris stopped and held his hands up as if to surrender.

"Did you hear?! I said what are you doing here?"

Morris wasn't able to answer before Sophia, sitting lonely on a bench, her eyes soaked in tears, held up her hand and called out to Sarah in her usual soft voice.

"We should call the police!" Sarah cried. "This has gone far enough!"

"Yes. Yes it has, Sarah," Sophia answered, her voice strained and broken.

Just then the occupants of the SUV showed up. Charley Garr and the Provenzanos all piled in looking for the two women.

"Here you are—what's he doing here!?" Garr snapped.

Sarah started to tell him how Morris had just shown up while Sophia, shoulders slumped and eyes bereft of any sparkle, only gazed back at Morris with what the old people from the war would refer to as the thousand yard stare.

Garr made his way to the front. He stood directly against Morris in what looked like a pretty good combat pose.

"Get…out," Garr growled. "Get your ass…out. Now."

Morris took a step back as a gesture but Sophia held up her hand and gestured to the former Ranger.

"Charley," she said softly.

"Sophia, this man can't be here. He doesn't work for a newspaper…he's nobody!"

"Charles," Sophia answered. "Everyone is…somebody."

Sarah moved to Sophia's side and sat next to Sophia on the bench. Her face began to sour as the tears started to flow.

"Sophia, what are you getting ready to do? Whatever it is, we can talk it through! We don't need this intruder!" Garr pleaded.

"I've talked enough, Charles. I want this to be over."

Garr wiped his brow, sweeping away what might have been a tear that had somehow escaped the prison of his eyes, eyes that guarded a locked room with uncounted bad memories huddled inside.

"Sophia," Sonny said coming forward. "Sophia…we said long ago…ya' know? We said we'd stand by whatever you decided. Okay?"

Connie Provenzano came and sat down next to the other two women. Taking Sarah's hand, she waited for what would happen next. Sarah had begun to cry freely as she held both Sophia's and Connie's hand in hers.

Morris said nothing. Even now he didn't know how to tell these people that he was not going to go to the authorities. There was so much coming out that he was not prepared for. So he waited. As soon as anyone showed any interest in anything he had to say he would say it. Anything other than the specter that had grown in his mind after last night's dream.

"Sophia…" Garr said. "Let's talk…alone…"

Sophia only stared back at Morris. Garr continued to plead

but finally Sophia slowly shook her head and held up her hand. Garr could only shake his head and stand off some to one side.

"He won't stop," Sophia whispered, her voice nearing collapse. "And he knows. Or he knows enough."

"I never intended to hurt anyone, Missus Tescovitz," Morris said.

"I know. But you were on to something that you didn't understand…but you've figured something out. That's why you're back. Am I right?"

He choked on his answer. Yes, he had figured some things out and right at this moment he was wrestling with something that scared the daylights out of him. But the last remnant of the old Jonny Morris held on for one more push…the only way for an old friend to say goodbye.

"I can't…help myself," he answered.

Sophia smiled wearily and turned her head in the direction of a row of flowers growing on a long table.

"Do you see these flowers, Mister Morris?"

"Yes," he answered slowly.

"Do you know what kind of flowers they are?"

"No…no I don't know much about flowers."

Sophia nodded. Sarah and Connie were holding onto each other, their heads almost together, tears falling freely. Sonny came over to sit next to his wife while Charley Garr stood off a short way, staring at the corner of the greenhouse.

Sophia rose and took a few soft steps towards the flowers on the table.

"These are Snapdragons. Have you ever heard of them?"

"Uh…yes, I have. They're very nice."

Sophia only gazed back at him.

"But you didn't come here to see Snapdragons."

"No Missus Tescovitz."

"You came here to see Walter."

"I came here to—"

"Do you know what an annual is, Mister Morris?"

"No. I mean, I don't remember what—"

"I know. You don't know much about flowers."

"No," Morris said shaking his head.

"Annuals live for a year. They live for a year…and then they die."

Morris nodded, becoming ashamed that he had ever done or said anything to hurt this woman.

"Do you know how old these flowers are?"

Morris could only shake his head.

"They're nine years old."

He knew there was a point to this but he had no idea what it was. He was so taken with the fact that he had a roomful of elderly men and women in tears or stone silent and that bothered him more than he could describe.

"How…can that be?"

"If you knew my Hav…I mean, really knew him. You would know the answer to that. But…being a reporter…you dig and you dig and you find things…things that don't make sense…so you start putting them together and you get a story."

Sophia stopped to take a breath, nearly having to sit down as her balance temporarily deserted her.

"Sophia!" Connie cried out. Sonny rose and tried to give assistance but she waved him off. She preferred to stand for now.

"Sophia! You're exhausted…ya' know? Let's go inside and sit down."

Sophia glanced at Sonny, holding up her hand again in her customary fashion.

"Too late for that, Sonny. We have already had enough heartbreak. And now we have one of our own that has been broken away from us."

"That was going to happen anyway, Sophia!" Garr answered sharply.

"Perhaps! But still…here we are. And here he is. I think… God is telling me something."

"Let her say it, Charley. Let her say it, ya know'? Let her say it before she gets worse."

Charley Garr, Sergeant in the Second Rangers, combat veteran who fought at Pointe du Hoc and Hill 400 and maybe a hundred other places suddenly became very small. He shrunk back and away from the conversation, hunkering down like he was expecting a bomb to go off.

"I'm gonna'…miss him," Garr said, the tears now falling from his face.

"Charles," Connie said. "Charles, come sit with us…!"

Connie held out her hand for Charley to come and take but he wouldn't.

Morris looked to Sophia.

"I don't think you meant to hurt anyone, Mister Morris. But now you need to be shown exactly…exactly what it is you're trying to dig into."

"I'm sorry Missus Tescovitz," Morris said, choking on the words. "I never meant to hurt you, or your daughter, or any of the others. It's not what I wanted. For you or your daughter."

There was an agonizing silence that followed. Morris was just about to tell everyone that he was going away and that there would be no story, no call to the authorities, no nothing. He would just go away and try to forget all the pain he had caused. But he was too late.

"Sarah?" Sophia said bluntly.

Morris stared back briefly.

"Yes. Sarah. She's your daughter right? Didn't you all tell me that?"

Sophia sat abruptly, her strength deserting her. The women on the bench had begun to hold each other very tight, like they were weathering a stormy sea in a boat that was taking on water.

"Yes, that's true. That's what we told everyone. But Sarah is not my daughter."

Morris didn't answer. He was stunned. Why would they make such a story up?

"Okay," he said slowly. "Why then—"

"Sarah is my sister!" Sophia shouted with what her voice would allow. She raised her head, defiant and uncertain as to the effect of her words.

"Your sister…" Morris murmured.

"Yes! My sister! My older sister!"

Morris was rocked. He froze up. His face, his voice, his mind, all shut down in a vain attempt to digest what he just heard. Suddenly the ghost that had bored its way into his head sprang to life. It came to the fore, shutting everything else out, killing everything until it was the only thought left in what was just a moment before a tangled mass of suspicions.

"Your…older sister," Morris said unbelieving. He glanced over at Sarah who was now looking back at him. She was too broken up to stand. She held his gaze through eyes blinded by tears that were falling freely, holding onto Connie Provenzano for dear life afraid of what would happen next.

Numbed, Morris took a step as he gathered the meaning of Sophia's words. Even though they were plain enough, he still fought against it. It wasn't possible. It was not in the realm of reality but it was the only explanation that made sense now as he started to think differently…perhaps for the first time in his life.

"Snapdragons." he said, gazing at the flowers poised just behind Sophia. "Snapdragons…your…sister. That means…"

He glanced at Sophia who said nothing.

"…that means that Walter…is….he is…"

Garr stood up angrily.

"Walter Johnson IS Walter Johnson! Got it!? Walter Johnson…Corporal! Second Rangers! F Company! There is no…—"

Garr now broke down completely. He was suddenly not an imposing figure. He was broken. Sonny too.

Morris took a step back attempting to rein in his reeling mind.

"Where is…Walter Johnson?" he asked numbly.

"You'll never see him…again!" Garr sobbed.

"He's right," Sonny said in a whisper, his heart breaking. "He took off to…start again, ya' know? He's gonna' start again…"

Morris started to shake his head. It wasn't possible. This kind of thing was not possible.

"Hav Tescovitz…found a way…a way…to…" Morris said, stumbling through his words.

"Yes," Sophia said flatly.

Morris was wordless, his craft having abandoned him. He was unable to refute what he was just told. That's when Sophia spoke again.

"My Hav was worried sick…about the effect…that this

would have on people…their families. Plus, he wasn't certain about his…formula. It worked well on the plants but people are not plants. So Hav tried to make it work for people."

"For people," Morris droned.

"Yes, Mister Morris. So, when Walter turned up with a terminal cancer, Hav wanted him to go first if he wanted. So…he did. Walter was a lonely man. His wife had passed a while back."

"Yes," Morris said, remembering some earlier research. "Celia…"

"That's right," Sophia said weakly. "But…there was something else. You see, during the attack…on Pointe du Hoc… Walter saved my Hav's life when the Germans threw a grenade into their…foxhole. Walter pushed my Hav aside and threw it out before it exploded."

Morris ran both of his hands through his hair. He didn't know what to say or what to think. He could only listen to Sophia as she filled in all the blanks.

"Then my sister…" Sophia glanced at Sarah who reached out for her. The two women clasped hands together briefly before Sophia continued. "It didn't work as well but it worked pretty well. We were all going to take it and then move away somewhere…one at a time."

"Because no one could know," Morris added.

"Yes," Sophia answered. "But at that moment, we also realized that…if no one could know…then maybe this wasn't right. Of course, Walter was…nineteen…or so already. And Sarah was around sixty."

Morris glanced at Sarah. She was shaking, her hands trembled and her tears had stained her face and worn out all the resistance in her.

"What…now, then? What happens next?" Morris asked, a little desperate to hear the rest.

Sophia took a seat at a lone chair that stood next to another small table.

"You see these flowers here?" she asked.

"Yes…"

"These are Busy Lizzies. They're annuals too. Do you know how old they are?"

"No," Morris said shaking his head.

"They're…ten? Sister?"

Sarah nodded.

"Yes, sister. Ten."

"I thought so. Yes, they're ten years old and still blooming…"

Sophia reached into the flowers and pulled out a flask that looked like it came from a high school chemistry class. It was quart size and contained a clear liquid, like tap water.

"This is…too much for Man to control," Sophia said weakly. "I've know it for some time now but it…it was hard to let go. It's all I have left of my Hav."

Then she turned to look at Morris.

"I burned all his notes last night."

Morris could only nod.

"And now this is all that's left," Sophia droned.

She waited a moment as if she was saying goodbye. Everyone had turned to look, watching her every move.

"There's no choice, don't you agree Mister Morris?"

The only answer he had was obvious. Still, she deserved it.

"No choice," he said in a hushed voice.

Sophia Tescovitz held his gaze a moment as if she was gauging the sincerity in his response. Then, still holding his eyes in her own she slowly turned the vial over and let all the liquid pour out onto the greenhouse floor.

"And that's that," Sophia said in a whispery voice.

The greenhouse went dead quiet.

"And you…leave Hall alone…!" Garr rasped.

"Yeah…ya' know? And leave the sisters alone. They never hurt nobody!" Sonny echoed.

"No one will believe you anyway, Mister Morris!' Sarah said, her words choked with tears.

Morris stood back, discovering some tears falling on his own face. Nodding his head, he started to back away.

"No…I don't want to hurt…anybody," he muttered. "I won't bother…anyone. I won't come back…again. I'm sorry…so sorry…"

He continued to back away looking at everyone for what he thought would be the last time.

"No one would believe me anyway…"

Sophia rose from her chair with great difficulty. Sonny and Charley Garr went to her aid and held her as she came to a standing position holding on to both men.

"I would…like to thank you for coming, Mister Morris." Her voice was weak and she was unable to stand unaided. But she still managed a thin smile as she spoke.

"You gave me…the inspiration I needed…to do what was needed. Even…if you didn't realize it."

"You'll leave the sisters alone, Mister Morris?" Garr asked.

"Yes sir," Morris answered, his voice little more than a hush.

"And Walter. You won't go hunting him down, right?"

Morris shook his head. He was dazed. Shell-shocked even. The specter that had descended on him after his last dream was more than a trick of the mind brought on by too much work and alcohol. Or even by simple obsession. It was real. Beyond everything he thought he knew. It was supernatural. And he couldn't tell a soul.

"The Patton book," Morris said weakly. "It was for Walter, wasn't it?"

Charley Garr nodded, his eyes unable to stop his tears completely.

"Because…Patton believed in reincarnation, right?"

"We thought it would help him, Mister Morris…" Sarah said. "He is going through a lot right now…we thought it would help somehow."

"Right…" Morris answered. "I hope it does."

Morris turned away and headed for the door. He was barely able to comprehend his surroundings. The truth had set him free in a way, but at the cost of catapulting him far from all that he was comfortable with. It all made a macabre sense somehow. The empty picture frame was kept as a keepsake because of the inscription on the back. The picture was gone because the fourth man in the photo was Walter Johnson Jr. Who at that time was Corporal Walter Johnson. No one on Story Road ever confessed this but Morris knew all the same. Then there was the book on Patton, the American general who believed he was incarnated and how Walter could speak like a veteran and know things teenagers didn't typically know, like how Hal Smith had actually saved Pittsburg in the 1960 series. Morris didn't even know that. Finally, his dark dreams of warfare and the Four Horsemen came into focus, how he was always unable to see Johnson's face but somehow he seemed to know who he was. It was his waking dilemma come in a dream, clawing at his walls of disbelief, trying to tell him the truth. But he wasn't ready to listen. He wasn't able to listen. It was all an overwhelming assault on the senses, a rush he could not withstand.

No one says 'Krauts,' anymore, he thought.

When he reached the door he turned one last time.

"Sorry for all the trouble," he said choking back tears. "I won't...bother you anymore."

Then he turned and left. Back in his Chevy he turned onto Story Road and pointed the car home. His thoughts were owned not by a passion for a story anymore or even the route home. His thoughts had been stolen by the past and weren't returning for some time. He didn't play the radio.

13

The Story Road Ending

Two months later...

Jonny Morris whipped his Chevy into WXGI's parking lot in downtown Pittsburg. He sat for a moment, the Impala's engine humming and the radio blaring away as he thought back on his accidental discovery on Story Road. To add to the shock of that epic encounter in the Tescovitz greenhouse, there had been a phone message waiting for him when he got back to his apartment. WXGI was not interested in a second interview, they offered him an assignment on the spot. Of course, they mentioned the fact that he had received an excellent recommendation from Ron Faber of The Globe.

"The Atlas Town Globe," Morris sang when he got the message.

So he was on his way, turning a corner in his life and he wasn't looking back. He was excited again. He felt alive. The big things in his life had finally become small things. His passion reignited, he was ready to push his journalistic flair into overdrive. But the old Jonny Morris was not going on this ride. He had moved on, leaving for parts unknown. His replacement was starting out with a new mindset and new goals. He was no longer interested in stomping over someone to get a story or to get to second base. The new Jonny Morris no longer believed in the ends justifying the means.

How can a pig write about a King in a golden castle? He would tell himself. So he still hunted angles on scent, he was still roaming for the real story but with a view that he wouldn't lower his morals to get his name in print. It felt good to be home again.

He was there when the terrible news came home to Atlas Town about the favorite son Jimmie Wilkes. He had been killed in Afghanistan when his unit was ambushed in the mountains. They brought his body home and held a service at Memorial Park. The same park where Wilkes had played such brilliant baseball when he was in high school and later, when he had graduated and moved on to softball. He had been Jonny's teammate and friend since the sixth grade. Jonny was there at the Wilkes' home with Phil Grier as they paid their respects and then tried to console a family they had known practically all their lives. Now a family of broken hearts. Tears were everywhere.

With Wilkes' passing, Morris' story on the vets finally emerged. Of course he wouldn't write about the Secret of Story Road as he referred to it. But maybe that wasn't the real story anyway. Maybe the real story was what was all around the edges, the small stuff that went unnoticed. He would write that instead and let the secret lie in its unmarked grave. It was painful but Morris' old fire was lit. His writing spilled from his hands onto a sweaty keyboard like floodwater over the sandbags. It was sharp. It spoke from the heart and it took no prisoners. He knew it was good because he was angry when he finished. Faber liked it and wrote him to say so. Morris offered it to the Globe, free of charge. When Faber accepted Morris felt the lifting of a terrible weight from his shoulders. Now he could deal with the ghosts from dark dreams and nightmares that plagued him, a narrative that concealed a story that couldn't be told and all the anguish over a crashed personal life. He could sleep again. He could get on with his life. And he could let the secret slip away, unknown to anyone save the players themselves and the former reporter from the Atlas Town Globe.

In time, what happened in Smicksville would be rationalized a thousand different ways. But the horror and soul breaking experiences of the war gave way to the last crowning drama, a bittersweet drink that everyone had to drink. Watching Walter Johnson drive away the last night he saw everyone, to leave behind everyone who meant anything to him in this whole world, never to be seen again. It was almost as if he went MIA in the war. Though Morris might watch for him to show up in a ballgame here or there, that would wither before long. Gradually, Walter Johnson would be devoured by fading memories and the eventual passing of everyone on Story road. He would be every bit the ghost from Morris' dreams.

And just like that Morris' world came together. All he had to do was let go of everything and it all came back, with interest, as if delivered by a divine tide. Now, just like Walter Johnson had asked in his dream, Morris was sure where he had to go. His new job would be the most exciting he had ever held. Jonny Morris was about to be deployed as a Contract War Correspondent for the parent company of WXGI.

Now I don't have to be dreaming to feel the insides of a foxhole, he told himself.

Morris listened to the radio for a moment longer, the memory of recent events slowly fading. The radio blared on, playing *Brand New Day* by Sting. He thumped the steering wheel to the beat of the song.

Brand new day, he thought.

But there was still a hole in his life. Lorraine was gone and Morris was not over her. Now that he was embarking on a new phase of his life the old fallbacks of softball, beer and loud music no longer kept the flood water from coming in. Maybe he could have a second chance too. Tonight he would be the one showing up unexpectedly just like she had at Memorial Park that day. She had to say yes. Christmas was coming.

And the Mazeroski Magic was back.

He listened to the last strains of the music fade away. Then, almost reluctantly, he shut the engine off, killing the radio and with an energetic grunt he grabbed his laptop and bounded up the nearby steps, disappearing inside. It was his first day. He didn't want to be late.

The ending to Morris' article for the Atlas Town Globe

A wise man once told me that people feel the need to forget about wars and those that fight in them so they can move on. He called it a 'self defense mechanism.' If people are unable to forget they remain locked in a soul breaking past. This man was a combat veteran speaking about our society's willingness to lose touch with and then forget about all the lives lost, first in World Wars and now everything from UN interventions to the new executive war, fought on the whim of one person exercising political privilege. Now conflicts burst upon the earth like the plague brings bleeding lesions to the face.

Is it really a self defense mechanism or is it a trick we play on ourselves to provide excuses for remaining on a path that is fraught with peril but is preferred due to its familiarity? If progress is change, as some say, why haven't we changed this? Maybe we do need to isolate our minds from the past so we are not burdened with the memory of what and who was lost. But if we continue to stumble down the same roads time and time again, aren't we in need of a reaction that is more proactive? If a people remembered such a thing, wouldn't they be less likely to repeat it? Just like the youngster who, on a dare set about assaulting a hornet's nest, would that youngster remember that? Would he do it again?

Atlas Town just buried one of their own the other day. Smicksville buried one of theirs last Fall. These two men fought in wars that were over sixty years apart. And it's gotten to the point that they don't even call them wars anymore. We don't even have the courage to call it what it really is. Is that part of the defense mechanism? Or is it part of a deception mechanism?

I am not going to allow the deception mechanism to operate with me anymore. I will remember. I may find a special way to deal with the pain, the pain of losing a close friend of many years. His family will have a much more difficult time doing the same thing. But to slowly obliterate the memory, to let it fall into disrepair, only to view it more and more cynically over time is the greatest disservice we can render unto those that went and fought. It is also the greatest disservice to those that will fight in the next generation, the kids that are playing baseball in high school right now, selling newspapers, joining the Boy Scouts. We commit them to the same future because we don't want to remember, or we choose not to remember, and so we demand to have it repeated over and over again. Not me. I choose to remember. Because whether it's Jimmie Wilkes of Atlas Town or Hav Tescovitz of Smicksville, all these men are One of Us. And we should not let them be taken away just to be forgotten about in a generation or two. And if we get into another war, or another conflict, then at least we won't be sending our young men and women off to some foreign land to fight for someone else because we forgot what it's all about. - Jonny Morris

Epilogue

A Soldier's Farewell

The old Pittsburg-Ohio line still runs. It just doesn't go to Pittsburg anymore. One of the cars has an open side and that is where a lone passenger sits. As the train clicks and clacks its way heading west this man recalls a past much different than the present. The people he loves but may never see, it almost seemed to be a similar fate suffered by those that were killed and buried in French cemeteries, cemeteries in Luxembourg, in jungles in the Far East, islands in the Pacific…in oceans. But he was still alive. He had to go on. It was the only way to honor those that stood by him and wished him well that last evening he saw them. He was supposed to live a life that he had missed out on. That's what they wanted.

He thought about what he was going to do the next fifty years. How he was going to live, sell himself with a new identity. He wasn't sure but he thought he might have to leave the country. That wouldn't be too bad. He just didn't want to do it. If he was getting a second chance then why couldn't he spend it the way he wanted? He knew soldiering. He could do that again. But he had already done that. Rifles, grenades, tactics, it was all far back in his brain. He liked it there. He wasn't too keen in bringing it back to the front.

But there was also baseball. He had been a pretty good pitcher in the barn storming days. Maybe that was the adventure to be had next. Trade in the rifles, hand grenades and tactics for gloves, bats and fast balls. Maybe he would make the All Star team. Maybe he would be in the World Series. And wouldn't that be the best way to say 'Thank You' to Sergeant Garr, Sonny Provenzano and Hav? He couldn't think of a better one.

As his thoughts soared out across a wide open land, the train rattling its way along, his thoughts were interrupted by a buzzing near his head. He looked to one side and then saw a bee that was suddenly interested in him. It buzzed about him like it knew him. Walter Johnson held out his hand so that the bee would land on it, which it did. As it crawled about on his palm he turned his hand this way and that so it could travel a little.

"You again..." he mused.

Then the bee stung.

He watched while a corner of his palm turned a bright red, with a small dark spot in the middle, like a pencil point, where the bee had stung him. After a moment he turned his hand outwards, towards the open section of the car and let the bee fly away. It vanished in a blink, leaving him with a lonely and uncertain heart.

"Right behind you," he whispered to himself. Then he put his head back and invited his memories to take him to a dream while the irregular rhythm of the train headed for a setting sun.

"Hall," he mused. "Short for Hall of Fame…"

Back in Smicksville, Hav Tescovitz's annuals were in bloom.

Again.

CPSIA information can be obtained
at www.ICGtesting.com
Printed in the USA
LVHW051046281221
707248LV00003B/155